Praise for *A Bad Day for Sorry*

"Crime fiction hasn't seen a character as scrappy, mean, and incredibly appealing as Stella in a long time."

—*Entertainment Weekly* (rating: A–)

"Markedly original . . . Littlefield uses words, not drawings, but this is as graphic a crime novel as you'll find this side of the thriller subgenre. The story's compelling, the dialogue perfect— and Stella is one of the most memorable characters of this summer or any other." —Jay Strafford, *Richmond Times-Dispatch*

"An abundance of violence is leavened with humor and heart in this debut novel in what I hope is the start of a new series."

—Hallie Ephron, *The Boston Globe*

"*A Bad Day for Sorry* is another of the year's best debuts, a standout mystery distinguished by its charming protagonist and her compelling voice. We don't get many characters like Stella in mystery fiction, but we should. She's fresh and sassy and an awful lot of fun to read about."

—David J. Montgomery, *Chicago Sun-Times*

"Sophie Littlefield shows considerable skills for delving into the depths of her characters and complex plotting as she disarms the reader. . . . Littlefield keeps the plot churning with realistic action that doesn't let up. . . . Littlefield's exciting debut should be the start of an even more exciting series."

—Oline Cogdill, *Sun-Sentinel* (South Florida)

A BAD DAY FOR SORRY

· · · · · · · · ·

SOPHIE LITTLEFIELD

Minotaur Books
New York

A THOMAS DUNNE BOOK FOR MINOTAUR BOOKS.
An imprint of St. Martin's Publishing Group.

A BAD DAY FOR SORRY. Copyright © 2009 by Sophie Littlefield. All rights reserved. Printed in the United States of America. For information, address St. Martin's Press, 175 Fifth Avenue, New York, N.Y. 10010.

www.thomasdunnebooks.com
www.minotaurbooks.com

The Library of Congress has cataloged the hardcover edition as follows:

Littlefield, Sophie.
    A bad day for sorry / Sophie Littlefield. — 1st ed.
        p. cm.
    ISBN 978-0-312-55920-5
    1. Abused women—Fiction. 2. Middle-aged women—Fiction.
3. Abusive men—Crimes against—Fiction. 4. Missouri—Fiction.
I. Title.
    PS3612.I882B33 2009
    813'.6—dc22

                                                2009007906

ISBN 978-0-312-64323-2 (trade paperback)

First Minotaur Books Paperback Edition: June 2010

10 9 8 7 6 5 4 3 2 1

For the Blob, who always knew I could do it.

Acknowledgments

Endless thanks to: Lisa, Lynn, Trish, and Cyndy for all those years of friendship and guidance; my brother, Mike Wiecek, for sticking with me and cheering me on; my agent, Barbara Poelle, for seeing something special in my words; and my editor, Toni Plummer, for helping me make this book the best it can be.

Thanks, also, to Craig McDonald, for teaching me the handshake and many other industry secrets; to my Northern California MWA friends, for the warm welcome and for showing me the ropes; to David Rotstein, for creating a perfect cover; and to Frank Borelli of Borelli Consulting, for explaining gun stuff.

And finally, thank you, T-wa and Sal, for tolerating the demands of this new gig—I sure like having you two around.

Prologue

Whuppin' ass wasn't so hard, Stella Hardesty thought as she took aim with the little Raven .25 she took off a cheating son-of-a-bitch in Kansas City last month.

What was hard was making sure it stayed whupped.

Especially on a day when it hit a hundred degrees before noon. And you were having hot flashes. And today's quote on your Calendar for Women Who Do Too Much read *Find serenity in unexpected places*.

"Fuck serenity," Stella said. And she shot the trailer.

ONE

. . . .

Stella knew from experience that Roy Dean Shaw wasn't a particularly brave young buck. But then, the ones who smacked their women around rarely were.

Hunting him down was going to consume a sizable chunk of her day off, and Stella was plenty annoyed. She only took Sundays and Tuesdays off from the sewing machine shop, and lately her sideline business was eating into her free time. Today, for instance, she'd had to cancel an appointment down at Hair Lines—cut and color—for the second time, and she hadn't done laundry all week.

It didn't help Stella's mood any that menopause had kicked into high gear now that her fiftieth birthday had come and gone. If widowhood had given Stella license to explore her authentic self, menopause stood under the window yelling at the bitch to come out and rumble. She felt like biting the heads off kittens—though that might actually be an asset today, given the talk she needed to have with Roy Dean.

A month ago, shortly after their first meeting, Roy Dean

had called to give her his new address. It was one of the rules: all of her parolees were required to inform her of any change in their personal information. Besides address and phone number, they were required to report all their income sources and what they did in their leisure time and, most important, any new relationships with the fairer sex.

Reporting back to Stella was not optional, but her parolees were usually anxious to comply. First meetings with Stella tended to have that effect.

Second meetings—if a parolee was dim-witted enough to require one—put any lingering doubts to rest.

Stella wasn't bound by all the bureaucratic red tape that *real* parole officers had to wade through. She didn't have to fill out paperwork. She didn't report to a boss. She didn't have to appear in court. And she could make the parolees tell her any damn thing she wanted to know.

She couldn't, however, always make them tell the *truth*. Stella had no doubt that the address Roy Dean had given her, on Cedar Street in Harrisonville, existed. She'd even lay odds that Roy Dean or one of his relatives had lived there at some point.

But a punk like Roy Dean would never give her a fact if he could spin her some fiction instead. It was in his blood.

After a late breakfast of Pop-Tarts slathered with peanut butter, Stella made a halfhearted effort to get the laundry started, and paid a few bills from the bottom of the stack. Then she set out to track down Roy Dean.

She found a lead an hour later in a dank and yeasty booth in the back of the High Timer. The place was little more than a squat shed at the intersection of a couple of farm roads five miles out of town, but it was popular with local bikers, and Jelloman Nunn was exactly where she thought he'd be, enjoying a lunch of Polish sausages sizzled in the deep fryer and a mug of Busch. Jelloman was happy to see her, folding her into a hug that mashed her face against his greasy leather vest and tickled her forehead with his long, scratchy gray beard.

He was even happier to tell her what he knew. Jelloman, it turned out, had been to Roy Dean's new place to extract payment for some weed, and Roy Dean had been sufficiently reluctant to pay up that Jelloman was irritated. So he made sure to give Stella fine, detailed directions. There were a lot of turns at landmarks like "the busted-up Esso station" and "a refrigerator somebody dumped"; Stella copied these carefully into her case notebook, which she then accidentally set down into a pool of spilled beer and had to dry off with a borrowed bar rag.

Her notebook was in sorry shape already, with a big coffee stain on the current page, and tomato sauce gluing several of the previous pages together. The tendency of her working papers to meet with misfortune dictated that every new case got its own notebook. Stella liked to pick them up in the school supplies aisle at the Wal-Mart when they went on sale. This particular one had a Happy Bunny logo and "It's all about me. Deal with it" written on the front.

Todd Groffe, the thirteen-year-old boy who lived two doors down and spent most of his free time finding new ways to be a pain in the butt, had informed Stella that Happy Bunny was over, a dead trend. Probably why the notebook was in the half-off bin at Wal-Mart. Luckily, Stella didn't spend a lot of time worrying about trends. "It's all about me"? That tickled her plenty—maybe she ought to tattoo it on her arm or something.

Stella tossed some money on the bar to cover Jelloman's lunch, and endured another boozy squeeze and a loud kiss on her ear. Back in her Jeep, Stella laid the notebook out on the passenger seat to dry, and tore out of the bar's dirt parking lot fast enough to spin gravel.

Nothing like a drive in the country to settle a person's spirits.

Stella's Jeep, a sweet little green Liberty with chrome aluminum wheels and a sunroof, had been her husband Ollie's pride and joy. He bought it new less than four months before he died and never let Stella drive it once. Ollie said she didn't know how to handle a car that sat up off the road like that, so she kept driving the crappy little old Neon that Ollie himself had creased along a guardrail after a few too many beers coming home from a fishing trip.

Once Ollie was gone, Stella sold the Neon to a neighbor's teenage daughter for a few hundred bucks and drove that Jeep like it had fire in the wheel wells. It never failed to light her up to take it out on the highway, with her favorite music cranked, rural Missouri flying by outside the windows.

"Love is like a cloud holds a lot of rain," Emmy Lou sang as Stella drove, and she hummed along. There was just nothing in the world like old Emmy Lou's drank-me-some-razor-blades-along-with-my-whiskey voice to smooth out Stella's own rough edges and ruffled feathers.

And today was turning out to be that kind of day. It wasn't just the hot flashes and the mood swings, either. Stella wasn't anybody's poster child for the Serenity Prayer on her best day, but thinking about Roy Dean's pretty wife Chrissy sitting in her living room trying not to cry, wearing long sleeves on a hot day to cover up the evidence of her husband's displeasure— well, that just made Stella's heart hurt.

Emmy Lou launched into "Sweet Old World." Stella sang along, squeaking on the high notes. Emmy Lou had no trouble taking her alto voice up into soprano territory, but Stella's own voice hunkered somewhere south. "Not much of a range" was how her junior high choir teacher put it, before making Stella a prompter, her only job to stand in the wings holding up cards during the performances. Well, screw Mrs. Goshen— Stella figured she'd sing any old damn time she wanted now.

Somebody so warm cradled in your arm
Didn't you think you were worth anything

Stella drove past fields bright with late-spring corn, the plants not much more than ankle high, and tried to get her thoughts in order. Worrying about things that were out of your control was a waste of time on a good day, but when you were on your way to meet the kind of trouble that was probably armed and definitely dumb, it was an especially bad idea. Clear thinking, that's what was called for.

Stella eventually found the road. A mile of cracked asphalt and weeds gave over to gravel and finally to a pair of uneven ruts that caused the Jeep to bump and lurch.

Roy Dean's trailer hideout was down at the end of the rutted dirt road, close enough to a buggy, brackish little cove of the lake to smell the water, if not see it. Not exactly prime real estate. On the other hand, not a bad spot to hang your hat if you were hoping to avoid encounters with folks you'd rather not see, like the law, for instance, or that crazy bitch from hell your wife sicced on you.

For kicks, Stella gave the Jeep a little extra gas and held on tight, flying over the hillocks and shallows of the road until she landed on the patch of cleared earth. She hit the brakes and spun in the dirt as she pulled up in front of the trailer and turned off the ignition.

It was worse than she'd expected. The trailer seemed to be leaning on its foundations. The wood lattice that someone had nailed around the bottom had come loose, and pieces of it lay in the weeds. The siding had once been white, but that was a distant memory; rusty streaks leaked down from all the seams. One of the windows had been boarded with a sheet of plywood, but that too had separated from its moorings and hung by a single nail.

Parked next to the trailer was a truck Stella recognized, having recently followed Roy Dean so they could have their first conversation. Last time she saw the truck, it had been parked in front of a liquor store at eleven thirty on a Monday night. Like Roy Dean, the truck was hard on the eyes and didn't look very reliable, with its dented tailgate and rust spots and low-hanging tailpipe.

Stella didn't plan on needing it, but she got a gun out of the locked steel box bolted to the floor of the Jeep, just in case. There were currently two weapons in the box: her dad's old Ruger .357 flat-top, and a cheap little Raven .25 semi-auto that she'd picked up on a trip to Kansas City six months back, when she'd tracked down a missing high school principal. The asshole had cleaned out his bank accounts and left his wife to face eviction while he moved into his waitress girlfriend's apartment in Blue Hills. The gun was a little bonus that Stella had taken off the guy, along with a tall stack of cash he'd kept in the kitchen cabinets, and his wife's good jewelry. Stella felt sorry enough for the girlfriend to give her back some of the cash before breaking a couple of the man's fingers and working out a payment plan. The ex-principal, now a Best Buy salesman, sent his ex a tidy little sum every month.

Stella made sure.

For today's visit with Roy Dean, she chose the Raven. She checked the magazine and chambered an extra round, then slid back the safety. The gun was a little short on firepower—it wouldn't drop someone the size of Jelloman, for instance, barring one hell of a lucky shot—but Stella liked it for little jobs where the power of suggestion was her main weapon.

As she stepped out of the Jeep's lovely air conditioning, heat and humidity hit her like a warm wet washcloth full of buckshot. Stella took a minute to stretch and peeled her shorts away from her thighs before crossing the dirt yard. She rapped her knuckles on the door and waited. There was something about the front doors on trailers; they never seemed to fit snug in their frames, so you always got a rattle when you knocked. That alone would keep Stella from ever living in one. That and the old twister problem—one tornado out for a joyride and you were history.

Stella heard movement inside the trailer. Banging around and cursing, mostly. After a few minutes of that, the door popped open an inch; a bloodshot eye peered out and then the door promptly slammed shut again.

Stella sighed and put her weight on the hip that didn't cause her trouble, and settled in for a wait. This wasn't the first time she'd had to roust someone from a trailer, and there wasn't a whole lot to it, once you took a moment to assess the particulars of the situation. She'd already seen that the rear of the trailer backed up against a brambly thicket of bush honeysuckle, so if Roy Dean hauled his skinny ass out of a window or door on the back side, he'd have to make his way along the side of the trailer, battling the shrubs the whole way, and come out one side or the other. If he picked a window on the front side, he'd be stuck wrassling his way out for a few moments. Either way, shooting into the dirt at his feet ought to do the trick.

Minutes ticked by, and still Roy Dean didn't appear. Stella heard the sound of heavy objects being pushed around. Incredulous, she demanded, "Roy Dean, you aren't trying to barricade yourself *in* there, are you?"

There was a pause, a few moments of silence. Stella could almost picture Roy Dean knitting those scraggly eyebrows together, pursing his lips and thinking hard—as hard as he could, at any rate.

"Well . . . what if I *am*?" he finally said, his voice muffled and echoey inside the trailer. "What are *you* gonna do about it?"

Stella couldn't believe it—the little asswipe was *still* mouthing off to her. After all the effort she'd put in. After laying it all out for him—with extra care, given his evident slow-wittedness—and explaining both what he'd done to get her attention and what the consequences would be of any further mischief. It was bad enough that she'd got the call about him yesterday—one of her sources said she had spotted a fella that looked an awful lot like Roy Dean at the concession stand of the Latham County Speedway, pulling on the long blond ponytail of his companion hard enough that she was crying and trying to get away, while he just laughed—but to give Stella lip? When she'd driven all this way? On her *day off?*

Stella sighed again and leveled the little Raven about two feet to the right of where she figured Roy Dean to be. She thought about the calendar sitting on her kitchen counter, with its pastel flower borders and its encouraging sayings, and she realized that she was no longer a member of its target audience.

"Fuck serenity," she said, and shot the trailer.

She wasn't sure whether the bullet would make it through— no telling what-all they used to line the walls of these things— but judging by Roy Dean's startled yelp and the string of cursing that ensued, the shot had apparently made an impression.

"I'm shooting out the windows next," she called, just to speed things along.

Sounds of the heavy objects being pushed out of the way were followed by the door being flung open and there stood Roy Dean in all his glory, sweating and panting hard, grimy boxer shorts hanging off his bony hips, a filthy white tank top leaving most of his pale chest exposed.

"Shit, Miz Hardesty, cut it out. Okay? Look, I'm invitin' you into my home, you don't need to go shootin' no more."

Stella lowered her gun hand to her side and let the Raven hang there casually. She could go from full dangle to aimed and ready to shoot in about a tenth of a second. That was a trick she'd worked on most of last winter when business was slow at the shop—sitting on her stool behind the cash register and practicing her draw, tucking the gun into the drawer when the bell at the door signaled a customer's arrival.

She'd also taught herself to spin the thing on her finger just like Gary Cooper in *High Noon,* but that trick was strictly for her own enjoyment. She didn't mind having a little flair, but she wasn't an idiot: guns, after all, were serious business.

"You got any coffee on?" she asked as she shouldered her way past Roy Dean. Inside it didn't smell any too fresh, and the dining table and chairs were all bunched together to the side. Presumably they had been part of the barricade that Roy Dean had been erecting to keep her out.

Roy Dean snorted, but as he circled the tiny kitchen he kept to the edges, his eye on her gun hand. Good. She liked them scared.

"It's almost one," he said. "Who the hell drinks coffee in the afternoon?"

"Me, as a matter of fact. But I guess I'd settle for a Coke."

"All's I got is beer. Coors or Coors Light."

"Coors *Light,* huh? You wouldn't be entertaining any *ladies,* now, would you, Roy Dean?"

"What? No, I, uh, I ain't gone anywhere near Chrissy."

"Can it, lover boy. Make no mistake, if you so much as look at Chrissy crosswise I'll know before you have time to scratch your balls. And then I'll, you know, probably come around and shoot 'em off or something."

Roy Dean's face darkened like a Fourth of July thunderstorm, and he leaned back against the Formica counter. The boy's knees were probably feeling a little wobbly, if Stella had to guess. She suppressed a smile.

"I'm through with her," he snapped. "I *tol'* you that."

"Yeah, you did, but if I recall we were kind of far along the convincing path before you managed to choke that promise out."

Stella had been surprised that Roy Dean had lasted as long as he had on the day she taught him a lesson. Some guys folded before she even got started—especially the ones who had heard the rumors about Stella being an insane dominatrix. When she started unpacking her bag of toys, some men turned into blubbering masses of terror, ready to talk sense without much exertion on Stella's part.

Early in her justice-delivering career, the thought of being suspected of favoring kinky sexual practices was intensely embarrassing, especially since the source of the rumors came about for only the most practical reasons. Being five feet six, overweight, and out of shape, Stella had managed to pull a muscle in her lower back the first time she tied up a recalcitrant jerk at gunpoint. She almost shot him by accident as she staggered around, yelping in pain. There was also the fact that the knot-tying skills she learned in Girl Scouts weren't up to the task: the same guy, as Stella waved the gun around wildly, managed to get his wrists free. It was only slightly reassuring that he immediately fell over as he tried to run away, having forgotten that his ankles were still bound.

Stella realized she had to make some changes. She started a fitness program, but she knew she also needed to find a more reliable way to subdue a man. She had a vague notion of learning some paramilitary restraint techniques that might rely more on finesse than brute force, but Google searches for words like *restraint* and *shackle* kept popping up bondage sites.

Stella had never seen anything like the photos featured on

those sites. The gear was fascinating, in a creepy kind of way. In the photos, lovely young ladies looked quite pleased to be trussed up like roasts ready to go in the oven. That's when she had an inspiration: why not try the same thing on her targets and see if it got them under control?

Stella's first purchase was a spreader bar and a yoke, which worked out better than she could have hoped. The solid metal bar had restraint cuffs at either end; once fastened they kept the legs in a spread-eagle position. Stella didn't skimp: she went for the most expensive model she could find and made arrangements with the vendor to bulk up the padded cuffs with an extra-sturdy locking mechanism.

The yoke worked in a similar fashion. The bar had padding at the neck and wrist restraints. Stella had to fasten these herself, but generally by the time the object of her attentions had maneuvered himself into the spreader bar, a lot of the fight had gone out of him.

For a while Stella had her eye on a custom-made Saint Andrew's cross, an arrangement of two-by-sixes that could be bolted onto the wall, with rings for restraining purposes in a variety of positions. It was well made, finished in a choice of mahogany or natural stains, by a very nice man in Ohio, who offered to drive over and install it himself.

At that point, however, Stella figured she was going a little overboard. All she really needed, after all, was to get these guys settled down enough to have a rational discussion.

Sometimes the discussion was a little one-sided. Stella did not care to be yelled at or called names—she'd had enough of that with Ollie—so she bought a selection of gags with balls or bits or rings that fitted into the mouth and kept the wearer nice and silent. Efforts to talk usually just resulted in drooling, so Stella bought a stack of cheap burp cloths at the Babies-R-Us and added them to her kit.

Roy Dean had required the full treatment. He'd shut up briefly when Stella rose up off the floor of the passenger side of his truck in the darkened liquor store parking lot, aimed a gun at his temple, and told him they were going for a drive. Stella kept the gun on him all the way out to an abandoned barn she sometimes used, but Roy Dean kept up a string of ugliness as he drove. He kept hollering right up to the moment when Stella strapped the gag behind his head, and then he glared at her malevolently and fought against the bars and restraints. It took some work with a length of rubber hose and a hammer handle, and a brief poke with the electric shock baton, until she finally judged Roy Dean rehabilitated.

When she finished up with these guys, she had a little speech she delivered while packing up her supplies. In it, she reminded the man she was about to send back into society that if anything bad were to happen to her, there was an ever-growing army of women who owed her, and who were willing to pursue vengeance on her behalf; women who, like her, had once had very little to lose, and therefore viewed the whole risk-and-return equation somewhat differently than the average person.

Some righteous scary bitches, in other words.

Roy Dean seemed like he got the message, but not even a month later here he was making a new woman cry. Stella was pretty sure it hadn't gone any further, but she was worried that Roy Dean was the sort of woman-smacker who truly believed down in his bones that it was his God-given right to settle every disagreement with force, that it was a woman's job to absorb a man's disappointments and frustrations in the form of taunts and put-downs and thrown punches.

Sadly, this was the type who was most likely to pick up again where he left off with some other poor woman. Which was why Stella was here today. Without proof of the incident at the speedway, she'd limit today's visit to a warning, but it would be Roy Dean's last before she dialed up their next encounter to a whole new level.

"You want a beer or not?" he demanded after starting half a dozen protestations and finally giving up.

"I don't think so. Tell you what, let's sit down and have this chat so I can get back on my way and you can get back to your knitting, or whatever it was you were doing when I interrupted."

Roy Dean didn't look too happy about it, but he lowered himself into one of the dinette chairs, never taking his eyes off Stella. She propped open the trailer's front door, so as not to miss any small breeze that might happen to wander by. Roy Dean had the blinds down in the trailer, no doubt trying to keep the place cool, but without an air conditioner it was a losing proposition. Stella almost—for a fraction of a second—felt a little bit sorry for him.

The moment passed.

She sat down on the chair across from him and leaned her elbows on the table, resting her gun hand casually on the sticky surface.

"So you got you a new girl," she said conversationally. "What's her name?"

"She isn't—I don't got—"

"Aw, sugar, don't try to keep secrets from Auntie Stella," she said. "You know I'll find out."

Roy Dean stared at a nail-bitten thumb. "There *ain't* anyone."

"Mmm–hmm," Stella said slowly. She let the silence stretch out in front of them, letting him cook in his own juices. Nervous wasn't a bad way to keep these boys.

"Well, that's real good," she finally said, keeping her voice friendly. "I always say, it's good to let a little time go by after a tough breakup. You know? You've got to give your heart a chance to recover. Who needs a rebound relationship, all that drama? Nothing but trouble. Am I right, Roy Dean, or am I right?"

Roy Dean shrugged and mumbled something that might have been assent.

"Hey, Roy Dean," Stella said, like she'd just thought of something interesting. "I ever tell you about my returning customer special?"

Roy Dean froze for a moment, then slowly shook his head, still not looking at her.

"Well, it works like this. First time around, I look at a guy and I say to myself, 'Stella, what are the odds we can make a decent citizen out of this moron who's been beating up on his woman?' I look him over good and I try to find it in my heart to give him another chance. I believe in second chances, I really do."

After staring at his thumb miserably, the temptation evidently became too much for Roy Dean, because he stuck the thing into his mouth and started gnawing at the nail. Stella tried to suppress a wave of nausea at the sight.

"But if that same man—the one I gave a chance to, the one I didn't nail when I had his dick in a vise—if that man gets a little full of himself and decides to pick up on his old tricks with a new lady . . . well, then I tend to lose all my patience."

She leaned across the table and waited until Roy Dean flicked an increasingly terrified glance in her direction to continue. "Roy Dean, you know that tire pile out back of Vett's body shop?"

Roy Dean took his thumb away from his mouth long enough to moisten his lips with his tongue and choke out a "yeah."

"Well, a couple years ago, a man—a preacher, if you can believe it—came back for my returning customer special. He was smart enough not to bother his ex-wife, she and I made sure of that. But get this, he wasn't smart enough to stay away from the lady who played the organ at the noon service. Moved her right in with him and everything. Now I'm not saying she was any kind of smart to hook up with him, but still, stupid ain't a crime. Oh, I'm sorry, here I am babbling on, taking up all your valuable time. . . . What I mean to tell you is . . ."

She leaned even farther across the table, keeping her finger nice and easy on the trigger, though she was pretty sure she wouldn't be needing it today, and whispered, "That preacher's in about six pieces buried under that tire pile."

She lowered herself slowly back onto the chair, gauging the effect her news had on Roy Dean. There was a fair amount of truth to the story—all of it, in fact, right up to the tire pile.

Stella didn't kill the man, though. She had only one death on her hands, and she meant to keep it that way. Killing Ollie had been a case of special circumstances—she was pretty sure that when Judgment Day arrived and she was called for her audience with the Big Guy, He would understand.

Still, there were other ways to skin even the most stubborn tomcat. When the preacher took up his old ways on a new lady, Stella merely switched tactics.

Whenever a garden-variety restraint-and-reckoning first visit didn't do the trick, Stella got creative. In this case, the preacher's hypocrisy reminded her of a story she'd read in her English class at Prosper High School, and she slowly and carefully burned a scarlet A on the preacher's chest with her electric prod.

If she remembered her lessons properly, poor Hester Prynne lettered in Adultery. The preacher, Stella figured, earned his for Assholism. But at least now he was a retired Asshole. Taking his shirt off was probably all a lady needed to see before she took off running.

Roy Dean left off his thumb mid-gnaw. The color drained from his face, and he blinked rapidly a few times.

"No'm," he said, pure sincerity. "I'm off women, and if I ever take them up again, you can bet you won't have no trouble from me."

"*She* won't have no trouble from you," Stella clarified. "That's what you meant, right?"

Roy Dean nodded and gulped air.

"Okay, good. Well, now, I'm glad we got that out of the way, but since I'm here I thought I'd ask about something a friend of mine saw down at the speedway."

Stella watched carefully, especially Roy Dean's eyes, tracking to see which way his glance darted, but he didn't look up. "Well, I been there. Same's about a million other folks. But I ain't taken no *woman* there."

Stella leaned back in the dinette chair, disappointed. The online criminology course she was taking from a college based in Idaho had offered up a bunch of theories about how to tell when somebody was lying. Apparently, liars looked down and to the left when they spoke. They also tended to touch their faces and turned their bodies away and showed emotions only in their mouth, not their eyes.

What a bunch of crap.

"Dang, Roy Dean," Stella said. "I wish I could believe you. But I don't, I just don't. I mean, you're all twitchy like—"

"You got a damn gun pointed at me!"

"Yes, I guess that's right. Thing is, if I put it away in the truck, and come back in here all nice and friendly, it's not going to be much of an incentive for you to say any different, is it?"

Roy Dean started to say something, then apparently realized the futility of the argument and just shrugged.

"Well, how about this," Stella said, pushing back her chair and standing, giving her bum hip a shake. "You know I'm a friendly kind of person, right, Roy Dean? I got a lot of friends, all over the place. And not just in Prosper, either. They're all over Missouri, and I got a few in Kansas and Arkansas. . . . I even got one gal all the way over in Ohio. And these nice friends of mine, if I ask them to keep a special watch out for you, maybe let me know how you're doing, since I can't really spend *all* my time babysitting—well, I'm sure they'll be glad to keep me posted."

Roy Dean's chin hung lower, his lower lip jutting out.

You can run, Stella telegraphed with her expression, but you can't hide. She stood and pushed her chair back in under the beat-up old table. "Roy Dean, you ever figure on getting a real job? You know, one with a paycheck? Benefits?"

Roy Dean's spiky eyebrows rose up in surprise. "I done that, already, Stella. That's what got me in this whole mess with you in the first place."

"Really?" Stella paused at the door of the trailer, interested. "How'd you figure?"

"Well, when I was on at the Home Depot, I got this promotion, see? Thirty-five cents an hour, and Chrissy thinks suddenly we're all moneybags, took herself over to Fashion Gal and bought her that leather jacket."

"And this is a problem . . . . how?" In truth, Stella figured she knew where this was headed, and felt her fingers tighten on the frame of the screen door.

"I tol' her we couldn't afford that! Bitch wouldn't listen, started in on me about a few times I went out after work, while she just keeps spending my money, one fucking thing after the next—"

The Raven, as Stella raised it up and pointed at him, got his attention. Stella could feel just a faint tremor along her arm, down to her trigger finger. It would be a real shame to shoot Roy Dean by accident. And that's what it would be, if she was provoked like that. An accident. But bad things happened every day.

"You listen to me real clear," she hissed. "I know about that jacket. That's the one Chrissy had on when she came to me the first time, 'cept she couldn't get the sleeve over her sling. Roy Dean, you know what irony is?"

Roy Dean, eyes fixed on the gun, shook his head and swallowed hard.

"Well, it's when the outcome of events isn't what you'd guess from what all leads up to it. Like Chrissy, see, she told me she had been saving for that jacket since last fall. She said on double coupon day she'd take whatever she'd saved and put it in a jar, and finally she had enough to buy the jacket. Only the same day she buys it, she gets her arm broke and she can't even wear it proper. See? Irony."

Roy Dean fixed his gaze on the floor and refused to look at her. "Or another example might be us talking here," Stella continued. "Getting everything all worked out, me spending my valuable time shaping you into a productive member of society and all, and then you say one stupid little thing and I have to shoot you dead. That would be ironic."

She slowly lowered her gun arm, gave Roy Dean a final glare, and left.

She was still shaking a little as she bounced along the rutted track, pushing the Jeep harder than it cared to go, taking the turns fast enough that the wheels threatened to lift up off the road.

That jacket. That damn jacket. She'd listened to Chrissy's tearful story with sympathetic fury, but only later did Stella figure out that it reminded her of something that had happened a week before she finally took care of Ollie once and for all.

It was an unremarkable Tuesday afternoon three years ago. She'd come home from the grocery with a bunch of daffodils. Jonquils, her mother had called them. Pat Collier used to grow them in every bare spot in her yard: under trees, along the fence, between rocks. Her mother was never happier than when the flower bulbs pushed their shoots up through the last of the snow, when the tight-rolled buds flung themselves open on a sunny early-spring day.

They had fresh-cut bunches for two bucks sitting in buckets of water outside the FreshWay, and Stella brought one home, thinking of her mother the entire time. Pat had been gone two years by then—pancreatic cancer, mercifully quick. As Stella was reaching up to the top shelf for her mother's old white scallop-edged pitcher, Ollie came stomping into the kitchen, scratching his wide ass. He took one look at her flowers lying there on the counter and demanded, "Where the hell do you get off spending my money on shit like this?"

She'd started to tell him it was only two lousy dollars, started to say she'd been thinking about her mother that day, missing her, but before she could get any of those thoughts out, he'd taken a whack at her that sent her toppling off the step stool and left the pitcher lying in a dozen pieces on the floor.

By the time she got back to the highway, Stella had herself almost under control. She slowed as she approached the cluster of gas stations and fast-food joints before the entrance ramp, and after a split second's consideration, eased into the drive-through lane of the Wendy's. Not on her diet, but she hadn't missed a workout for weeks, so that had to be a few thousand calories she'd worked off.

As the line of cars made its slow trek around the parking lot, Stella got her gun locked back up in the box. By the time she got up to the order screen, her fury had simmered back down to its usual bubbling simmer.

"Number three," she said. "And a chocolate Frosty. Better make it a large."

Stella visited the bottle of Johnnie Walker Black before her date, just to make sure there was enough left for a powerful belt before bed. She unscrewed the top and inhaled—held it—then replaced the cap with a mild sense of regret. She was running low—and that was an errand she couldn't put off. Johnnie was a staple item in Stella's pantry.

But she never drank before her standing Sunday night date with Todd Groffe. It would be bad form, since he couldn't join her, being thirteen and all.

Todd let himself in the front door without knocking at a little after seven. "Damn them damn girls," he said by way of greeting.

"What'd they do this time?" Stella asked, getting a couple of cans of Red Bull out of the fridge and tearing open a bag of Flamin' Hot Cheetos.

"Got in my dresser and got my damn boxers and they're wearin' 'em around the house over their clothes and shit. And Mom thinks it's cute so she won't make them take 'em off. She's all like taking their pictures and stuff."

Todd's twin sisters were six. Stella, like everyone else in the world besides Todd, thought they were adorable. Todd's father wasn't in the picture anymore, and his mother, Sherilee, worked long hours during the week and brought work home on the weekend. They lived in a little house a few doors down from Stella, and Sherilee had a hard time with the upkeep on the place, not to mention paying the mortgage.

But on Saturdays Sherilee got the girls a sitter and took Todd out on the town. Stella admired her for that. Sherilee took her son to Burger King, to action movies, to play paintball. They went to Wal-Mart and played laser tag and mini golf.

Sunday night it was the girls' turn, and Todd came over to Stella's. They shared a secret passion: they were both *America's Next Top Model* junkies. Stella TiVoed the show, and she and Todd ate junk food and critiqued the outfits and the judging and tried to figure out who was really nice and who was just pretending to get along with the other girls. Meanwhile, Sherilee took the girls to Disney movies and Pizza Hut and Fantastic Sams and Sears.

Tonight, though, Stella had a hard time concentrating on Tyra and her crew as they shuttled the models through a photo shoot in what looked like a muddy jungle. Her thoughts kept going back to Roy Dean and his insolent, stupid expression as he denied that he was seeing a new girl.

She had a bad feeling about this one. He might turn out to be one of the ones who required creative thinking, a step up to an intensified program of discouragement.

Stella didn't relish this aspect of the job—the turning of the screw, the dialing up of the pressure, the creation of new varieties and levels of pain. She understood that there were people in the world—plenty of them—who got their kicks from hurting others, who experienced a rush of pleasure to see other human beings contorted in agony. Heck, if she were to advertise for an assistant—someone to wield the whip or rubber hose or cattle prod or pliers or lit cigarette so she could keep her hands clean—she'd probably have applicants lined up out the door.

But her business didn't work that way. Stella knew too much about pain—the kind inflicted on the innocent, the defenseless, those whose worst sins were bad judgment and displaced loyalty. And she'd pledged to stop it. Not every abuser, everywhere—there were simply too many. But if it was in her power to help a woman in Sawyer County, she did so. And gradually word reached sisters and cousins and best friends and acquaintances further afield, down through the Ozarks and up to Kansas City and over to Saint Louis and—as the months grew to years and Stella learned how to turn vicious and conscience-deficient men into cowering repenters—across state lines.

Stella picked off the sons-of-bitches one by one, leaving their women free to breathe easy, to live without dread as their constant companion. And now this sideline threatened to over-take her real job, the shop she'd inherited from Ollie, supply-ing the women of Prosper with sewing notions and keeping their sewing machines in good working order. Every time she thought she'd earned some time off, a new woman would show up, terrified or battered or both, but finally ready to make it stop. And Stella knew what kind of courage that took—and she never turned a client away.

Though she did daydream about the day when the world straightened itself out, when the last abuser met his doom and she could go back to selling sewing machines and thread and needles full-time. Keep her highlights fresh and her nails done. Work in the garden. Bake banana bread.

Go on an occasional date with a real man.

Todd yawned and zapped the TV off with the clicker. He grabbed a last handful of Cheetos and jammed them all in his mouth at once. While he was chewing, Stella collected the

Red Bull cans and folded the crocheted afghans and brushed a few crumbs off the couch.

"See ya," Todd said, wiping his orange fingers on his baggy shorts.

"Thank you very much for inviting me, Miz Hardesty," Stella said.

"Yeah, whatever. Bye, Stella."

Stella waited a few moments after Todd left, then eased the front door open and watched him skateboard down the street to his house, holding his helmet loosely by the strap, pushing off with his foot and leaping up onto the curb and back down with grace. She waited until he slipped into his own front door, using the key he wore on a shoelace around his neck, before she went back inside.

Just two doors down, but the world was a dangerous place. Anything could happen.

Good folks had to look out for one another.

One of the biggest rip-offs in the universe had to be when the pleasant buzz you took to bed with you at midnight turned itself into queasy can't-sleep at 5 A.M. Where the hell did all that lovely sparkle go?

Stella had drained the Johnnie. She hadn't really intended to, but some nights were like that. Some nights were for thinkin' and drinkin', when it seemed like you couldn't do one without the other.

Stella rarely drank in the days before Ollie died. She'd figured that someone in the house ought to stay sober, and Ollie frequently wasn't up to the job.

The Johnnie thing—she'd discovered Johnnie Walker Black a few weeks into her new life as a widow and was so grateful for the way it took the edge off that she started spending more and more time with the bottle. There was a stretch there, four or five months, that didn't bear recalling—even if she could remember anything through the whiskey haze.

But these days her relationship with Johnnie was more measured. Once Stella took up exercise, jogging around the neighborhood and dragging Ollie's barely used Bowflex out of storage, she didn't need the alcohol-induced numbing as much. Just the nightly drink, or occasionally two . . . except for the rare night when two didn't do the trick. When she needed an extra layer of fuzzy loveliness.

If only she could skip the early-morning sleeplessness that always followed.

In those pre-dawn hours Stella sometimes amused herself by imagining how she would do in the joint. It was luck more than anything that had kept the law from investigating her sideline business, but her luck couldn't hold forever. Eventually, one of her parolees would decide to roll the dice and turn her in. Or the long arm of the law would somehow get wise enough to catch her in the act of rehabilitating a subject. Either way, questions would be asked. Leads would be followed. And when that happened, odds were good that Stella would be headed for jail.

Stella wasn't sure she much cared. Life with Ollie had been worse than anything the prison system could dish out. Life without Ollie was better, but it was still lonely. Becoming a stone-cold enforcer had changed her, taking away any desire she'd ever had to play nice just to fit in. She called it like she saw it now. Cussed when she felt like it. Didn't back down.

Jail didn't scare Stella. With an assault conviction or two, she figured her reputation would precede her. Her nickname would be some variation on Hardesty, probably "Hard-ass." Of course you didn't get a handle like that for free; she'd probably have to shank somebody on the first day or something.

But then there was the matter of all the pairing-off that happened in women's prison. She'd seen a TV documentary on the subject. Diane Sawyer, Stella's favorite journalist, spent the night in jail, wearing a prison-issue jumpsuit to interview the inmates. Stella couldn't believe how matter-of-fact the women were about their sex lives. And how creative, too, making sex toys out of bits of junk stolen here and there.

Unfortunately, Stella was pretty sure she didn't have any latent lesbian tendencies, so all that prison action wouldn't do her much good. It was a shame, too, because the documentary made it clear that even the homelier ladies had opportunities for love.

Stella was no beauty queen. Despite the hours she spent on the Bowflex, her muscles were still protected by a generous larding of extra pounds. Then there were the gray roots, the facial hair in odd places, the breasts heading to the equator.

But on TV she'd seen it with her own eyes: gals who didn't have anything on her—hell, downright old, ugly gals with no access to a blow-dryer—enthusiastically reporting all the lovin' they were getting. Diane didn't back down, either. She listened with polite interest. She didn't judge. Stella admired her for keeping her cool.

Diane, who made even prison duds look elegant, hadn't

seen fifty in a while herself, but she had a sort of mature sensuality that implied she'd done more in the sack than most people even dream about. She probably had mind-blowing sex five days a week.

Stella figured she might miss sex more if it had been any good when she had it.

Fucking Ollie. That thought, never far from her mind, and in a thousand different contexts, brought unexpected tears to Stella's eyes as she lay there in the bed she'd once shared with him. This time, it was simply because he'd been such an incredibly worthless lay. All those years . . . all that bad sex. That wasn't even in the top five reasons why he'd deserved what he got, but still, Stella found herself immensely sad to think of how many times she'd lain in this bed with Ollie laboring over her like a man stuffing fiberglass insulation between roof joists on a sweltering day.

Of course, it wasn't like he had an overabundance of insulation to work with. That wayward thought cracked Stella up a little, so that when she did finally manage to fall back into a brief but deep sleep, she did so with a smile on her face and tears dried to salty tracks on her cheeks.

TWO

. . . .

Monday went by slowly. Stella roamed the shop floor restlessly, her head throbbing and her mouth cottony. She ordered a pizza for lunch and, after promising herself she'd eat only half and take the rest home for leftovers, nibbled it down to a few crusts over the course of the afternoon.

Hardesty Sewing Machine Sales & Repair did the same languid business it always had. There had been a steady trickle of customers when Ollie ran the place, and there was a steady trickle now. The only difference was that Ollie used to fix the machines himself; now, a man came in and picked them up once a week and returned them a few days later, running better than Ollie had ever managed.

Stella made small talk while she handled the day's few sales, and tried to keep herself awake by dusting and polishing and straightening the stock, until it was finally time to close up and go home. After a dinner of an apple and half a bag of carrots—penance for the pizza—Stella fell asleep watching

CNN, woke up after eight dreamless hours, and switched to *Good Morning America.* For a while she was content to watch Diane Sawyer sideways, checking the tourists holding signs, as she always did, for anyone from Missouri. On the rare occasion when one of her fellow Missourians made it all the way to Rockefeller Center, Stella felt both proud and wistful; the farthest east she'd ever been was a high school trip to Philadelphia, back when they still had the Liberty Bell out where you could see it close-up.

Diane had on a fungus green jacket today, and a section of her hair, the part that was supposed to fall coquettishly above one eye, was doing something a little strange, winging out at an angle. "Not your best look," Stella murmured at the television. But kindly: she could relate.

Stella decided it would be a day of hard work. She had a banana for breakfast and got to work in earnest. She put the laundry in the dryer and collected all the dirty sheets and towels and the remaining dirty clothes and sorted them. The sight of the color-coded piles made her feel pleasantly efficient.

She'd been a competent homemaker. As a young mother, she'd kept a spotless house, dressed her daughter Noelle in clean, pressed little outfits, with her hair in ribbons to match. She'd baked elaborate cakes for church fund-raisers, slipcovered all the furniture herself, vacuumed the drapes regularly, and dusted twice a week.

Now, with two businesses to run, she'd let the place slide. Usually it didn't bother her. In fact, it still felt decadent and rebellious. Occasionally, though, Stella spent a whole day cleaning the place from top to bottom.

Today would have been such a day. Except that around ten

thirty, the doorbell rang. Stella peeled off her yellow rubber gloves and set down the bucket of soapy water and the brush she'd been using to scrub the kitchen floor, and answered the door.

Chrissy Shaw stood on her front porch wearing a strappy purple top that showed off her pillowy breasts as well as the fading bruises along her shoulders and upper arms. She crossed her arms over her chest and shifted from one high platform sandal to the other, her face swollen from crying.

Stella's heart sank. She hadn't expected to see the girl for a while. Usually, her clients stayed away after a job. She didn't take it personally—they usually just needed to distance themselves. Not everyone was as comfortable dishing out Stella's brand of justice as she was. No matter how relieved they were with the results, it could be a messy business.

When a client came back this quick it usually meant something had gone wrong.

"Is Roy Dean bothering you?" Stella demanded, holding the door wide for Chrissy to enter.

"No'm," Chrissy mumbled. She had on tight denim shorts that barely covered her jiggly rear, and she tugged at the fringed hems as she clopped past Stella. She trailed some kind of perfume that smelled like it came out of one of those peel-and-rub ads in *Cosmopolitan* magazine—a little musky, a little papery. Could be the girl had just spritzed on a little over-much to cover up skipping today's shower; Stella employed that technique herself from time to time.

Chrissy walked into Stella's living room and lost her momentum. She turned to the couch, the love seat, Ollie's old La-Z-Boy and considered each one, but couldn't seem to make up her mind. She pressed the back of her hand to her forehead and managed a pathetic little whimper. Chrissy was in her middle twenties, but if you didn't know better you might guess she was eighteen.

"Hell, sugar, don't matter where you plant your butt, we'll still be having the same conversation," Stella said. "Tell you what, while you're deciding, why don't I get us some iced tea."

When she came back with the tray a few minutes later, Chrissy had slumped low in the love seat and was leaking tears down her plump cheeks, pale blond hair sticking to her sweat-damp skin. Her wide blue eyes were ringed with smudgy mascara.

"Oh, dear," Stella said. "I know it seems bad now, but whatever Roy Dean's done, it's nowhere near the worst problem someone's come here to talk about. Nothing I can't help you fix, anyway."

Chrissy wiped her nose along her knuckles and sniffled. "Yeah? Well, guess what, I think this time I might a brung you a problem you ain't had before."

Stella sat down on the couch and picked up a long silver spoon off the tray and gave her glass of tea a swirl. Oh, these girls. Every one of them sure they had a new story to tell. Honestly, it tried her patience sometimes, until she remembered what it felt like to be in their shoes. When you were the one getting smacked around, trash-talked, cheated on, and generally treated worse than any man would treat a tick-infested hound dog, then yeah, your story seemed like the most singular piece of news on earth.

"Is that right, dolly." Stella screwed down the lid on her

impatience and settled in to hear the whole story. "Well, you tell me all about it, and then we'll figure out what to do. But here, wet your whistle before you get rolling."

Chrissy accepted a glass of tea but set it down on the table without sipping. "Roy Dean's gone and run off."

"Now honey, he isn't gone, he's just been staying out at a trailer down close to Shooter's Cove," Stella said, wondering if the girl had been foolish enough to go looking for him. Sometimes, even after suffering all manner of abuse, her clients had second thoughts. "But there's no need to go stirring things up."

"Ain't Roy Dean I care about, Stella—only just he's taken Tucker. Came and took him yesterday morning. Told me he wanted his hibachi back and when I went around back to get it, I guess that's when he got Tucker 'cause when I came back inside they was both gone." Chrissy snuffled and dabbed at her eyes, smearing her makeup further.

"Oh no," Stella said, setting her own glass down and jerking to attention. "That does change things. Shit!"

"Yeah," Chrissy said, and her glum expression slipped further and a shadow of terrible worry flashed across her doughy features. "That's about the size of it."

Stella excused herself, making sure that the plate of Oreos was in Chrissy's easy reach, and called Sheriff Goat Jones from the kitchen. She was one of only a handful of people with direct access to the sheriff's mobile number, and that was a result of her only case that had gone terribly wrong, a failure from which Stella would never entirely recover.

Two years back, Lorelle Cavenaugh went missing less than a week after she came to Stella for help. Stella spent forty straight hours searching for Lorelle on her own before calling the sheriff. She invented a story about them being third cousins and Lorelle leaving a terrified message on her machine, which she had just happened to erase, and which oddly didn't show up in the phone company records.

By the time they found Lorelle, stuffed head-down into a rain barrel at Jack Cavenaugh's fishing cabin, Stella had promised herself that she'd never again let anything get in the way of a woman's safety. Not even if it meant danger to herself, or exposure, or bringing in the entire sheriff's department.

Goat Jones told her she had more stick than a cocklebur after she hounded him to widen the search and ignored every order he gave her to stay away from him and his men while they scoured the county. He called her a few other things, too—the words *bulldog* and *no-sense* and *damn stubborn fool* came to mind.

Goat said he'd be right over, grousing only a little that she wouldn't give him any details on the phone. Stella peeked in at Chrissy, who was nibbling morosely at a cookie, and hightailed it to her bathroom, where she got out the modest arsenal of beauty products that she kept in an empty Jif peanut butter jar, and went to work.

It wasn't that she was fixing up for the sheriff, exactly. Because that would be ridiculous. For one thing, their work generally put them on opposite sides of the law. That alone made the man, if not exactly an enemy, certainly not a person she should be fraternizing with.

And anyway they didn't run in the same social circles. Goat was a regular at the Friday night poker game at the firehouse—

the same game Ollie had played in for years, the game all of Ollie's old friends still belonged to. Not that it was fair to paint them with the same brush as her dead husband, but they had become a little standoffish since she nearly stood trial for killing Ollie.

Goat got himself invited to the game as a sort of law enforcement courtesy. His deputies, Ian Sloat and Mike Kutzler, had been playing for years, and it wouldn't have looked right to exclude Goat, even though he was still a newcomer to the area. He had lived in Prosper for only a couple of years, having been hired in to replace old Sheriff Burt Knoll after he died of a heart attack while cheering on his grandson at a go-kart race.

Most of the poker players had lived in Prosper for decades, if not their entire lives. They were courteous to Goat, but maybe "friend" was too strong a word; outside the poker game, she knew they didn't barbecue together or bowl in the same league or even jaw too long if they ran into each other at the Home Depot. Still, at the rate of four hours a week for two years, that was . . . oh, hell, a few hundred hours anyway that Goat and her late husband's drinking buddies shared each other's company, and in Stella's book that made Goat guilty of poor taste in the company he kept, if nothing else.

Stella splashed cold water on her face and slapped her cheeks a few times in an effort to get a little color into them. She leaned in close to the mirror and didn't like what she saw: it had been a while since she'd taken a pair of tweezers to her eyebrows, and they seemed to have made expansion plans on their own. The battle she was waging on her wrinkles, armed with the jumbo tub of Avon Anew Clinical Deep Crease Concentrate that her sister had sent her last Christmas, didn't seem like it was trending in her favor. The wrinkles were still there, and if she wasn't mistaken, the ones around her eyes had hatched a plan to reach down and shake hands with her laugh lines.

Stella scrambled through the Jif jar, tossing aside shampoo sample packets and emery boards and a dozen lipsticks in unflattering shades—she was a sucker for those Clinique gift-with-purchase deals—until she found the tube of Avon Radiant Lifting Foundation. Another gift from Gracellen. Praying it hadn't passed its sell-by date, she squeezed a little onto her finger and dabbed at the worst spots on her face.

Her hair had escaped its barrette and sprang out in an unruly mass. That was entirely Stella's fault. For most of her life she'd been vain about her thick, wavy light brown hair, keeping it trimmed and conditioned and blown dry. She'd just gotten in a few bad habits in the last couple of years, that's all. Missing yesterday's appointment with Jane over at Hair Lines hadn't helped any.

She grabbed her hairbrush and yanked it forcibly through, ignoring the pain. Unfortunately, taking out the tangles also served to play up the line of demarcation between her gray roots and the shade that Jane had mixed up at her last visit.

Stella was overdue for a goodly amount of maintenance work.

She gave up and put down the brush. She made a face at the mirror, figuring she'd done all she could on short notice.

At the door to her bedroom, she had a thought, and dashed back to the bathroom. She dumped the Jif jar out in the sink and found what she was looking for at the bottom of the pile: a small bottle of White Diamonds. She sprayed behind her ears and on her wrists, sniffed deeply, and added one last spritz down her bra.

In the living room Chrissy had made a sizable dent in the Oreos. "Good girl," Stella murmured, helping herself to one. "Got to keep your strength up."

Naturally, Goat knocked on the door just as soon as she had the whole cookie in her mouth. Stella backhanded the crumbs off her lips and swallowed hard as she went to open the door, managing to get the thing stuck in her throat. She had to cough out a greeting.

"Goat," she gasped, holding the door wide and gesturing him in. "Good of you to come." A bit of cookie lodged stubbornly and she hacked some more.

"You okay there, Dusty?" Goat asked, but damn the man, he didn't look so much concerned as amused. Light streaming through the picture window bounced off his shiny bald head and sparkled up his bluer-than-blue eyes, and he gave her one of his sideways grins. "Want me to whack you on the back a time or two?"

"Don't you dare," Stella said with as much dignity as she could manage. "Please sit."

She reclaimed her own spot on the couch and sipped primly at her tea. Once she'd cleared her air passage so that she could talk without spraying crumbs, she gestured at Chrissy, who had managed to get herself more or less into a sit-up-straight position in the chair to greet the sheriff.

"Chrissy, you know Sheriff Jones, don't you, dear? And Sheriff, this is Chrissy Shaw. She's one of the Lardner girls. Out Road Twelve, the soybean Lardners."

There were two strains of Lardners in town. The soybean

Lardners were the wrong ones to hail from, if you had any choice in the matter. Ralph Lardner was a lazy mountain of flesh who did more sitting on his ass and ordering his boys around the farm than he did actual labor, and the family skill set lent itself more to quick-and-dirty methods rather than true craftsmanship, so the Lardner sons were constantly patching the siding on the barns and resetting leaning fence posts and attacking late-season weeds with industrial-strength fungicide in watering cans, killing off their mother's flower garden at least once a year.

The other Lardner in town was named Gray. Ralph and Gray were distant cousins, but it would take degrees in both history and math to trace out the exact nature of their blood relationship. The lineage had split long enough back that Gray's side had managed to build a modest fortune buying up rich land along Sugar Creek on the south end of town. While Ralph's crew mined stony, hard-packed dirt for a bedraggled crop every year, Gray had to just look at his land sideways and it seemed happy to send up burgeoning fields of corn, alfalfa, prizewinning squash—whatever he had a mind to grow.

Ralph's boys seemed bent on following in their father's sorry footsteps. His girls, on the other hand, tended to marry the first boy who asked, just to get off that unlucky land.

"Pleased to make your acquaintance," the sheriff said, shaking Chrissy's limp hand with exaggerated care before settling his lanky frame into Ollie's old La-Z-Boy.

Damn, but the man was tall, Stella couldn't help thinking for the thousandth time. Had to be six foot four, with acres of muscle running along his broad shoulders visible even under that homely tan uniform shirt. In his spare time, Goat had what was generally viewed as a strange hobby: he liked to lash his kayak to the top of his pickup truck and drive to any of the hundreds of put-in spots along the northern shore of the Lake of the Ozarks, as close as twenty miles away as the crow flies. Then he'd spend the day paddling around the inlets and channels and bights along the jagged shore.

All that paddling clearly built up a man's physique.

"Nice to meet you, Sheriff . . . sir," Chrissy said, a rosy blush stealing across her pale, full cheeks, and she looked at the carpet rather than at Goat. Stella might have thought the girl was shy, but she knew better: stammering uncertainty was the blood-dictated response that all the Ralph Lardner kin had to the law. She guessed that the idea was that if your pa or brothers weren't guilty of something at this particular juncture, odds were good that they had just come from or were plotting to soon commit some sort of law-skirting activity.

"Chrissy's a good girl," Stella said, hoping to head off any conclusions Goat might be tempted to draw.

"Oh, I'm sure she is. I'm sure you are," he repeated, giving Chrissy a reassuring smile.

"I suppose you're wondering why I asked you over," Stella said.

"Well yes, Dusty, I am, but I'm also wondering if you're planning to offer me a glass of that tea."

"Oh!" Stella felt the blood flow to her cheeks as she hauled herself up out of the couch. "I meant to, I'm sorry, I just, ah . . ."

She retreated to the kitchen to fetch another glass, cursing under her breath. Damn, damn, damn. She had the hardest time keeping her wits about her when Goat was around, and that annoyed her plenty. She possessed, after all, a slick and hardened criminal mind; she'd committed any number of misdemeanors and felonies. She generally stayed icy cool in sticky situations, so why was she such a stuttering mess around the man?

It wasn't like she was afraid old Goat was going to put two and two together anytime soon. Those who knew her business weren't talking. Those who suspected . . . well, they weren't talking much either, and Stella figured they all had their reasons: some didn't want to end up on her bad side; others figured the world was a sight better place if she was left in peace to do her job.

Of course, there was the small and niggling problem that Goat, she suspected, was far smarter than he let on. And eventually, someone was going to break the time-honored rule of small-town living and engage in a little conjecturing with him—outsider or not. When that day came, it would be the sort of reckoning that would make all of her previous brushes with the law look like playground entertainment.

Yet another reason to spend as little time with the man as possible.

"Here," she said accusingly, thrusting the glass at him.

"Well, I suppose I'll just pour myself," Goat said, accepting the glass. He reached for the pitcher, raising his pinkie in an exaggerated fancy-schmancy pose. "Don't you exert yourself none, Dusty. Am I allowed to have a cookie, or are those just for the ladies?"

Stella picked up the plate and smacked it down in front of him. There were only three or four cookies left. Poor Chrissy had eaten most of them—who could blame her? "And stop calling me Dusty."

"Why's he call you that, anyway?" Chrissy stage-whispered in a perfectly audible voice, still keeping her eyes cast down.

"'Cause he hasn't got any manners, I guess," Stella said.

Goat laughed. "That's not right. It's just 'cause she's a bad old Hardesty. Get it—'desty,' 'dusty.' She's not like a regular gal, Miss. Why, she frequents disreputable taverns, cusses a blue streak, probably chews tobacco when nobody's looking. Can't exactly call her 'Rosebud' so—"

"That's enough," Stella said sharply, and she must of put a little extra mean-it in her voice because suddenly everyone was very quiet and Goat slowly lowered his iced tea glass to the coffee table and gave her a long, studied look.

"What I mean to say is, I think I'm a little old for some juvenile nickname, so if you don't mind, you can just start calling me Stella, like every other person in this town. *Goat*." Maybe it wasn't necessary to add that last bit, but Stella was steamed enough to go for it.

"Well, why d'you call him *that*?" Chrissy asked the carpet. Clearly, she was no student of conversational subtext.

Stella sighed. "Now, hon, why don't we just lay this whole names business to rest. We got plenty else to talk about here."

"No, Miss, I don't mind answering," Goat said, but he kept his gaze trained steady on Stella, and by the wicked sparkle in his eyes Stella could tell she'd managed to get his ire up. Smart, she chided herself, way to provoke the law when she needed him most. "See, when I got divorced, my first wife saw fit to tell everyone that the problem was that I'm as randy as a—"

"Stop right there," Stella snapped. Chrissy might be one of the dimmer bulbs in a family that wasn't lit up bright with smarts to start with, but Stella didn't think it was right to take advantage of her gullible nature with any sort of teasing. Not to mention the terrible day the poor girl was having. "It's just that the sheriff has been stubborn from the day he was born. It was his own mama who gave him that nickname."

"What kind of stubborn?" Chrissy asked, darting shy little glances in the man's direction. *Her* mama had obviously not gotten around to teaching her that it wasn't polite to talk about people right in front of them as though they weren't there.

"Well, the wrong kind, of course. Like a goat. You ever try to lead one around? Wherever you try to drag it, the goat figures it wants to be headed the other way."

"Oh. I see." Chrissy nodded. "Well, Sheriff, I imagine I'll just call you 'Sheriff Jones,' if it's all the same to you."

"That'd be just fine, Miss."

After that there was a brief silence while Stella's two guests stole polite glances at each other.

"Chrissy's husband, Roy Dean, has run off," Stella said. Time to get down to business. "He's been gone since yesterday morning. And he took little Tucker with him."

"Who's Tucker?" Goat asked.

At that, Chrissy's features, which had been schooled into her best approximation of mindful interest, melted into a blubbery puddle. Stella handed her the box of Kleenex she kept at the ready on the side table next to the couch; smacked-around wives often found it came in handy. "Tucker's my little baby boy," she wailed. "He's not even two years old yet."

"Oh, well, I'm sorry to hear that. But it's only been one day—"

"And Tucker ain't even his!" Chrissy continued to sniffle. "Roy Dean never paid that child any mind before. I don't know why he'd want to go and run off with him!"

Goat looked at Stella, eyebrows raised.

"Chrissy was married before," she explained. "To Pitt Akers, from the Akers over up south of Sedalia."

"But *he* wasn't the father either," Chrissy cut in, dabbing at her eyes with a tissue. She was getting herself under control a little.

"No?" Goat asked politely. "I think I might ought to start noting some of this down." He pulled out a little notebook and flipped to a fresh page. "Now, whose boy is your Tucker?"

"Well, I'm not *entirely* sure, see, because that was right about when I broke up with the fella I'd been seeing after Pitt and I split up, and there was this one night out at my cousin's—"

Goat held up a palm to stop her. "I guess I don't need to know that," he said.

"What Tucker is, is a child from a previous relationship," Stella clarified, hoping to save Chrissy a little embarrassment.

"That's right," Chrissy said, nodding. "That's exactly what he is."

"Now, had your husband been talking about taking any trips, going to visit kin, anything like that?"

"Oh, no sir, Roy Dean's not one for a lot of visiting. And his folks are all around here."

That was an understatement; Shaws were firmly rooted in Prosper. Some of them probably hadn't left Sawyer County in years. Roy Dean's daddy had a painting business he'd got from his own daddy, and now Roy Dean and his brother Arthur were on the books. Tucker, if Roy Dean'd taken more of a shine to the boy, could have looked forward to a painting career himself.

"Was there anybody he had a beef with?"

Chrissy shot Stella a wide-eyed glance, no doubt wondering if she herself counted. Stella gave her a tiny little shake of the head, hoping the girl would have the sense not to talk about the problems between her and Roy Dean. Assuming Roy Dean turned up, and Chrissy had the need to take care of him in some manner or other down the road, it wouldn't do for the sheriff to know too much about their relationship.

"Um, no," Chrissy said. "I mean, yes, he got into a fight now and then. He's kind of quick-tempered, I guess you'd say."

"Who's he fight with?"

"Well, just whoever's there when the mood comes on, I guess. I mean it's usually somebody says something Roy Dean don't like, when he's been drinkin' too much. Ain't that usually how it goes?"

"Can you give me a for-instance?" Goat sat with his pen poised and ready to go, but he hadn't written much yet. So far this wasn't a terribly unique tale that Chrissy was telling.

Despite its name, Prosper was not a place where people lived extravagant lives. Times had gotten hard in the eighties, and not improved much since. Besides farming, there was the pork-processing plant, and a sad little office park that had never been fully occupied. The businesses ran along the shabby side of legitimate. There was a used-office-furniture dealer, the headquarters of a regional fried-chicken chain, an outfit that installed prefab sheds in people's backyards, so they had somewhere to put all the junk that didn't fit in the garage.

Prosper had developed an undercurrent of dissatisfaction, of cynicism, that Stella didn't remember from her own childhood there. Fifty years ago, when she was born, rural Missouri still strove to live up to the wholesome ideals generated by the postwar era. Men like her father worked hard to buy a house, to get ahead. The American Legion hall and a few of the local churches had been built by volunteers during that era of civic responsibility. As Stella and her sister attended Prosper Elementary and played in the streets and parks and back yards of town, the world seemed like a safe and orderly place. Sure, Prosper had its town drunk, its ne'er-do-wells, its hard cases, but they routinely got their clocks fixed by Sheriff Knoll: after a lecture and a couple nights in the lockup, sheepish spells of better behavior nearly always followed.

Nowadays the distinction between the good guys and the bad guys was a lot blurrier, and it wasn't clear to Stella who was winning. She was almost tempted to feel sorry for Goat and his crew; she knew that they spent most of their time on patrol and traffic stops and trying to keep a lid on all the problems at the high school, a job that Stella figured parents ought to be helping out with. Sawyer County didn't extend down to the lake, so they were spared the job of patrolling the shore, but they got the traffic heading home, often drunk, frequently rowdy, and sometimes belligerent.

And with the mountains of procedural requirements in place these days, Goat and Ian and Mike didn't have the freedom to police the town the way they saw fit, as Burt Knoll had once done. Hell, they probably spent half their time doing paperwork.

It was a wonder Goat had never been tempted to go freelance himself, like she had.

"Well, Roy Dean likes go to BJ's after work some days," Chrissy said. "Him and Arthur and them all. Sometimes things get a little out of hand."

Goat wrote a few words down. "Bar fights, then," he said. "Anything lately?"

Chrissy shifted uncomfortably in her chair. A pale band of flesh muffined up over her shorts, her lively top not quite up to the task of covering it, and Chrissy tugged at the fabric ineffectively. "Well, maybe," she said. "A couple weeks ago he came home scraped up some."

"How so?"

"Well, a little worse'n some, not as bad as other times."

"I mean, what was the nature of Roy Dean's injuries?"

"Oh. One of his eyes was swoll up so he could hardly see out of it, and he got hit in the other one too, but not as bad—it didn't bruise up until the next day. He did something to his arm where he couldn't lift it up past his shoulder for a while. He was favoring it, said it hurt to lift anything. Oh, and he thought he was gonna lose one of his teeth. It went kind of loose on him, but you know, that seemed to take care of itself. And of course he was cut up here and there, not bad enough for stitches or anything."

"So a pretty good dustup, then," the sheriff said.

"Well, not the worst ever, but bad enough, I guess."

"And you don't have any idea who it was he got into it with?"

"No sir. Roy Dean don't like to talk about that kind of thing much. He just makes light of it. I put Bactine on 'im, gauze and bandages. Put some steak on his eyes, raw, you know, have him lay down and that helps."

What a fool waste of meat, Stella thought. But at least Chrissy was answering the sheriff's questions without mumbling too much—and without giving too much away about her marital problems. But if Goat had any sense, he'd be on his way to figuring out that part.

"You know men," she interjected, joining the conversation in an effort to distract him. "They don't have much to say when they're on the receiving end of a beating."

Oops.

Stella clamped her mouth shut, but the unfortunate remark had slipped out. Goat turned to her and gave her a long, searching look. She had to work hard not to fidget. It was like those blue eyes sent out some sort of low-level laser beam that burned right through her skin.

"Is that right," he said mildly.

Stella had a thought that she'd had before, and not a very comfortable one. At times it seemed as if Goat suspected a little too much about her sideline business. The sewing machine shop provided as much cover as she ought to need: Stella was there every Monday and Wednesday through Saturday, nine to six; Sunday and Tuesday were her days off, and then she made sure that folks saw her doing errands around town.

Her other business was the sort of thing that could be conducted in the evenings. *Late* evenings, if need be, which was often the case. Besides, it was word of mouth only—and her clients were very, very discreet. They passed her name along only to their most trusted—and desperate—friends. After all, they had as much reason to keep things quiet as she did. More, most of them.

"So I hear," she said, cool as she could. She felt little prickles of sweat pop along her hairline but resisted the urge to wipe them away. Fussing like that was a good way to signal you were thinking something you didn't want to let on—Stella had learned that from the online course.

"What about when men are the ones dishing it out?" Goat asked. Same steady gaze.

Stella shrugged. "Wouldn't know."

She looked straight at him and carefully blinked twice while she told this whopper of a lie. That same criminology course had advised that people who didn't blink at all might be lying, concentrating a little too hard at looking you in the face.

Although this might be a pointless lie. It wasn't exactly an iron-clad secret that Ollie had taken out his frustrations on her for the better part of her marriage. Neighbors heard sounds coming from the house, friends noticed the bruises, and even the most taciturn talked eventually.

Of course, lots of folks had talked when Stella went up in front of the judge, back when Goat was still just a deputy sheriff all the way over in Sedalia, and it was Burt Knoll who had answered a call from the neighbors and found Stella sitting in this very living room next to the body of her husband, wrench still in her hand.

Every person in town knew that Ollie was a wife beater, and plenty of them were prepared to say that he'd always been a cowardly bully, as well. The judge finally had to turn away the flood of would-be character witnesses who'd swear they'd seen Ollie kick a dog or backhand Stella in the car as they pulled out of the church lot after Sunday services. The judge did allow several to testify they'd clearly heard Ollie threaten to kill his wife.

But Stella was willing to bet that Goat didn't know everything. One of the holy commandments of small-town living was that newcomers weren't privy to local gossip, even if it was acknowledged truth. So he probably had to do a little guesswork to fill in the gaps. For all Stella knew, he was still wondering why old Judge Ligett had dismissed the case and sent her home in time for *Jeopardy*.

"All right then." Goat turned back to Chrissy. "Can you give me the exact date of this fight?"

Chrissy thought about it for a few moments. "No, I can't," she said apologetically. "It was probably a Friday, 'cause Roy Dean does his more serious drinking on Fridays, and I guess it was probably in April, but I don't know beyond that."

"Well now, Easter was, let's see, I believe it was on April twelfth. Was it before Easter or after? You remember that?"

Chrissy put on a look of tremendous concentration, pinching her bottom lip between her thumb and forefinger. "Well . . . we went to Easter dinner at Roy Dean's folks' place and I don't remember him being busted up in the face then, so I guess it must have been after."

"So that leaves, uh, Friday the twenty-fourth, and then you're into May. May first's a Friday. You think it was the twenty-fourth?"

More thinking. Chrissy's brow wrinkled with intense concentration. "Oh, Sheriff, I just don't know. I'm sorry, sir."

Goat reached over and patted her knee awkwardly. "That's all right, hon," he said gently.

Stella noticed the gesture with surprise. Goat was hardly a warm and fuzzy creature. She had never heard him use any form of endearment before, but maybe Chrissy's pathetic expression had swayed the stubborn man. A point for their team.

"And you're sure you don't know who he might have seen that night?"

"No."

"Do you think his brother Arthur would have been there?"

"Well, maybe. Sometimes they'd go together, sometimes not. You know how brothers are. Sometimes Roy Dean'd get mad at him for some silly little thing and not talk to him for a day or two."

Goat scribbled in his pad a little more. "How about since then? Any more fights? Did you overhear any arguments, maybe on the phone?"

"No, nothing like that," Chrissy said, a little too quickly.

Stella guessed she knew what that meant. Usually women came to her when there had been an uptick in the abuse heaped on them by their men. Sometimes there was a huge confrontation, but more often it was just that the abuse became more and more frequent until the women never had time to recover in between, to convince themselves that it was worth sticking around, that they'd imagined how bad it was, that things would change. In the end, one last straw, usually not so different from those that came before, would be the one that broke the camel's back and sent them to Stella's doorstep.

She peeked at Goat and saw he'd knit his eyebrows together in a look of consternation; Chrissy's quick denial hadn't got past the man.

Stella also noticed, before she had a chance to stop herself, that Goat had some fine-looking eyebrows: for a man who was out of the hair business on the top of his head, he'd got him some nice thick all-business brows with a rakish slant to them that made him look like the close cousin of a handsome devil.

Goat caught her looking. Winked at her.

Winked! Just when Stella figured she had a handle on the man, he'd go and do something like that, shake her foundations. Maybe that was his goal, to get her flummoxed enough that she'd let her guard down. As Stella blushed, he turned back to Chrissy.

"Any change in his work habits?"

"Well . . . I don't think so. I mean him and Arthur Junior been helping their dad on a job at Parkade Elementary School over in Colfax. It's a big job, so he's been gone regular, and he doesn't call me during he day less he needs something."

"Arthur Junior still on that job?"

"I guess."

"You haven't talked to him since Roy Dean left?"

"No . . . me and Arthur Junior, we don't get along so good. I can't ever think what to say around him. I don't guess he much likes me."

Stella narrowed her eyes. That was news to her, news she would have preferred Chrissy save for later. She coughed lightly, trying to signal to Chrissy to put a sock in it.

Goat didn't seem to notice. "I'll talk to him. What about their folks? Mr. and Mrs. Shaw. Have you talked to them?"

"No sir. I just usually wait until I see them. We go over for Sunday dinner once a month or so, and his mom and I catch up then. Roy Dean sees his dad on the job most days."

"But didn't his dad call around looking for Roy Dean yesterday when he didn't show up for work?"

"Well . . ." This time Chrissy glanced at Stella before answering. "See, it's not all *that* unusual . . . if Roy Dean or Arthur Junior take a day off here and there. . . . They cover for each other, you know? If one of them is feeling poorly or something like that?"

Stella couldn't help it—she rolled her eyes heavenward. Feeling poorly—yeah, she could guess what that was about. She had plenty of her own mornings when she was feeling that brand of poorly. *She,* however, went and opened up the shop, hangover or no. She didn't give herself a day off as a reward for misbehaving the night before.

Goat evidently got the drift. He gave those eyebrows a bit of a workout and cleared his throat.

"I see. Okay, why don't you tell me a little bit about your boy. Tucker, was it?"

"Oh, yes. Here, I got pictures." Chrissy sat up straight in her chair and grabbed her purse off the table. She dug in it and found a cheap little plastic flip book and handed it to Goat.

He paged through the book, taking a few moments over each photo. "Well, if he isn't a little dickens," Goat said, smiling, and Chrissy brightened.

He handed the book to Stella. Tucker was adorable, a big, chubby-handed baby who was laughing in nearly every picture. He had his mother's wide blue eyes and silky pale hair.

Stella glanced over at the fireplace mantel, where she still kept one of Noelle's baby pictures; her daughter had been a big, happy baby too, a good sleeper and nearly always contented.

Funny how they turned out.

Stella turned back to the conversation and noticed that Goat was watching her. "That your daughter in that picture?" he asked.

Stella nodded. She didn't plan to say anything more on the subject, but to her surprise she suddenly *couldn't* say any more, because her throat closed up and her eyes stung. Well, it was no wonder, was it, what with all this talk about missing kids.

Of course, Noelle was twenty-eight now, and she wasn't exactly *missing*; she just wasn't speaking to her mother.

"Tucker's eighteen months and thirteen days old," Chrissy said. "I got his fingerprints done at the Home Depot on Safe Kids Day. You want me to go home and get the card?"

Goat snapped his notebook shut and slid his pen into the ring binding. "Well, I don't see any need for that just now, Chrissy. I don't want you to worry too much about Roy Dean and Tucker just yet. There's all kinds of reasons why he might be gone, hear, and you've given me lots of ideas for where to look for him."

"You're going to start right now?" The longing in Chrissy's voice tugged at Stella's heart; the girl was desperate enough to get her baby back that she was eager to launch a hunt for her no-good husband.

"Might as well. I'll be in touch soon's I find out anything. You think of something, or hear from him, you call me." He stood, unfolding his lanky legs like a carpenter's rule, and took a card from his pocket and laid it on the coffee table in front of Chrissy. After a moment's hesitation, he laid a second one in front of Stella. "I suppose you might as well have one too."

He gave her that same long, studied, know-too-much look before he threw in a grin, nodded to Chrissy, and made his way to the door. Stella stood and watched him warily. "Thanks for coming so quick," she said.

"Anytime." He shut the front door with care, holding the handle so it wouldn't slam. Through the screen Stella and Chrissy listened to him start up his department-issue Charger and drive off.

"Well," Stella said uncertainly. "I guess that went about as well as it could have."

"He sure is *tall*," Chrissy said, "for a sheriff."

"Why, you known any short ones?"

"Short what?"

"Sheriffs, hon." Stella's opinion of Chrissy was taking a turn for the dumber, and she was sorry to see it. Dumb wasn't going to help find Roy Dean any quicker. Still, it could just be the stress of the situation. Poor girl had a lot on her mind, and besides, talking to Goat did weird things to Stella's own brain, so she supposed she shouldn't judge Chrissy too harshly.

"Oh! No. Well, there was Sheriff Knoll, of course, and he was about medium, I guess."

"Chrissy." Stella sat back down, scooted a little closer to Chrissy, and leaned in close. "This is important. What you told the sheriff, was that all true?"

Chrissy nodded. "Yes ma'am."

"Did you leave anything out?"

"You mean, like what he done to me lately? Yes, I guess I did." Chrissy lifted up her shirt, showed the shadow of a wide black-and-blue bruise that stretched across her rib cage. "He's got more careful about hitting me on the arms, 'cause sometimes it showed. Done this one with his fist though. And got me right above the butt, too, here."

"All since that fight in the bar?"

Chrissy sighed. "Yes, these ones . . . they're taking their time fading. I never do heal up very quick. But before that it kind of seemed like things might be looking up a bit, you know?"

Stella didn't say it, but she remembered well. How you'd go a week or two, a month, sometimes maybe three with nothing. Start thinking things had changed, that your man wasn't really so different from other guys, that he'd just come through a bad patch, that was all. That if you were just a little extra careful, a little more attentive, it would be different this time.

Until one day he saw fit to remind you.

"Okay. Well now, look. I want you to go on home and try not to worry, just like the sheriff says. If he calls you, you tell him whatever he wants to know. But then you call me up and tell me about it, hear?"

Chrissy nodded, only a little wobbly. "I just want Tucker back. I'll do anything to get Tucker."

"Me too, sweetheart. And I'm going to work hard to make that happen. We'll get your boy. But if Roy Dean comes back too, then we're going to be right back where we started. And we need to make sure that you're still ready to do what needs done. Do you follow what I'm saying?"

"Yes, ma'am. We're gonna whup Roy Dean's ass."

For the first time that day, Stella managed a smile. "That's right," she said. "That's the spirit."

THREE

. . . .

By the time Stella pulled into the Parkade Elementary parking lot, the day had moved into asphalt-melting, breezeless midafternoon. The place looked to be locked down tight as a drum, but there were a few cars in the lot, and Stella figured the handful of teachers and administrators still hanging around during summer vacation had themselves barricaded in with the air-conditioning.

Over at the far end of the parking lot was a white pickup with SHAW PAINTING spelled out in a mostly straight line in black stick-on lettering. It wasn't a bad-looking truck, maybe six or eight years old, with a recent-enough wash. A nice Dee Zee aluminum toolbox was bolted in the bed, and a utility rack had a variety of tools and ladders lashed to it, neat and orderly. Stella's dad always said you could tell a lot about a man's character by looking at his workshop. If he didn't respect his tools, according to Buster Collier, then he likely didn't respect himself either, and you could forget about him respecting anyone else.

Well, this sure as hell wasn't Roy Dean's truck, then.

Stella got out, lugging her water bottle—she was trying to be mindful of staying hydrated in this heat, and she figured the iced tea had worn off by now—and leaving the gun behind in the box. She took a discreet sniff under her arm: not too bad, considering that this was one of those days when you're sweating two minutes after you get out of the shower. This meeting wasn't any beauty contest, of course; but the morning's encounter with the mirror had Stella in a self-conscious frame of mind.

Stella ignored the VISITORS, PLEASE CHECK IN AT THE MAIN OFFICE sign and started across the campus. In addition to the main building, there were several others, a two-story gymnasium and a science lab and a long, low shed labeled FUNBEARS AFTER-SCHOOL CARE.

It was around the far side of this last one that Stella found Arthur Senior, up on a ladder painting the trim a creamy color a few shades warmer than white. In contrast, the old paint looked dingy.

"That looks nice," Stella said. "Amazing what a fresh coat of paint can do."

Arthur set his paintbrush carefully down on the pan that was attached to the ladder, and backed his way down. Once his feet were on the ground he squinted at her and wiped his hands on a rag he kept attached to his belt, then offered it to shake.

"Stella Hardesty, isn't it?" he said.

"Yes sir. Good memory."

"Well, you've had your face in the paper in the last year or two, if I'm not mistaken."

"Oh, that." Stella could feel a flush rise to her face. That had been a close call; she'd been hailed a hero for dragging Phil Rivka out of his burning house. In truth, she'd intended only to torch the garage and Phil's treasured Camaro, the one he bought the day after he sent his wife, Irma, to the hospital with series of injuries requiring overnight observation.

Luckily, even Sawyer County's crack fire investigation squad hadn't figured out how Stella got the blaze started in the first place, which was a good thing. Stella had refined her technique since then, and there was no longer much risk of her killing herself or anyone else with a botched attempt.

Despite Stella's protests, photos of her and a very dejected-looking Phil had appeared not only in the local papers but all the way up in *The Kansas City Star.* Goat himself had called to congratulate her on her heroics. And to apologize for having been out on another call during the rescue. "If I'd been there," he'd said in that inscrutable voice of his, "maybe we'd have figured what got that fire started in the first place."

"Guess you're a bit of a hero," Arthur continued, but he sounded more wary than admiring.

"No, no, not me. Hey, I was wondering if Roy Dean or Arthur Junior were working with you today."

Arthur didn't answer right away. He took a tin of Skoal out of his pocket and slowly opened it, then just stared at the brown-black shreds of tobacco inside. Stella stared right along with him.

Nowadays you couldn't find many fans of chew. Every doctor's office in the county had warnings posted—mouth cancer, throat cancer. And Lord knows the spitting and the chewing were nasty, vile habits; the black bits stuck between the teeth didn't do much for a guy's appeal.

But Stella had a soft spot for the stuff. Her dad used to treat himself to a chew now and then, out on the back steps where her mother wouldn't have to watch, and Stella's own first sweetheart kept a tin in the glove box of his truck, hidden from his parents. He'd have a chew sometimes after football practice when he and Stella went for drives in the country.

"Er, do you mind . . . ," Arthur said.

"No, no, go ahead."

Arthur took a healthy pinch between his forefinger and thumb, and tucked it expertly in the pocket between his cheek and gum. For a moment he closed his eyes and concentrated on the tobacco. Then he opened his eyes and breathed a sigh that conveyed a world-weariness far beyond his fifty or so years.

"Neither of my boys is working here today," he said.

"They take the day off?"

"Well, now, we don't really do like that. Wish I could say different, but the boys got themselves all involved in these side businesses of theirs, and I'm lucky to have them along more than a day or two a week."

"Side businesses? How do you mean?"

"Oh, this and that. Arthur Junior, he got on part-time at the Wal-Mart Tire Center, and he's been doing a program up at ITT on the weekends. You know, all the electronics they got in the cars these days, you practically have to have a degree in computer science to work on them."

"What about Roy Dean?"

Arthur didn't look at her but gazed out across the parking

lot to the fields beyond. Alfalfa, lush and low-growing, poked its purple-flowered stems toward the blistering sun. "Well, you know, Roy Dean, he's always got some idea or other. Last year he got himself hooked up with this multilevel marketing outfit. Nothing but a pyramid scheme, really. That didn't end up all that well, and we had words. Now he don't much tell me what he has going on."

Stella noted the sad note in Arthur's voice. Recognized it all too well.

"I understand," she said. "My daughter, Noelle and me, we don't talk much either. We had a falling-out, I guess you'd say, after her dad passed, and now she just lives thirty miles away in Coffey, but sometimes I feel like it might as well be the moon."

Arthur pursed his lips together and nodded slightly, and the two of them stood there in a silence that was plenty melancholy, but not uncomfortable: just two parents wondering where they'd gone wrong.

"I guess they just have to go their own way," Arthur finally said. "How old's your girl?"

"She just turned twenty-eight in July."

"Arthur Junior's thirty. Roy Dean's twenty-seven. . . . You know, when we were that age, we were settled down, raising kids. I think Gemma's about given up on having any grandkids."

"Oh, now," Stella said soothingly, "don't let's give up yet. You know the kids nowadays. They like to wait before they have children. Besides, what about little Tucker? Chrissy's boy?"

A smile flashed across Arthur's ruddy features, crinkling all the wrinkles around his eyes and his mouth and making him look ten years younger. "Ain't he a pistol? Aw, Gemma and I took such a shine to him."

"Eighteen months old, I think Chrissy told me."

"Yeah." The smile slipped, and the light flickered out of Arthur's gaze. "Thing is, those two, Roy Dean and Chrissy, they don't get on so well. I think Gemma's trying not to get attached, you know? If Chrissy goes back to her ex, why, she's not likely to bring the little guy around anymore, see."

"Her ex?"

"You know, that Akers boy, from up around Sedalia."

"But they've been divorced for years."

"Uh, well, the way I hear it, he didn't want the divorce. He's been after her all this time. They say . . ." He cleared his throat but didn't look at her directly. "They say he used to get a little *rough* with her."

Stella wasn't sure what to say to that.

"I don't mean to speak out of turn," Arthur said quickly, "and I know my boy's not easy to live with. Why, if Chrissy's been . . . *visiting with* the Akers boy, on account of Roy Dean being away from the home so much, it wouldn't be my place to blame her."

"Arthur," Stella began, then stopped, not sure how to say what needed to be said. "I wonder if you've noticed, that is, when Chrissy comes to visit, you might have seen, well, all manner of bruises and such—"

"I *have,*" Arthur said, his voice going sharp. "And if it turns out that Akers boy put 'em on her, why, I'd like to reckon with him myself."

This time he did look at Stella, but it was only a quick glance with those troubled eyes.

It was possible the man really believed what he was saying.

It was also possible he suffered from the same disease that afflicted so many of the people Stella encountered: *denial*. Stella had battled denial herself long enough that she knew the pathology well, how it could really take a toll on a person as they struggled to keep believing the unbelievable.

If Arthur Shaw had convinced himself to ignore the facts in front of him, Stella wouldn't judge him for it. They say most violent men follow paths that get set early in their own lives, that they'd been abused themselves and knew little else. Well, Stella'd bet a hundred bucks that Arthur Shaw had never raised a hand to his boys in anger.

Sometimes it just worked out that way. Sometimes you did your level best with a child, gave them all the love and direction you knew how, and things still didn't work out the way you wanted.

Stella tried again, cautiously. "But you don't think Roy Dean—"

"Oh, Roy Dean's a trial," Arthur interrupted, turning away from Stella and picking up his paintbrush again. "But he wouldn't hurt a fly."

"Oh," Stella said. "Huh." She thought about mentioning some of the convincing details Chrissy had shared about Roy Dean, then decided Arthur had punished himself enough for one day.

"Ah, well," Arthur said, making his way up the ladder again. "Sorry I couldn't help you more."

"No, you were—you helped plenty," Stella said.

"Just one thing. It ain't Arthur Junior causing anybody trouble," Arthur said without looking at her, picking up his brush and dipping it carefully in the creamy paint. "He's a good boy, just gets a little distracted sometimes."

"I'll remember that. You have a good day, now."

As Stella made her way back to the car, her heart felt like it had got weighed down and rode a little lower in her chest. She hoped Arthur Junior, at least, would not give the quiet man on the ladder any more cause to live by the lies he told himself.

When Stella pulled up in front of her house, the sun was casting long shadows across the lawn, and Todd was doing skateboard tricks in her driveway.

"Hey, Stella, park out on the street," he called. "I want to use your driveway." He did some sort of flip that involved him leaping into the air with his skinny legs out at a comic angle while the skateboard flipped both over and around in a circle. When he landed, with a crash so loud it was miraculous the deck didn't split in half, Todd teetered for a moment and then fell on his behind.

"Ow! Shit!"

"Watch your mouth," Stella said, but she did as he asked and left the car in the street. Better to have him flopping around on her driveway, leaving patches of his skin on the concrete, than in the street getting run over. She walked over and glared at the boy, not bothering to offer to help him up.

Todd examined his palm, which was scraped red and crusted with old scabs.

"I reckon you ought to put some Neosporin on that," Stella said.

"You got any?"

"I might, but am I your personal nurse? I don't think so."

"Aw, come on, I don't want to have to go all the way back—"

"Todd, you live *two doors down,*" Stella said, pointing.

Todd shrugged and got to his feet, as graceful and light as a dancer, and jumped back on the board. He wore his hair down around his shoulders, but it looked as if he'd cut it himself, and maybe he had. His mother had more than enough on her plate.

"Well, you got anything to eat?" he asked, wiping his bloody hand on his baggy shorts.

Stella rolled her eyes. "I guess. Come on in."

"There's a lady in your house," Todd said. He toed the end of his skateboard, and it flipped up into his hand. Not a bad trick, really.

"Yeah? Leave that filthy thing outside and wipe your feet. What kind of lady?"

"Kind of fat, but not too fat. Blond hair. Giant boobs."

Chrissy.

Inside, Stella called out a hello—no sense spooking the poor girl. Found her in the same chair from the morning, but she'd fallen asleep. Startled awake, Chrissy pushed at the strands of corn-silk hair that had matted themselves to her face with sweat.

"How'd you manage the lock, sweetheart?" Stella asked.

"Oh, I showed her your key," Todd said. "You know, under the pot on the porch."

"Todd," Stella said sternly. She'd shown Todd the key last winter when she hired him to water her plants during a visit to see her sister Gracellen in California. "You do not give strangers my key. You don't let strangers into my house. Hear?"

"Yeah, well, I—"

"She could be anyone. You know, an axe murderer or something."

Todd looked dubious. "Her?"

Stella bit down her unease. It was true that Chrissy looked about as dangerous as a toy poodle. It was also true that Stella had always managed to keep the unseemlier aspects of her work away from her home, but the day might come when some disgruntled asshole came around looking for trouble. She grabbed Todd's arm hard and gave it a yank. He had already passed her up in height, but she had the advantage of mass and bulk.

"Hey!"

"Listen up, cupcake, or no snack. You don't ever let anyone in here without me saying so. And if you ever see anyone hanging around, you go straight home and lock your doors and don't be coming over here until you see me back here in person."

"Christ! Okay, okay," Todd said. When she released his arm he rubbed at it and glared at her. "Isn't it almost dinnertime, anyway? Maybe we should skip the snack and have pizza or something."

Stella stared at the boy, shaking her head slowly. "Your mom get hung up late again?"

"Yeah, she called. She's got to pick up the twins at day care so she won't be back for another hour at least."

"What's for dinner?" Chrissy said, her voice sleepy. "And did you find anything out yet?"

Stella looked at the pair of them, back and forth, and wondered why the Big Guy had seen fit to deliver these pathetic, hungry souls to her house, when all she wanted was to put her

67

feet up and fix herself a giant Johnnie Walker Black on ice. Well, there was no rest for the weary, was there?

"Papa Martino's," she said. "You call 'em, Todd. Coupon's on the fridge. Get a large. Half combo and half whatever you want. Oh, get a dozen wings too, extra spicy."

"Fuckin' A!"

"And watch your damn mouth!"

While they waited for the pizza, Todd went back out on the driveway to flip his lanky, awkward body over the skateboard some more.

"I believe I'll go watch him some," Chrissy said, rolling forward off the couch. "He's something to see, ain't he?"

"Hold up there just a sec, hon," Stella said, settling down on the ottoman. "I've got something to ask you. Something of a personal nature."

"Sure," Chrissy said, bobbing her chin.

"It has to do with your ex," Stella said carefully. "Pitt . . ."

"Oh," Chrissy said, her face going a little pale. "It's that damned Internet, ain't it."

"The . . . Internet?"

"I tol' Pitt don't be takin' them dirty pictures, seein' as they always end up on the Internet."

"Pitt . . . took pictures of you?'

"Yeah, dirty ones." Chrissy sighed. "I didn't mention it 'cause I didn't figure it was, you know, important. And it ain't, neither—if I get Tucker back I guess I don't even care what-all anyone wants to put on the Internet about me."

"Um . . . were these, ah, recent pictures?"

Chrissy shrugged. "Well, yeah, I guess. I mean it was like, I don't know, March probably."

"You've been seeing Pitt."

Chrissy shrugged. "Not regular or anything. Just, you know, sometimes."

Stella heaved a sigh. "You know, back when you first came to talk to me, I told you that I had to know everything. Remember? Don't leave anything out, I told you, because every detail counts, even the ones that might not seem important at the time. Well, I surely wish I wasn't only finding out about Pitt now."

"I'm sorry," Chrissy said, staring down at her hands. "It's just . . . I didn't want you to think I was . . ."

She swallowed and Stella could see her eyelashes fluttering.

". . . a slut," she finished in a whisper.

Stella's annoyance shrank up to see the girl so remorseful. "Oh, wait, I'm not trying to judge here. I don't think that, I really don't. Only, it's been suggested that, uh, Pitt was the one who hurt you."

"Pitt?" The tremulous note in Chrissy's voice gave way to a snort of disbelief. "Pitt ain't but five foot three on a good day and a hunnert twenty. 'Sides, he wouldn't never hurt me. He's crazy about me. We'd prob'ly still be married if I hadn't taken up with his boss."

Stella nodded, trying to assimilate all these new details. "How'd Pitt feel about Roy Dean? And Tucker?"

"Well, he pretty much hated Roy Dean," Chrissy said. "Always threatening to come to the house one day and blow him away. And Tucker—well, he thinks Tucker might be his, even though I've told him a million times I was seeing someone else, and besides, anyone can see Tucker's going to grow up twice as big as Pitt. Ain't no way they're kin."

Stella felt a chill along her neck. Enraged boyfriend, denied not only his woman but the child he believes is his . . . men had certainly committed crimes for far less.

"People see what they want to see, sometimes," she said.

Chrissy's expression sharpened up. "Stella," she said dubiously, "you ain't actually thinking it was *Pitt* stole Tucker, are you?"

"Well . . . you said he went missing right after Roy Dean was at your house so—"

"But Pitt was there too. I mean, I'm really sorry I didn't tell you about it, but Pitt was over visiting that morning, and when Tucker fell asleep in his playpen Pitt 'n me went back to my room for a spell . . . and when Roy Dean came to the door, Pitt hightailed it to the guest bedroom to hide out."

Stella bit back another scolding. Honestly, the girl tried her patience.

"Is that it? Or is there anything else you need to tell me beside the fact that there was a *whole other person* present when Tucker disappeared?"

"I *said* I was sorry," Chrissy said.

"Yeah, okay . . . just . . . But why'd Pitt need to hide, considering that you and Roy Dean were split up? You're free to live your life any way you want now," Stella said.

"It's just what we did a couple times back when Roy Dean was still living at the house and he came home unexpected. I guess Pitt was still in the habit." Chrissy laid a hand over her heart. "Pitt's just a little sweetie, but he ain't the most ballsy man. He don't like confrontation."

Stella didn't bother to point out that desperation occasionally moved even un-ballsy men to act. "Was his car gone when you went outside looking for Tucker and Roy Dean?"

"He didn't have no car. He had a buddy drop 'im, and he was going to just walk back home. He's in those apartments over by the office park."

"Don't you think it's strange," Stella mused, "that he didn't call you later that day?"

"Well, I ain't got a cell phone."

"Or stop by? Just to make sure you were okay?"

"It wasn't like that, Stella," Chrissy said, crossly. "It was just casual."

It sounded to Stella like Pitt might not have considered it nearly as casual as Chrissy did.

"I'll go talk to Pitt," Stella said.

"Suit yourself," Chrissy said. Her mood was darkening by the moment. "But it's a waste of time, you ask me. It's Roy Dean we got to find. Maybe we ought to see what the sheriff thinks. Get up a search party or something."

"That's something to think about," Stella said, trying to hide her exasperation.

"But Stella . . . about them pictures. Can you do something?"

"Well, are they in digital format? Did Pitt put them on his PC? Does either of you have an Internet connection?"

"Ain't neither of us even got a computer, Stella. And they was Polaroids—Pitt likes watchin 'em develop."

"Well then, I wouldn't worry too much about them getting online. Listen, the pizza's going to be here in a minute. Why don't we eat—it'll help us think clearly."

As if on cue Todd came bursting through the door, trailing a young man in a Papa Martino's T-shirt who was carrying a suspiciously large thermal bag.

"Hope you don't mind," Todd said. "I ordered an extra pizza. I was hungry. You need to pay him. Don't forget the tip, okay?"

By the time she got the kitchen cleaned up and Todd sent home and Chrissy settled into the guest room, Stella could sense the prickles of a second wind starting along her spine.

Part of it was the whole bar thing, of course. Stella couldn't help it: she loved bars, loved the way folks came in and shed the first three-quarters of their day and settled into the final stretch, some of them weary, some of them desperate, some on the make, some—occasionally—even happy. Stella loved to sit on the sidelines and watch the squabbling and the mating rituals and the jealousy and the preening, the lively bubbling of humanity's stew.

She'd missed so much; Ollie never wanted her to go out at night. With his crazy jealous streak he didn't even like to let her wait on the very occasional male customer who came into the sewing machine shop. Since he died, Stella had decided she had some catching up to do, and she took herself out a couple times a month.

Tonight was a work outing, of course, but that didn't mean she couldn't have a little fun. She'd told Chrissy she was going to stop by Lovie Lee's divorce party, just to be polite. Lovie wasn't a client; she and Larry Lee had just grown tired of each other. Larry'd been living in the garage, which he'd fixed up with a waterbed and a couple of weight machines, for a few years. They were only making it official because Lovie had got tired of parking on the driveway. She wanted her garage back.

The party probably would have been fun, but duty came first.

Chrissy hadn't questioned Stella's lie—which Stella had told only because she didn't want to have to explain why her hunt for Tucker was starting out in a bar. She was afraid Chrissy might bring up the search party idea again. But deep in her melancholy funk, the girl just nodded and said she'd be fine, that Stella should go ahead and have a nice time.

Stella pushed the hangers back and forth in her closet, finally settling on a jazzy little teal number, a tank top with straps wide enough to cover her bra, which was a serious piece of equipment with a big job to do. The top had beads sewn along the neckline, a little sparkle to set off her earrings, which were a dangly crystal pair she'd got out of the Avon catalog Gracellen sent her.

She squeezed into her favorite jeans, which had a squiggly row of stitching on the butt pockets and molded everything into a tight-looking, if generous, package. She added slip-on black sandals with just a bit of a heel, sprayed herself with White Diamonds, and she was ready to go.

Stella peeked in on Chrissy, who was reading a copy of *Redbook* with the sheet pulled up to her neck. The fan in the window cranked along on high, cooling the bedroom down to a tolerable temperature.

"You gonna be all right, sugar?"

"Yeah, I guess. But every time I think about Tucker . . ." Chrissy's lips wobbled, and Stella was afraid she was going to bust out crying again. Earlier, it had taken half an hour to get her calmed down, and Stella needed to get on the road.

"Look here, honey," she said, sitting down on the edge of the bed and patting Chrissy's arm. "I'm doing everything I know to figure out where they've got to. And even if Roy Dean's a son of a bitch, you know he won't do nothing bad to Tucker."

Chrissy nodded, and Stella prayed hard she had just spoken the truth.

"Sheriff Jones is good at his job," she continued. "He'll be looking in the places I can't. And tomorrow, we're going to keep you busy at the shop, so now you've just got to put it out of your mind, and get some rest, right?"

Putting Chrissy to work had been one of Stella's better ideas: not only would it give the girl something to do, but it would free Stella up to work on tracking down Roy Dean and Pitt Akers. She didn't want to admit it, even to herself, but as the hours ticked by she was getting more and more worried about Tucker. Get a bunch of stupid assholes together and the first things they were liable to let slide was the women and children. At least women had a fighting chance.

"Thank you," Chrissy snuffled. "I just couldn't go back home."

Stella understood; having to go back to the empty house, with all of Tucker's toys on the floor, his crib, would just make her crazy. Chrissy worked part-time at an in-home day care in her neighborhood, and she didn't want to go to work either, and Stella guessed she could understand that too. She wouldn't be much good to the other kids, frantic with worry. A quick call to Chrissy's employer had straightened that out.

Stella headed first for the apartments across the street from the Prosper Industrial Park, a sad L-shaped complex of prefab buildings that had never been fully occupied in its ten-year history. The apartments had been there even before the industrial park was built, and hence had time to accumulate a nearly full complement of divorcées and down-on-their-luck entrepreneurial types and drifters and general underachievers—anyone who found the idea of a cheap, boxlike one-bedroom apartment with drafty aluminum windows appealing.

She found Pitt's place easily enough in the last of the evening twilight. He had a ground-floor apartment on the back side, which enjoyed a fair amount of privacy on account of a bank of Dumpsters. After knocking and trying the door, Stella set down the Tupperware spaghetti tote she used to store her lock tools and shone her mini Maglite in the crack between the door and the frame, where indifferent construction had left a hair's-breadth gap.

"Oh, didn't your mama teach you nothing," she breathed—Pitt hadn't used the deadbolt. Stella was a little disappointed at the lack of a challenge; she'd spent a few recent slow afternoons at the shop making herself a set of shims using tin snips and some rinsed-out Bud cans, and she was eager to try them out.

Still, there were advantages to keeping it simple. Stella slipped her old Macy's card—long since canceled but kept for occasions like this one—into the door jamb. Then she slid a pair of quart-size Ziplocs over her hands and let herself in.

She stood for a moment in the living room, listening for sounds and glancing around. The door to the bedroom was open, and the cramped kitchen was visible through a pass-through. A shape darted past her, nearly giving her a heart attack, but as it bolted under the couch Stella realized it was just a cat.

She snapped on the lights. Illumination did little to improve the surroundings—scuffed white walls, dingy gray carpet, tired plaid sofas—but at least Pitt kept the place clean. There was no cat smell; Stella even detected a faint scent of Clorox. "Might oughtta have kept this one, Chrissy," Stella murmured as she started looking around. "Knows how to clean."

If she'd planned on any serious digging, she would have splurged and used a pair of disposable latex gloves from the box she kept under her bathroom sink, but they were so danged expensive compared to the Ziplocs. Worrying about fingerprints was probably ridiculous anyway; Stella highly doubted whether the crime scene techs would be coming down from the county seat in Fayette anytime soon to go looking for Tucker. Still, anything worth doing, as her dad used to say, was worth doing right.

There was little to see. Pitt, it appeared, had been leading a monklike existence since divorcing Chrissy, aside from his Polaroid collection, which Stella found in an envelope on his bureau. One glimpse convinced her she didn't need to see any more of that, but she slipped the packet into her pocket anyway—one less thing for Chrissy to worry about.

Other than the racy photos, scouring Pitt's place was about as exciting as watching paint dry. A couple of Costco uniform shirts hung in the closet. Tightie whities and V-neck T-shirts and over-the-calf athletic socks were neatly folded in the drawers. Pitt owned an impressive collection of household cleaners—409 *and* Windex, among other things—but nothing seemed out of place.

As she turned to leave, the cat appeared, one cautious paw at a time, from under the living room sofa, and stalked imperiously into the kitchen, where it lapped at a full water bowl. Watching the cat, Stella noticed something she'd missed earlier; there was not one but two very full bowls of cat food set out on a vinyl place mat on the floor. One had a small dent, a few of the little orange triangular nuggets having spilled to the floor, but the other was mounded high and undisturbed.

"Looks like your master wanted to make sure you had plenty to eat," Stella said, "while he was away. Where'd he go, anyway?"

No response. Typical. Stella left without saying good-bye, having confirmed that she was still a dog person; she wanted a pet that *interacted* a little.

So it looked like Pitt had left town for a while. Interesting.

Stella returned her spaghetti box to the back of the Jeep and hit the road, thinking that in the morning she'd have to try to find out where Pitt had gone. She made the drive to BJ's Bar with the window rolled down, despite the damage it did to her well-sprayed hairdo. Sometimes you just had to feel the wind on your face.

On her way from the parking lot to the front door, she patted her hair back into place and hitched up her bra straps, getting everything settled where it was supposed to go.

BJ's wasn't a place Stella visited unless it was in the line of duty. It was a little rough even for her. It wasn't that she was afraid; get the meanest cuss drunk, and his reflexes would go to hell and he'd be no match for her, especially with the Raven in her purse. It was just that it wasn't all that much fun to hang out in a place where optimism was in as short supply as overtime pay, tempers were thin, and old grievances lay thick on the ground.

Things went quiet when Stella walked in. She ignored the pool tables at the far end of the long, narrow room, the few square wooden tables where customers sat in twos and threes, and headed for an empty stool at the end of the bar near the bathrooms.

BJ's wasn't much to look at. You could tell before you put a hand on the bar or a table that it would come away sticky. Some of the wooden chairs didn't match, and the bar stools were popping their brass studs and losing the padding on their vinyl seats. The walls were decorated with an assortment of titty posters and neon beer signs, some lit, some busted. A single framed softball photo gave evidence that at some point Big Johnson had gotten it into his head to sponsor a team, an event that must have caused the league a fair amount of consternation.

Big Johnson himself wandered down the bar to greet Stella. There was a waitress on duty as well, but she was on the floor with a tray, plonking down pitchers and trying to avoid having her rear end pinched any more than was necessary.

"Stella," Big Johnson said, leaning his muscular, hairy forearms on the bar in front of him. Big Johnson had moved to town and bought this place after serving in the first Iraq dustup, and he already had his nickname then. Naturally there was some talk of whether it just referred to the fact that he was a solid 240 on a six-three frame, or whether there were further reasons, but if he'd shed any light on the question, Stella hadn't heard about it.

She might not have minded finding out for herself, actually. But there was that delicate issue of dating people in the workplace—and as long as Big Johnson kept attracting the kind of clientele that was hanging around the joint now, the bar was likely to continue to be on Stella's professional rounds.

"B.J., good to see you. Been a while."

"Yeah. Last time you were in here, lessee, you dragged out one of my best customers, and he don't come around no more."

Stella felt herself blushing, but she doubted he could tell in the dim light.

"Yes, well—I just wanted to give him his Christmas card. Forgot to mail it and I'd been carrying it around in my purse. You know how that goes. Far as him coming around here . . . well, I hear he's not partying much these days."

Big Johnson gave her a ghost of a smile and a twitch that might have been a wink. "Aw, we ain't missed him much. What're you drinking tonight?"

"Let's see." Stella pretended to think it over, tapping her nose with her forefinger and glancing along the shelves behind the bar. "Well now, I guess you better make it Johnnie Black with a Bud back."

Big Johnson went off to get the drinks, and Stella glanced down the row of drinkers at the bar. There he was, and she didn't even have to go chasing him down: Arthur Junior was keeping company with a brassy redhead, the two of them giggling over something, their noses almost touching. Interesting. Last Stella heard, Arthur Junior had hooked up with a gal from Ogden County, but she hadn't been a redhead. Oh, well, he was known to have quite a few smooth moves; probably the reason Gemma Shaw despaired of having any grandchildren off him anytime soon.

Any *legitimate* grandchildren, that is.

Big Johnson came back with the drinks and set them down in front of Stella. "You know," he said, clearing his throat and looking somewhere over her shoulder, "I don't believe I ever got your Christmas card either, now that you mention it."

Stella raised an eyebrow. Could it be? Was Big Johnson actually *flirting* with her? Her stomach did a little back-and-forth slide, and she felt heat rise to her face. The light was mercifully low: one of life's funny truths is that the worse the lighting in a bar, the better a lady tends to look.

"Oh." Nice—*idiot,* she scolded herself, but couldn't for the life of her think of what else to say.

"Yeah . . .'course, I didn't send any myself, this year. You know, the holidays snuck up on me and what-all, had my brother's family come stay . . ."

Big Johnson trailed off and cleared his throat again, backed off the bar, and still didn't look her in the face.

"What I mean to say, though," he said, grabbing a rag off the sink and taking a wild swipe at the stretch of bar in front of him, "was that if I *did* send cards, I woulda sent you one."

Then he was off, practically jogging down the bar to where customers were hollering for him.

Well. Dang. Now that was interesting. Stella took a biggish sip of her whiskey and then a nice long cool drink of her beer, the foam tickling her upper lip. There was something going on with B.J., that was for sure.

It was nice. But it wasn't quite exactly the mmm-hmmm-yeah that generally signaled powerful attraction to Stella.

She thought about it some more. Waited a few minutes to see if a reaction was just sneaking up on her. But no: Big Johnson, sweet as he was, didn't light any roaring fires under her. Which was just too darn bad, because there wasn't exactly an abundance of suitors lining up at her door.

Truth was, ever since Ollie died, Stella had been pretty reluctant even to think about men—except for the ones whose skulls she was knocking together, of course. Those thirty years of paying for a single grievous mistake in the man department had put her off her feed a bit.

But . . . it *had* been three years. Long enough for even Stella's rusty, ill-used parts to start clamoring to get put to use again. Hell, she was a grown woman; there shouldn't be any shame to admitting, at least to herself, that she'd started thinking about sex again. Checking out butts at the Home Depot, spotting an appealingly crooked smile or a snazzy goatee or a nice tan . . . harmless, right?

Unfortunately, there was only one man in a hundred miles in any direction that really got her engines purring, and that was—damn it—the one man who was absolutely, positively, off-limits, the one who could send her world upside down and not in a good way—the kind of way that would have her serving time at the Sawyer County jail up in Fayette.

"Hey, Mrs. Hardesty."

Stella jerked out of her reverie and turned to face the man who had spoken to her. Well, well.

"Hello, Arthur Junior."

"Dad said he saw you out on the job."

"Yes—yes, I did bump into him there." Stella turned to Arthur Junior's companion, who was standing behind him looking bored and teetering on her spike-heeled sandals. It appeared that Arthur Junior's date was accustomed to deficits in his manners, but Stella believed in starting every relationship off on the right foot. "Hello, dear. I'm Stella Hardesty. My, you have lovely hair."

That got the gal's attention. She lifted her chin and flashed a smile. Had a darling little gap between her front teeth, nice skin, a smattering of freckles. "Hello, ma'am. I'm Silver Mason. Pleased to meet you."

Ouch—that goddamn "ma'am." When was that word going to ease on out of the language?

"Mason . . . would that be the Masons out Route 12? I went to school with a couple of the girls."

"No, sorry, I'm from Saint Louis. I came out here for work. I'm an intensive care nurse over at Lutheran."

Arthur Junior frowned impatiently. "I just figured I should find out what your interest in the family was, Mrs. Hardesty."

"Well now, Arthur Junior, I wouldn't say it's the whole family, exactly, just your brother Roy Dean. He seems to have gone missing, and I was wondering if there was any chance he might've taken something along with him that doesn't belong to him."

The cast of Arthur Junior's expression shifted, and Stella could see plain as day that a variety of emotions were doing battle on his face. A twitchy little tic appeared at the edge of his jaw, and his eyes narrowed to slits. After a few moments he turned to Silver.

"Darlin', I'm afraid this is going to take a few minutes. Just some boring business shit. Would you mind if I talked to Mrs. Hardesty alone for a bit?"

Silver gave him a sunny smile. "Oh, that's fine. I'll go watch the darts for a bit."

They watched her walk away. Silver had a nice little figure, a narrow waist and ample curves; for a fleeting moment Stella felt wistful remembering the long-ago time when she could still sashay her way to a man's attention.

"You might think about hanging on to this one," she said. "Looks nice, talks nice, gainfully employed . . ."

"Yeah. So listen, I don't know what my dumb-fuck brother's gone and done now, hear? I've got no part of his dealings. He stopped showing up on Dad's job about a month ago, won't answer my calls or nothing. Hell, he hasn't even been out for Sunday dinner, and Mom's about to hit the roof. To be honest, Mrs. Hardesty, I ain't seen him for two, three weeks now."

Stella evaluated Arthur Junior. She was inclined to believe him. The criminology course said she should look for facial tics, perspiration, and fidgeting—all things that were tough to see in a dark bar.

"Now, Arthur Junior, there's a chance you could be lying to me, sweetie, and I'd have no way of knowing it. I wonder if I mentioned that the thing Roy Dean took off with is needed in the worst way by a friend of mine. No, now, I'm not saying you know anything about this mess—and I'm not saying you don't. You may have heard . . . when it comes to my friends, I take their needs pretty seriously."

The faint little flicker in Arthur Junior's eyes clued Stella in: he'd heard. She didn't know how much he knew, but it looked like it was enough. There were days when it paid to have rumors floating around about how you'd ruined a numbskull's day with a bit of old-fashioned violent reckoning.

"I hear you, Mrs. Hardesty." Arthur Junior bit his lip but didn't take his eyes off her face. "What is it you think Roy Dean took?"

Stella considered her options. She generally had a policy against revealing any of the facts of a case unless absolutely necessary. And given her new information about Pitt Akers, along with Roy Dean's general lack of affection for Tucker, it almost didn't seem worth stirring up a fuss over such a long shot. Still, time was critical, and she couldn't see any reason not to get as many eyes looking out for Tucker as possible.

"A little boy," she said. "Chrissy's boy, Tucker."

Arthur Junior said nothing for a moment. It clearly wasn't the answer he expected to hear. He frowned, the lines appearing on his forehead making him look a lot like his father.

"Why would he go and do *that*?"

"I really don't know. I'm just trying to connect with anyone who was with Tucker right before he disappeared. And your brother was there, at Chrissy's, picking up some belongings he'd left."

Arthur Junior took a deep breath and let it out real slow. He stared off at Silver, who was chatting with a couple of local gals over by the dartboard; then turned and looked back down the bar at the assembly of drinkers.

"Look here, maybe we better go somewhere else to talk. Let me just get rid of Silver. If I give her my keys, can you run me home after?"

The evening was shaping up to be full of surprises. "That would be no problem, Arthur Junior," Stella said.

While he left to make his arrangements, she sucked down

the rest of the whiskey and beer. Didn't make any sense to waste it.

"Anywhere particular you got in mind to go?" Stella asked, once they pulled out of Big Johnson's parking lot in the Jeep.

"Yeah. Head out Old State Road Nine."

"You gonna clue me in where we're headed?"

"In a bit."

Stella nodded to herself and drove along, well within the speed limit. She was drive-safe, her BAC adequately low due to her sizable frame and the big dinner she'd had and a tolerance maintained with a healthy daily dose of Johnnie Black, but there was still no sense calling attention to herself.

A bright slice of moon lit up the road with a soft glow.

"I'm older than Roy Dean by two years," Arthur Junior said after a while. "Bigger, too. Taller, at any rate. But do you know, by the time I was ten Roy Dean would sneak up on me and take me down when I wasn't lookin'."

Stella nodded. Now the boy had decided to talk, it was best to let him unroll his story at his own pace.

"Now that's the kind of thing you just hate when you're a kid. Specially if your friends know about it, getting your ass kicked by your kid brother. So I made it a project to beat the crap out of him. And you know what? I never did. See here?"

Stella glanced over; Arthur Junior had pushed up his short sleeve to reveal his shoulder, but Stella couldn't make much out in the dim light in the Jeep. "Hmm," she said anyway.

"Fucking *bite* marks. I got him down, got his arm pulled

behind him one day, had half a mind to break it I was so mad, and he bit me. Mom wanted to take me to the hospital, but Dad said I was just going to have to learn to fight back. Now that was plenty humiliating, let me tell you. And Roy Dean just standing there grinning at me the whole time."

"Your folks didn't punish him?"

"Well, sure they did, but the thing was, wasn't much you could do to Roy Dean that would make any kind of difference. I think they took him off TV for a month, but he didn't care—he just invented new kinds of trouble to stir up. When he got bored, Roy Dean used to sit out back on this split-rail fence Dad built behind the vegetable garden, and when a rabbit or something would come by he'd shoot it with his slingshot. He wasn't much of a shot, but he just kep' at it and kep' at it, and now and then he'd get lucky and hit one. Thing'd drag itself off and Roy Dean would follow, and if he caught up, he'd stomp the thing dead with his boots. I'll say one thing for my brother—he ain't got a lot of quit in him."

Stella thought of little Tucker and got a very bad feeling in her gut. On the off chance that Roy Dean *had* taken him, she prayed he was keeping his temper under control.

"Arthur Junior, I gotta tell you, you're not painting a very pretty picture of your brother. But what would he want with a little boy that isn't even his?"

"I have no idea," he said, "and that's the truth."

"You could have told me that back at BJ's," Stella pointed out. "Not to sound ungrateful, but if you don't know where Roy Dean is, there's other holes I could be digging in. Why exactly did you want to go for this here drive?"

"Because I believe I know where Roy Dean has been spending his time lately, and it ain't no kindygarden, see what I'm sayin'? It's bad news, serious bad news—no place to be haulin' kids into. If Chrissy's kid *is* with Roy Dean, then somebody needs to do something."

"Jeez, just what is this place anyway? Some kind of strip joint?"

"I believe I'll just show you. Turn off on Methaney there."

Stella glanced at Arthur Junior; his arms were folded across his chest and he had an angry set to his jaw. She did as she was told.

She hadn't driven Methaney in years. A couple of decades ago, someone still farmed soybeans out here, but the soil didn't give up much, and the fields lay mostly unworked and fallow, sowthistle and carpetweed taking over.

"Drive slow," Arthur Junior said, his voice a near whisper, "and don't stop."

After a half mile or so, they drove by a hand-painted wood sign that hung by chains from a couple of posts driven into the ground next to a gravel turnoff. In big block letters, it read BENNING SALVAGE. Five yards into the turnoff, a tall set of steel gates was locked tight with a heavy padlock.

"Oh," Stella said. "The junkyard. That's what you wanted to show me?"

"Ain't just a junkyard," Arthur Junior said, his voice low. "Drive on by, and when you get down to the T down there, turn around and come back. But don't stop, hear? Don't be lingerin'."

The boy was spooked, that was for sure. Wasn't any way anyone could hear them out here, but Stella didn't bother to point that out. Driving past the property, she spotted lights on in a little prefab house up on a berm shaded by a couple of twisty scrub oaks. A few pickups and sedans were parked out front. Further back on the property, sodium vapor lights on blocky steel poles illuminated other buildings and sheds. And beyond that, cars—acres of cars in various states of body condition and decomposition, skeletons of wrecks and rusting carcasses whose innards were being stripped a little at a time to patch up other cars. All along the edges of the property ran a chain-link fence topped by razor wire. Nasty to look at, especially since some of the barbs caught the moonlight just right and glinted shiny and menacing.

She figured there was a mean dog or two not far off. It wasn't just junkyards that had them—in Stella's experience every family compound out in the sticks had a few flea-bitten curs, bred to meanness with stick beatings and fights over scraps of garbage. When one got hit by a car or lost a fight or mangled a leg on a trap or fence and had to be put down, there was always some scrawny mutt bitch around ready to deliver a new generation of hardscrabble pups.

She turned back to Arthur Junior. "I knew a Benning or two. One of 'em was just a few years behind me in school."

"That woulda been Earl. He's probably about forty-five—he's owned the place since his dad passed. But he has a partner. You know—an associate. Don't know his full name but he goes by Funzi. Comes down from Kansas City with some of his guys and stays for a few days now and then; I think he has a place down on the lake."

"*Funzi*? What is that, Italian or some such?"

Arthur drilled her with that gaze again, and this time Stella did turn and look at him. In the moonlight his face looked pale as milk, his eyes deep sockets. And the boy looked scared shitless. "Uh-huh. Italian, like Alphonse. Mrs. Hardesty, you know what Italian means up in Kansas City, don't you?"

Stella made the turn, a gentle curve on the scruffy remains of a farm road, and started back. The junkyard was on the driver's side of the Jeep now, and she watched carefully as it rolled by. No signs of life anywhere, but the light in the windows of Benning's house showed sheer curtains pulled shut. A blue flicker from one window probably meant a TV. Big one, no doubt—seemed like the humbler the dwelling, the fancier the TV these days.

"What are you trying to say, Arthur Junior? Benning's mixed up with some sort of Cosa Nostra shit? The Family comin' down here to the Ozarks for a little R and R?"

"It ain't funny." Arthur Junior's voice was suddenly sharp. "You don't mess with those boys."

"I didn't say it was funny, but you got to admit—I mean, I've never seen any godfather types around town, you know? Haven't been any horse heads turning up in folks' beds or anything like that."

She could feel Arthur Junior's gaze fixed solid on her face. "If you get to tangling with these guys, you'd damn well better be as good as they say you are," he said coldly. "You have no notion what they're capable of. I told Roy Dean, I begged him not to get mixed up with these guys, but he just can't say no to a quick buck, not ever."

Stella didn't say anything until the junkyard was in her rearview mirror, and then she put a little steel in her voice, just like she used to when Noelle was a teenager sassing her about one thing or another.

"Now listen here, Arthur Junior. Unless Roy Dean took Tucker, there's no reason for me to do so much as give Benning and his pals a cross-eyed glance. I'm real sorry your brother ain't got a lick of sense, but he's not the one that hired me, so I'm not going to go rattling any cages just for kicks."

"I didn't say—"

"So if you know anything about Tucker you aren't telling me, any reason I should worry about him and Roy Dean, then you need to come clean and tell me exactly what's going on. Won't do anybody any good for you to keep giving me these little pieces of the picture, hear? Otherwise, your brother's a big boy—he's on his own."

"I don't know anything about Tucker, like I said," Arthur Junior said, his voice flat and resigned. "Only . . . maybe you could just listen to me and, I don't know . . . give Roy Dean some advice, or, or, like *convince* him, maybe . . ."

Stella glanced at the dashboard clock: after eleven already. There was no way she was hiring on to talk sense into a blockhead like Roy Dean—she knew firsthand how futile such an effort would be. Still . . . she was a little bit moved by Arthur Junior's fraternal loyalty. Sticking up for a sibling like that—well, that showed character. And character was rare enough that it might merit a few more minutes of her time.

Heading back to a bar to finish this conversation didn't make much sense, though, and that only left one place she could think of. She turned back on Old State Road 9 toward town.

If Arthur Junior was surprised to end up at Denny's, he

didn't show it. Stella had the hostess seat them in a corner booth away from the handful of other customers. When the waitress came, Stella waved the menus away and ordered them both a Grand Slam and coffee. Any remnants of her earlier buzz were long gone, and she meant to ensure that she and Arthur Junior were alert for the rest of the conversation, and not fainting from hunger.

She dug out the fresh notebook she'd tucked into her purse before leaving the house. This one had a Hannah Montana cover, with silvery foil and sparkles on the gal's picture. Hard to believe that Billy Ray Cyrus was old enough to have a teenage daughter; seemed like just yesterday Stella was dancing around the living room to that tune of his, laughing at Noelle as she shook her little-girl booty.

Once the waitress set their coffee down, Stella wrote the date and "Arthur Shaw, Jr." and "Denny's" at the top of the page and said, "I get that you're worried about your brother . . . now shoot."

Arthur Junior took a deep breath. "It's cars, see, Mrs. Hardesty. Roy Dean jacked a car way back in high school, and he got caught and did some juvie time for it. But I guess the bug bit him good. He's always been wanting a better ride than he's got, even though he's not willing to work regular to get it. Long about last January he comes to me and says some pal of his says they can make good money stealing cars from up in Independence and Kansas City and taking 'em to salvage yards to sell for parts. So I guess Roy Dean and him do this for a while and then Roy Dean comes to me and says, why don't he and I team up? Takes two, see, because you drive up there together and then one guy watches out while the other one gets the thing started, then you got to drive your own car back along with the one you stole."

"I thought you boys don't get along," Stella said. "Why would he want you to go in on this thing with him?"

"No'm, we don't generally, but the way I figure it is, Roy Dean knew he could trust me. I'd never rat him out or anything. That ain't the way we're raised. Plus, I think his friend was wanting to always take the bigger half of the haul, it being his contacts and all."

"What do you mean, contacts?"

"Well, there's four, five salvage shops in the county. More if you're willing to drive a ways. But not all of 'em will take a car without title, you know? And those that will, you gotta kind of build up a relationship with them, just like any other business. And if you really want to make some good money, you got to know what they're looking for. See, there's makes and models they need parts for more'n others."

"Sounds like you know quite a bit about this, Arthur Junior, for a guy who didn't want to get tangled up in it."

Arthur Junior hung his head, looking sheepish. "Well, thing is . . . Roy Dean, he just wouldn't let it drop. And you should've seen Mom. Roy Dean, dumbass that he is, tells her we're going to start a fucking body shop together, fix up cars and resell 'em. Excuse my language. Sorry. And Mom was so happy, you should've seen her. . . . All she ever wanted was for Roy Dean to stay out of trouble, and here he's got her thinking he's gonna go straight and that I'll be there making sure he keeps his nose clean."

Stella remembered the weary look in Arthur Senior's eyes

when he talked about his boys. "What did your dad think of all this?"

Arthur Junior stirred his coffee with a spoon, eyes downcast. "Dad . . . well, I think he quit believing anything Roy Dean said back when we were kids, but you know, he just wants Mom to be happy."

"That's a female affliction for you," Stella said with feeling. "Trying to believe one thing when all the evidence points in the other direction. If women weren't so darn bent on fooling themselves . . . well, I guess that's another subject. Go ahead, tell me the rest. Did you join up with Roy Dean or didn't you?"

"I . . . well, I hate to admit it to you, Mrs. Hardesty, but I rode up to Independence with Roy Dean a couple times. I don't know what I was thinking, maybe that I could talk him out of it or something, but—I mean it was just so damn simple. People leave their cars right out in the open without even locking the doors, and do you know how easy it is to hot-wire them? Especially pre-ninety-five, ninety-six, all you have to do is go under the steering column and get at the wires and touch them together. It's not hardly rocket science, and Roy Dean always was good with that stuff, and the thing is these aren't new cars. These are like old Camrys and whatever. It's almost like a victimless crime, because with a car that age, people are done paying it off and the insurance company writes a check and, you know, they just go and get another car."

Stella didn't have much to say to that, especially because breakfast arrived. "Grand Slam," the waitress said cheerfully, sliding it under Stella's nose, "and . . . Grand Slam."

Arthur Junior stared at his plate with little interest.

"Anything else I can do for you right now?" the waitress asked.

"No, sweetie, but thanks—I think we're set." Stella smiled despite herself. There was nothing in the world better than eggs cooked in pools of butter, bacon finished off in the deep fryer, and pancakes swimming in puddles of syrup. Even late at night—especially late at night—breakfast was Stella's absolute favorite meal.

"If I ever end up on death row, this is what I'm ordering for my last meal," she said, and dug in energetically.

Arthur Junior stared at her with a look bordering on horror.

"What?" Stella mumbled around a mouthful of eggs.

"Nothing. It's just—I mean—what I hear and all, I can't believe you can talk that way. If they can ever pin half the stuff on you that people say you done . . ."

Stella swallowed and set down her fork. This was a bit delicate. She knew what people said—that there were bodies buried all over the state, men who'd met their bloody end at Stella's hands. The truth was that despite beating, interrogating, threatening, and torturing her parolees; despite leaving them with scars, broken bones, burns, post-traumatic stress disorder, even the occasional missing limb—despite all of this, she hadn't killed a single parolee, no matter how blackhearted and irredeemable he was. Other than Ollie, but she figured she'd earned that one.

But there was no percentage in quelling the rumors. They were, after all, largely responsible for her effectiveness: a man who believed her next visit would bring a bullet to the forehead was far more likely to behave.

"You shouldn't go listening to everything you hear," she

said carefully. "I really lead a pretty laid-back life. You know, what with the shop, and—and my garden and all."

"Well, if you're going to tangle with Benning and them, I hope at least some of it's true."

Stella nodded. "All right. Let's just say that maybe some of the ass-kicking part's true."

"And look, if you do talk to them, you can't—I mean you *really* can't bring me into this."

"Okay. Noted. So we got you and Roy Dean making a little extra cash at the chop shops. How often were you doing this?"

"I only went a couple times, back in March, and then I told Roy Dean I was done. I'm getting my certification. I don't want to mess that up. He got all pissed off and then he tells me we don't have to take the whole car anymore, that Benning's given him a list of what he wants, shit like GPSs and DVD players, speakers, xenon headlights. Says we can do two or three or more at a time, but we might have to go up to Kansas City. Man, I didn't like that. I hate the fucking city. But Roy Dean kept on me until he talked me into going around and meeting Benning. Told me if I didn't like it once we talked to him, I could leave off and he'd quit too, even told me he'd go back to helping Dad out. Like he's any help to Dad. Anyway, like some kind of dumbass, I went."

Stella wrote a few notes with one hand and forked up hash browns with the other. "Okay, so you went with Roy Dean out to the salvage yard? When was that?"

"I don't know, maybe end of March, start of April, somewhere in there. So he wants to go over there late at night, and I ask Roy Dean why we can't go during the day and he's like, no, we got to go when Benning's associates are there. How do you like that, 'associates,' my brother the damn fancy talker. Should've told me something. So anyway we get there and honest to fuckin' God they got this guy down at the gate waitin' for us. Comes out with a flashlight and shines it in our faces and talks to Roy Dean before he'll open the gate, and he calls someone on his cell phone and tells us to go park up by the shed and I'm like, what shed, and Roy Dean tells me to shut up and so that's when I realize he's been here before, because he drives up past the main area back to this prefab storage building, but I'm telling you, it ain't really any kind of shed. I mean you could park a couple of tractor-trailer trucks in there, but it's pretty much empty except this one area they got done up kind of like a living room—they got a carpet scrap on the floor, some recliners and whatnot, a table . . . and some computer stuff. Couple of PCs and printers and faxes and all that. Mini fridge . . . anyway, I don't know what to think of this whole thing, but Roy Dean walks right up to Earl Benning and high-fives him and already I'm getting scared, 'cause the other guys sitting around there, man, it's like *The Godfather* or something."

"What do you mean? These guys . . . they were Italian? They were armed? They were wearing tuxedos?" Stella was fascinated, despite herself.

"No, just—well, I'm pretty sure they all had guns. Some in plain sight and I figure some hid. Roy Dean 'n me, all we got's my .22 in the rack in the truck, and we didn't bring it. This guy standing with his hand on the table, I figure him for in charge, and sure enough, later I find out it's Funzi, even though none of 'em ever talked direct to me or Roy Dean."

"How long were you there?"

"Not long. I was trying to signal Roy Dean, you know, like let's get outta here, but he's acting like some kind of hot-shot, won't even look at me. So Benning's all, you've done some good work for us, and Roy Dean's just pleased as shit to hear it. Like he's a fuckin' big dog, you know? And he starts saying that's nothing, he and me can do double, triple that kind of turnaround, and I'm starting to sweat but I don't want to say anything because, like, you argue with these guys you end up regretting it, right?"

"Yeah. Swimming with the fishes in the East River," Stella said. She was dubious.

"Huh? Whatever. Roy Dean says he feels like he's ready for more responsibility, and isn't there some sort of work for us? Says he's willing to relocate. I mean, beat that! So then I'm like, come on, Roy Dean, we need to get going and Benning's like, you got some sort of curfew? And Roy Dean laughs like it's the funniest thing he's ever heard, but when we're back out in the car, out through the gates with that guard guy locking the whole thing up behind us, he nearly rips me a new one. Tells me I just blew our chance to get somewhere in the organiza-tion, and I tell him he's full of shit and to make a long story short he dumped me out a mile from home and I had to walk and that's the second-to-last time I seen him since."

"So you told him you didn't want anything to do with his . . . activities."

"Yeah. I mean, I got this ITT course and once I get my certificate I'll be making good money anyway, and I don't have to go to the city or break any laws to do it."

"Straight and narrow," Stella agreed, spreading jelly on her toast, which had gone cold. "Not the worst idea in the world, when you get down to it. So what do you think, Roy Dean went back with these Mafia goons or whatever they are and got busy doing their errand-boy work? Or what?"

Arthur Junior shrugged. "I don't know. I mean, I was freaked out enough I asked around. You know, a couple guys I know that are into . . . some shit. And Benning's name came up a few times. Guess he's got his fingers in drugs, least that's the rumor, except it's hard to know because he's the—what do you call it?—the middleman. He isn't selling at the street level or anything."

"What kind of stuff?" Stella asked, her apprehension growing. "Pot? Prescription?"

"Mostly pot," Arthur Junior said. "I guess there's a bunch of Vietnamese down south Ozarks as are growing it indoors. Them Vietnamese know the hydroponics and all that shit. But far as I can tell it's not getting resold around here. Somehow it goes up through Benning and disappears, up to the city or who knows where. I mean, if Funzi and them really are mob, it could be Saint Louis or Chicago or who the hell knows— they're all connected."

"Hmm," Stella said. As little as she knew about organized crime, she had trouble believing that Arthur Junior knew much more. But the thought that the mob could have its tentacles here in rural Missouri—it was a possibility she'd never considered. "What else?"

"Well . . . I don't know about this one, but this guy I know works on one of the riverboats. He says they're running a skim operation on a lot of the mom-and-pop slots. You know, you got your low-end casino hotels, like that? Not a lot of oversight. Supposedly these guys, not Benning but some of Funzi's guys, they come around and take a regular payout, and I guess that goes up through the organization, too."

"So you're telling me that Benning's place is, what, like some kind of mob playhouse?"

Arthur Junior frowned. He'd barely touched his food. The eggs were congealing, and the bacon grease had solidified. "Mrs. Hardesty, all due respect, I think you're not taking this serious enough. I think Benning's place is kind of like the conduit for all their local operations. You know, out all over the county—maybe up along the river, where the gambling is—through Funzi, up to Kansas City and then who knows."

Stella thought that through. *Conduit*—now there was a ten-dollar word. Much as she hesitated to admit it, Arthur Junior was a shinier penny than she'd expected. Which made his anxiety that much more striking. A dumbass gets scared, you can chalk it up to cowardice or sheer stupidity. But a guy like this . . .

"Tell me, Arthur Junior," she said, voice low and serious. "What do you think has happened to your brother? I mean, leave off for a minute whether he took Tucker or not."

Arthur Junior shook his head. "I think he figured he could outsmart Benning. Roy Dean's played both sides of everything since we were in grade school. Hell, he double-dealt me out of my allowance more times'n I can remember. So I guess he probably talked them into giving him some sort of job, running packages—"

"By which you mean drugs," Stella interrupted.

"Drugs, sure, or maybe those stolen car parts, load 'em into a truck or something, drive them to some central location. Or money—it's not like they deposit all that cash down at Sawyer

County Bank, you know? Roy Dean can be convincing. So if he started that in April, that's a couple of months he could have been trying to work his way up until one day he figures he'll just keep a little for himself or hold back some of the load to resell or something. I mean, if there's an angle, Roy Dean'd find it."

"But—what then? What are you thinking?"

"Mrs. Hardesty," Arthur Junior said miserably, pushing his coffee cup in a circle on the table, "I'm thinking it's possible he got himself killed, the dumb shit."

Stella sat with that a minute, considered the angles. Sure, she'd read lots of crime novels; they were her favorite. But that was the kind of thing that happened in L.A. or New York—if it really ever happened at all. Would anyone bother to kill a local loser over a few hundred bucks worth of swag?

"Seems kind of . . . ruthless. You know: overkill."

Arthur Junior was silent a moment, but then he looked Stella in the eye and said, "Some might say the same about your methods, Mrs. Hardesty. I guess it's all a matter of perspective."

Well. Now that was saying a mouthful. Stella resisted the urge to protest, and wondered. Was it really possible the mob had taken up residence here, not ten miles from where she was born and raised, without her knowing?

She had to talk to Goat. If anyone knew anything about it, he would. But how was she going to pull that off without tipping him off to everything else?

"Go back to the Tucker thing for a second," she said. "You can't think of any reason—any at all—he might have had for taking him? Getting back at Chrissy, maybe?"

"No, that's just crazy," Arthur Junior said. "It's not like he was all that fond of the kid. I never saw Roy Dean give him a second look, anytime they were over at Mom and Dad's. I just don't think he'd go in for the inconvenience, diapers and feeding him and all, when there's other ways he could've messed up Chrissy's life easier."

"I'm inclined to agree with you, but Chrissy thinks Roy Dean might've took Tucker with him. He came over to the house on Saturday morning, and there was a, call it a short discussion, and then Chrissy got called away for a bit, and when she got back they were both gone, and Roy Dean's car, too. And the diaper bag." Stella didn't mention the fact that another, equally viable suspect had hidden naked on the premises during this exchange, before making a stealthy and unexplained exit. No need to cloud the issue.

"Well, I don't know. Maybe Roy Dean figured, if he was in trouble, they wouldn't off him in front of the kid, or something."

"Damn it all," Stella said, with conviction. "Look, Arthur Junior, this has been a lovely meal, but I'm afraid we got to hit the road here. Tomorrow's gonna start early, and at my age, it takes a while to get my beauty sleep in."

She threw some money down on the table and stood up.

"Yeah," Arthur Junior said, giving his untouched meal a forlorn glance as he followed her. "Only I don't think beauty sleep's gonna help this time."

FOUR

. . . .

Y ou sure you got all that?" Stella asked, watching Chrissy's stubby fingers, with their sparkly lavender nails, move over the keys of the old cash register. It was nearly nine o'clock, Hardesty Sewing Machine Sales & Repair's official opening hour, though the street outside wasn't exactly overrun with eager customers.

"Um-hum. Unit price, then that dept shift key. Then dept number and, um, PLU . . ." She tapped the keys slowly and deliberately until the drawer popped open. "And personal checks okay if I know the person."

"Not if you know the person, Chrissy, if you *trust* the person. There's a difference, remember?"

Chrissy knit her eyebrows together. "I still don't get how I'm supposed to know if somebody's going to *try* and write a bad check. I mean, there's been times I've wrote one and never even knew it, 'cause I just didn't tote up how bad off we were in the account."

"Well, think, sugar. Like, you wouldn't take a check from Crandall Jakes, now would you?"

Chrissy's eyes widened. "Oh no I wouldn't. That man lets his dogs get knocked up and then drowns the puppies, I know it for fact. Don't even *try* to find 'em homes."

"Well, yeah, but . . ." Stella considered trying to explain that it was Crandall's two stints at County for tax evasion and social security fraud that were more to the point.

"What do you suppose he'd want to buy here, anyway?" Chrissy continued, looking around the shop at the walls hung with racks of sewing notions, the quilting and embroidery machines set up with sample scraps of fabric under the presser feet, the racks of books and patterns.

"Forget him, he was a bad example. Oh, Chrissy, just use your judgment. I won't be gone all that long anyway."

"Okay." Chrissy hitched her feet up on the rungs of the stool and patted the stack of magazines Stella bought her at the 7-Eleven. "I'll just read and maybe dust a little and be fine here."

"I know you will, darlin'."

"Wouldn't it be just great if they got Tucker up in the trailer out there?" Chrissy asked with a little smile. "Like if maybe Roy Dean asked 'em to babysit while he did some errands for Mr. Benning and them all? Heck, you know how men are, they're prob'ly feedin' him those little powder sugar doughnuts and lettin' him watch pro wrestling."

"Uh . . . yeah, that would be nice," Stella said, slinging her big old brown leather purse over her shoulder. It was a little heavier than usual today since she'd taken the precaution of

adding the Ruger. She'd picked it more for luck than anything—it reminded her of her dad, though she'd never seen
him fire it. She'd cleaned and oiled it when she got home from
dropping Arthur Junior off, listening to the radio and thinking. "But don't go getting your hopes up, hear? We got to be
ready for the possibility we're in for a bit of a haul here, remember, like we talked about?"

Chrissy nodded but refused to look at Stella. She used a
long lavender nail to scratch at the sales tax chart taped to the
counter and pursed her sticky pink-glossed lips. "I know, I just
said it would be *nice*. You know."

On the drive to Benning's Stella wondered if she'd done
the right thing, soft-pedaling the information she'd wrung
out of Arthur Junior last night. She'd told Chrissy that she'd
run into someone at the divorce party who told her Roy
Dean was just helping out some friends of Mr. Benning with
some business that might include trips up to the city, which
could explain why he was away. Stella allowed as to how
Benning's business might not be on the proper side of legal,
but that didn't faze Chrissy in the least, seeing as how her
brothers and cousins and uncles had already done a fair job of
setting her expectations for the conducting of business firmly
in gray territory.

Stella hadn't mentioned Arthur Junior's fears that Roy
Dean might already be dead. Chrissy, convinced as she was
that Roy Dean had her son, would no doubt make the intui-
tive leap straight to real, frightening danger for Tucker. And
Stella needed the girl to stay calm, if only so she didn't have to
stay home and babysit her.

She also didn't tell Chrissy about the visit to Pitt Akers's apartment. Stella was more than a little concerned about the empty rooms, the cat food stockpiled with what looked like several weeks' supply. She'd snuck a look at the National Center for Missing & Exploited Children web site while Chrissy was busying herself at the cash register, and she didn't like what she saw, not one bit. All those sweet faces—all those big trusting eyes—and the terrible facts: "Last seen with her mother's live-in boyfriend . . ." "Last seen with his non-custodial mother . . ." If Pitt truly believed the boy was his, who could say what lengths he might go to?

It was better not to give Chrissy any more to worry about than necessary. By leaving the girl at the shop, Stella hoped Chrissy would pour all her attention into selling a few packages of elastic or fetching fixed-up machines for the ladies who came to collect them. And if she messed up the day's receipts or rang up a package of straw needles as a box of silk pins, well, that was just part of the cost of doing business when you were breaking in new staff.

That particular thought was still on Stella's mind as she pulled into Benning's. No guard today; the big metal gates had been folded back, leaving the dirt entrance clear, and a couple more cars were pulled in the area between Benning's trailer and the start of the rows of ruined and wrecked cars and parts.

She eased Chrissy's '96 Celica into a space between a dusty late-model pickup and a fenced-off dog run. Chrissy's car, with its rust-spotted panels and rear bumper attached with a length of steel cable, was Stella's ostensible reason for the visit, though Stella didn't intend to need one. She meant to see if she could just deal straight with Benning, especially since it wasn't too likely that his friends from up north would be hanging around the yard on a Wednesday morning when very little was stirring, including the drooping black walnut trees lining the fenced edge of the property, their branches looking like they were ready to give up from the heat.

As she turned off the ignition, the radio guy announced it would get up to a hundred again.

Stella wasn't too excited about that, but as she walked around the front of the car, the fevered braying that went up in the pen next to her indicated that the dogs, at least, didn't intend to let a little heat and humidity keep them from their duties.

Stella considered herself a dog person. Years ago she'd brought home a stray, a little dog that was at least part beagle, with some mystery elements mixed in. She'd named the dog Buttons for the spots that ran along her soft belly, but when Ollie took to kicking Buttons for no reason at all, Stella gave the dog to a family on the other end of town, crying all the way home, and swore she'd never put a pet in harm's way again. Besides, there was Noelle to think about; even if Ollie never hit the child and mostly ignored her, it wasn't good for a child to see acts of violence carried out right in front of her. While Ollie did most of his wife-beating when Noelle was asleep or out of the house, he kicked Buttons any old time he felt like it, no matter who saw him.

Stella had been meaning to get a dog ever since Ollie died, but she'd been waiting for things to calm down a bit so she'd have time to raise a pup up right. Unfortunately, her side business had remained strong, with a new client showing up every time she thought she'd finally hit a dry spell, and it was beginning to look as if Stella would just have to bite the bullet and get herself a broke-in dog. Not the worst thing in the world, of course; Stella had a fair amount of hard miles on herself, and she wouldn't hold that against any potential canine pet.

But the huge, angry beasts throwing themselves against the fencing just inches from her hip were another story. With the boxy snouts and barrel chests that indicated pit bull blood, they had their dog-lips bared and their snapping teeth exposed, and the ruckus they were sending up had an edge of crazed fury to it that Stella knew only too well came from a particular dog-raising philosophy.

It took mean to breed mean. Always had, when it came to dogs. Unlike men, who'd produce a bad apple now and then even in the best environment—like Roy Dean, for instance— it was near impossible to raise up a mean dog if you just gave the thing a little attention and didn't take to abusing it.

The pair in the cage, though, with their quivering, muscled bodies and drooling vicious grins, appeared to have developed appetites that were downright terrifying. Stella could imagine the huge jaws clamping down on unprotected flesh, the fore-arms scrabbling for purchase as they went in for the kill, and she backed away from the fencing.

"Aw, now, they wouldn't hurt nothin'," an amused voice said behind her.

Stella turned and found herself face-to-face with Earl Benning.

"What can I do for you today, young lady?" he continued, and then a curious thing happened: his eyes, which had been all squinty in the bright sun, opened a little wider, and the smarmy grin snapped off his face as though someone had knocked it down with a plank. "You're Stella Hardesty, ain't you."

So much for the whole "just looking" ruse. Oh, well, Stella wasn't one for subterfuge. Down and direct, that did the trick more often than not.

"I am. And you're Earl Benning, am I right?" She jutted a hand out, but after Earl just kept staring at her face, making no move to shake, she finally withdrew it.

"You used to be a brunette, I think I remember," he said. "Had a tight little figure, too."

Stella hadn't been planning on a tea party, but Earl's manners were a little much even for the circumstances. "I'm *still* a brunette," she said, touching a hank of her hair. "I paid good money for this. And as for my figure, I seem to remember there was a little less of you a decade back, too."

"Nah, I'm talkin' about back when you first married Ollie. Course, I was still a kid then, but—mmm, *man,* you sure used to fill out your blouse."

Stella, who was almost never at a loss for words, gulped air. What the hell? If it was just a matter of filling out her shirt, well, she could probably manage two for the price of one these days. She'd been a 34C when she walked down the aisle. Now she was a 40DD. But she doubted that was exactly what Earl Benning had on his mind.

"Thanks, I guess," Stella said. "Course, I don't recall ever checking out your package, so even if I wanted to now, which I don't, I wouldn't be able to do any comparin'. Look, this is real fun and all, but if you're fixin' to ask me out I'm not interested, and besides I got some other stuff to talk over with you."

The expression on Benning's face darkened from amusement to something a sight more cruel. "Ain't it just my bad luck," he said. "Here I was wondering if you were free for the prom. All right, what is it that I can do for you today, Stella *Har-des-ty?*"

The way he enunciated each syllable of her last name gave Stella a chill that started around the bottom of her spine and snaked its way up her back, shivering along her nerve endings. She was glad to have extra insurance in her big purse.

"How about if we take a little walk?" she asked. "That okay?"

"I suppose that'd be all right," Benning said. "Gimme just a sec here."

He pulled a walkie-talkie-type device off the worn belt that hung low beneath his drooping gut and muttered into it for a minute.

"Why don't we take this way?" he suggested, replacing the walkie-talkie and giving his pants an upward tug.

Stella followed without a word. They walked down a gravel lane through rows of automotive refuse that were arranged in rough rectangles. Most of the cars either had the front or back end caved in, or had taken a T-bone to the side. Some had apparently died of a series of unfortunate encounters, damage extending all the way around. A few looked as if they'd succumbed to old age. In the distance, a yellow front loader was moving scrap toward a towering pile of crushed cars.

"Let me get right to it," Stella said. "I'm looking for Tucker Lardner. Little boy, eighteen months old, just a baby, really."

Benning glanced quickly at Stella, his eyes narrowed; something flickered within their flinty depths. "No babies around here," he said quickly.

"Just hold on," Stella said, watching him carefully. "I ain't saying there was. What I know is, Tucker disappeared last Saturday with Roy Dean Shaw. Now, I don't have any business with Roy Dean. Don't even care where he ended up, though I wouldn't mind knowing just so's I could, you know, cross all the t's and dot the i's on this."

"Cross the t's, huh," Benning echoed, muscling his expression back into indifference. "I ain't seen Roy Dean since, since ages, and I *definitely* ain't seen no kid."

"Well, okay, like I say, I'm really just looking to find the boy. Now, there's some talk that Roy Dean was doing a little work for you and some of your, ah, business associates. That's none of my concern, either. Hell, looks like a nice place you got here, all this . . . stock, and whatnot."

"You like my place, do you?" Benning laughed, a short, percussive sound that was almost a bark. "Well, now, that's a nice compliment, coming from a businesswoman such as yourself."

Stella kept walking, keeping her eyes on the gravel and clumps of weeds on the ground in front of her, but her heart did a little speed-up. "You mean my shop," she said. "The sewing machine shop. I did some nice business last year, but—"

"That ain't what I mean, Stella *Har-des-ty,*" Benning said, his voice going low. He leaned closer, conspiratorially, so that their shoulders brushed as they ambled along, and Stella had the weird thought that they must look like lovers strolling together. "I mean your *other* business. Course, I don't know what sort of numbers you got on that. You know, expense ratios and receivables and all that. Yeah, surprising, right," he added, giving her a little poke in the ribs. "My daddy didn't raise no dummy. Didn't get to be the biggest salvage outfit around by letting it run itself."

"Clearly, you're no dummy," Stella agreed. "Though I'm not sure what you're talking about with—"

"Can it, Stella. Let's just get this said. I know what-all you do, and if I wanted, I could get a lot more information pretty quick. You know, in the form that might be useful for law types. See where I'm going? I run a nice, tight shop here, but I don't like the idea of anyone coming around snooping into my business, any more'n you probably like someone coming around doing it to you. So here's what I propose. I don't have any idea where Roy Dean is. Yeah, he's brought a few cars around, and we buy now and then, but I run a clean shop and if he can't provide title, I take a pass. So I haven't seen him in what, two, three weeks. I can check the books if you want to know what we last bought off him, though seems like it was an Odyssey, front-end collision, if I'm not mistaken. As far as that boy, I didn't even know Roy Dean had a kid. It never came up."

"He doesn't. Tucker's his wife's. Chrissy's."

Benning shrugged and nodded. "Well, there you go. No reason for him to be hauling the kid around anyway, then. Wish I could help you, but looks like we're just a dead end for you."

Benning took a left and led her down a rough section of road that veered back toward the main lot. Stella glanced behind her shoulder and could just make out the edges of a shed big enough to fit Arthur Junior's description past the fields of cars and several structures holding various parts suspended from metal gridwork. Reluctantly, she followed Benning.

"You say 'we,'" Stella said. "Who all you got working here, anyways?"

Benning shrugged impatiently. "I got a part-timer most days. Chuck Keltner, you probably know his mom, and a guy moved up here from Morrisville. Not full-time, you know, no benefits or nothing. Mostly it's me for the big stuff."

"Yeah, see, way I hear it, you got some out-of-town interest, too."

Benning said nothing, but Stella could sense him tense up next to her.

"Some friends of yours maybe bringing you in on some other avenues," Stella continued. "Look, like I said, it's no concern to me. You want to grow a little pot patch on your back forty, whatever. Just trying to keep this a two-way flow of information, hear what I'm saying?"

"If I knew anything, I'd tell you," Benning said, his voice soft. "But you're way off the mark with that last comment. Yeah, I got some friends come down from the city from time to time. We go out on the lake, fish a little. Play cards. Hunt or whatever. I don't know who's been giving you your information, but let me tell you, the biggest thing around here is maybe a little weekend party from time to time, and if someone stuck their nosy face in and saw something that wasn't there, well, that would be their problem, see where I'm going?"

"I think I see," Stella said, keeping her own voice low. "Anytime you had a bunch of visitors after hours, maybe taking the party over to some of your other facilities on the site, why, you're just eating pretzels and playing Crazy Eights. That about the size of it?"

"Yeah, I'd say so," Benning said, nodding. "Now you're getting it. Roy Dean's not exactly on my A-list, and we sure don't have no little kids around when we party, so I guess that's about all I can do for you today. Unless you want to see if we can find something to fix up that rust bucket."

They had arrived back at Chrissy's car. The sun had climbed higher in the sky, and the heat shimmered inches above the opaque, faded paint on the car's roof and hood.

"I appreciate the offer," Stella said as the dogs hurtled across their pen, braying and crashing into the fence, "but I think I've changed my mind about it since talking to you."

"Yeah? How's that?"

"Well, this little ride don't look like much on the outside," Stella said. "Lots of miles, just like I got. But under the hood? That's a scrappy little engine. Gave me plenty more get-up-and-go than I was expecting."

"That so."

"Yeah." Stella got in the car and rolled down the window. She gave Benning her sweetest smile as she stuck the key in the ignition and fired up the little Celica. "Sometimes you just can't tell from looking how much trouble your ride's going to give you."

Hardesty Sewing Machine Sales & Repair shared a parking lot with China Paradise, a generally decent restaurant run by the eternally grumpy Roseann Lu. When Stella pulled into the lot at eleven thirty, she figured the three cars already parked there were Roseann's customers, getting an early start on the lunch special.

In her shop, though, she was surprised to find Chrissy with not one but two customers, Lila Snopes and a second woman in her sixties, both of them talking at once. Chrissy's wide, pale blue eyes darted from one to the other, and when she saw Stella she blurted, "Oh, I'm so glad you're back! We got us a situation here!"

Lila turned away from the counter and, at the sight of Stella, pursed her features into a frown that caused the many wrinkles around her smoker's mouth to focus in like arrows. "Not a situation, just a case of the customer is always right," she said primly.

"Hello, Lila," Stella said. She noted a heavy resemblance in the woman's companion: same steely, severe bob haircut, same pronounced chin and flaccid cheeks. "And this must be your sister."

"I'm Delores," the woman said, nodding.

"I called Delores to tell her you were running the binding two-for-one," Lila said. "I love the wide stuff for quilts. I'm stocking up."

She pointed to the counter, where packages of binding were piled up high. Her sister had her own pile. There were probably thirty packages between the two of them.

Stella took a deep breath and said, "Sorry, ladies, but I'm not running any specials. I think there's been some misunderstanding."

"That's what I've been trying to tell them," Chrissy stage-whispered in a singsongy voice.

"No misunderstanding I can figure," Lila said. "I was in here at ten and I bought two packs of the inch and a half. Kelly green. And your girl here charged me for one. So I says, you charged me for one, deary, and she says no, that's no mistake, that's what you told her to do."

"I said no such thing!" Chrissy said. "I said I was just doing what Miz Hardesty told me, and it wasn't my fault the cash register wasn't ringing up the numbers right."

"Well, you took my money, didn't you?" Lila said, the jut of her chin taking on an even more stubborn set. "Way I see it, that means you agreed on the two-for-one."

Lila's sister nodded along to everything her sister said, and Chrissy's face was getting blotchy and red. "Now let's just slow down a minute, ladies," Stella said. "This is Chrissy's first day on the job, and she's still getting used to our . . . system. I don't think—"

"I did drive up from Quail Valley," Delores said primly. "Seein' as you had the special."

Stella tapped her foot on the floor. Did the math in her head. "Okay," she said after a minute. "How's this. Twenty-five percent off. That's the best I can do."

"Well . . . how about you throw in one of those serger books I know you ain't sold in two years," Lila sniffed. "And maybe you ought to consider getting some more qualified help."

Chrissy went very still for a moment, and Stella was trying to figure out how to diffuse the old bitch's comments, when she noticed something interesting.

A deep purple flush was creeping upward from Chrissy's collarbones, and her eyes had narrowed to slits. She slowly drew herself up to her full height and drew in a breath, and then she made her hands into tight fists before extending her fingers out like a boxer getting taped for a fight.

"Excuse me, lady, what did you just say?" she demanded, her voice very soft.

Lila put her hands on her hips and glared back. "Just that seein' as you're not even able to run a simple cash register or add up a purchase, maybe Stella here ought to—"

Chrissy's hand shot out so fast that Stella jumped. Chrissy made a crisscross motion in front of Lila's face, snapping her fingers twice.

"Lookie here," she said, voice full of menace. "I have had a very bad couple of days. I have sat back and took what assholes like you have been dishing out for way too long, and I'm about sick of it. I am *not* dumb. I am *not* helpless. And I'm not taking any more shit. I'm done, and I'm about to get very, very pissed off and I'm tellin' you now I don't think you want to be around when that happens, hear?"

Lila's eyes went wide, and she gripped the handle of her handbag hard. Her sister shifted slightly so she was standing behind Lila.

"Um, now . . . ," Stella began, but realized she didn't really feel like scolding Chrissy. This anger of hers might not be such a bad thing. In fact, it just might be something they could use.

She grabbed the book Lila wanted from the rack and slipped it into a plastic merchandise bag along with the binding tape. "You got a deal," she said, and gently pushing Chrissy out of the way, rang up the sale and quickly counted out the ladies' change.

Lila Snopes took the bag and the change without comment. She shoved the money in her purse, and the two old ladies scuttled out of the store without a backward glance.

When they were gone, there was a long silence. Chrissy

stared at the shop door and took a few deep breaths. After a few moments she turned to Stella with a nearly placid expression and handed her a Post-it note.

"I took a message for you," she said.

Stella squinted at the note. In curvy lettering was written: "Call me on my cell."

"That's great," she said. "Thanks. Call who?"

Chrissy looked at her in surprise. "Well, the sheriff, of course."

Stella's heart did a little rollover, but she kept her expression neutral. "Oh. 'Cause see on the note, it just says . . ." She pointed to the Post-it. "Never mind. When did he call?"

"He didn't call, he stopped by. After that lady was here the first time. Maybe an hour ago?"

"What did he say? I mean, besides to call."

"Well, mostly he told me not to worry. But you know what, Stella? I've been thinking. I think y'all ought to stop trying to make me feel better. I mean, I'm Tucker's *mama*. I need to know what all's going on, so I can help find him."

Stella hesitated. She admired the girl's guts and was relieved to see Chrissy provoked out of her listless funk. But her instinct was to tell Chrissy to stay out of it. It wasn't just that she'd always worked alone—there was also the promise she had made to herself after Lorelle Cavenaugh died: that she would never do anything to endanger a client again.

Chrissy was still a client.

Letting Chrissy anywhere near Benning and the rest of them—or letting her tag along on the hunt for Pitt Akers—was insanity.

"Anything else?" she asked carefully.

"Sheriff Jones asked where *you* were. Oh, you know, I guess I could have given him your cell phone number. I didn't even think of that."

"That's okay. He's got it," Stella said. "Did you tell him?"

"Tell him what?"

"Where I was. You know, out at Benning's."

"Oh, no, I didn't. 'Cause you remember, you said—"

"I remember. But when it's the sheriff who's asking—no, scratch that." She had been about to tell Chrissy that, despite her earlier warning to keep Stella's errand a secret, the sheriff was an exception. But that wasn't really true. As much as Stella was sort of wishing she'd been back in time for his visit, she wasn't ready yet to fill him in on her search.

She needed to find out a little more about Benning's side dealings. After her visit, she was more inclined to worry about that angle: there was something about the way Arthur Junior had reacted when she mentioned Tucker. Earl Benning was shiftier and meaner-looking than she remembered, that was true; and yet when he kept insisting he didn't know anything about Tucker, there was an element of something resembling fear in his eyes, a nervous quality to his voice.

Enough to make Stella think twice. Just because she couldn't figure out *why* Roy Dean might have taken Tucker to the salvage yard didn't mean it hadn't happened. Some men, she had learned, didn't always need good reasons to do bad things.

Earlier, as she left Benning's, Stella had taken a good look at his house. A recent-model silver Camaro was parked in front of a glossy black Ford F-450, and around the side a pair of Sea-Doos were loaded on a trailer. On the other side of the house, on a larger trailer, a sweet blue and white closed-hull Ski Nautique was pulled up under a carport. On the porch, a long-legged bleached-blond gal in a bikini top and a pair of cutoffs lounged in a deck chair.

Cars, boats, toys, and women . . . none of those came for free, at least not for a man like Benning.

Stella needed to find out where the money was coming from. That would lead her to the business Earl and his friends were conducting. And that information, with any luck, would lead her to Roy Dean.

And from there, just maybe, to Tucker.

But if she went to Goat now, with nothing but a hunch, he was bound to go in and ask a bunch of questions and give Earl plenty of time to cover his tracks. While Goat was going through channels, talking to judges, getting search warrants, their chances of getting Tucker back would be slipping away. It was times like these that reminded Stella how convenient it was to be on the more casual side of law enforcing. Luckily, she had a few contacts who would help her get the information she needed without having to involve Goat.

On the other hand, if Pitt Akers had Tucker, waiting was exactly the wrong thing to do. In the case of family abductions—not that Pitt was family, but the man evidently imagined himself to be—early days were critical, and they needed to get on his trail before he had a chance to take the boy so far away that no one could find him.

Stella felt her veins go icy at the thought, and the images of lost children from the Internet flashed through her mind. She'd never forgive herself if she waited too long, if Pitt was even now driving out west to California or down to Mexico or up to Canada, Tucker sitting in a wet diaper and wailing for his mother.

"Stella, you okay?" Chrissy asked, peering at her carefully. "You look like you're about to faint there."

Stella forced a smile. She crumpled up the Post-it note and made a rim shot on the wastebasket across the room. Tomorrow—if she was no closer to finding Tucker by tomorrow, she'd tell Goat everything. "I'm good. Come on, Princess. Let's eat."

After a no-worse-than-usual lunch of lemon chicken and greasy chow mein served with a bare minimum of chat by Roseann Lu, which Chrissy consumed with gusto befitting a far tastier meal, they returned to the shop and Chrissy set to pacing back and forth. Stella had an inspiration.

From the back room, where she kept spare inventory and cleaning supplies and Costco-sized containers of pretzels and beef jerky, she brought out a large cardboard box. "Fran Colvin started this back when we had that teacher in here doing the quilts," she said. "Poor Fran, she died before she could finish it."

"Got that chicken bone in her throat, didn't she," Chrissy said, coming to take a look.

"Yup. Anyway, how about I teach you how to do this?"

Chrissy hesitated. "Ain't there something I can do that's, you know, for Tucker?"

"But that's just it," Stella said. "We'll make him a quilt. And when he gets home, you'll be able to tuck him in under it."

"Oh," Chrissy said. For a long moment, Stella wasn't sure she was going to go for it. The girl had a far-off look to her, part longing and part grief and a fast-growing part nail-spitting fury.

The thunderclouds building in Chrissy's pale eyes worried Stella. The last thing she needed at this point was a loose cannon.

"All right," Chrissy finally agreed. "Let's do it."

Stella explained the basics, then started working the phone, dialing trusted friends—many of them former clients—all over the county, and out to the far edges of the state, to let them know about the missing little towheaded boy last seen wearing denim overalls with a baseball embroidered on the bib. If Pitt—or Roy Dean, for that matter—stopped for a burger or a bathroom break or to pick up a pack of diapers, there would be a lot of women on the lookout, women whose lives had taught them to be observant and resourceful. It wasn't an AMBER Alert, but it was a start.

She also called a few people who had access to official-type information, the type of information that wasn't generally available to the average citizen.

Between calls, Stella showed Chrissy how to cut the fabric using a ruler and rotary cutter. The rotary cutter looked like a pink-handled pizza wheel, but its blade was razor sharp and easily sliced through several layers of fabric at a time. When the patches were cut, Stella taught Chrissy to join them into blocks, lining up seams and trimming the thread tails, then pressing the finished blocks at the ironing board. When Chrissy held up her first nine-patch, a homely, uneven affair of blue and brown fabric, she smiled faintly.

"*I* made that," she said. "Damn!"

Stella rested a hand on Chrissy's shoulder. "Tell you what," she said. "Sewing's good therapy. There were plenty of times when I didn't feel much like dealing with my life. You know?

And I'd sit there at my machine—probably sewed a million miles in seams, just thinking about things."

Chrissy looked doubtful. "This is okay and all, but I'd still rather be *doing* something," she said. "Not just sittin'."

Stella thought how Chrissy had looked just yesterday, puddled in the chair in her living room, eating her way through her worries. She was amazed at the girl's transformation. She'd got some fight back in her. Telling off the dreadful sisters seemed to be just what she needed.

Chrissy reminded Stella of herself, in a way, on the day when she'd finally had enough of Ollie's abuse and made the transformation from passive victim to hell-for-leather avenger.

Nobody had told her, that day, to sit down and relax. Nobody had offered to help her set things right, either. Maybe it was a mistake to try to settle Chrissy down, to keep a lid on her newfound anger . . . but at the same time, Stella couldn't figure out any way to include her without putting her into danger. And that was something she simply wasn't willing to do.

She wasn't going to let another woman get hurt—or killed—on her watch. She had to do the job alone.

"I hear you," she said, not meeting Chrissy's gaze. "But really, there's not a lot we can do today. Until we start hearing back from these folks, we just got to be patient."

"Who all'd you call, anyway?"

"Oh . . . just friends, here and there."

"Stella." There was reproof in Chrissy's voice. "I know you think I couldn't hear you fishin' around for stuff you ain't supposed to know, but I *am* sittin right here not ten feet from you. And I got young hearing. Now, who was it?"

"Well . . . the DMV, for one," Stella said, giving in. She supposed there was no harm in letting Chrissy in on some of her strategy. "I wrote down some plate numbers out at Benning's. I want to see if they're all registered to him direct."

"They just gonna tell you that?" Chrissy asked.

"Well, not exactly. But I got a friend . . ."

"Uh-huh." From her expression, Stella could tell she'd made the leap.

"Friends that owe me favors, actually."

"That's good with me," Chrissy said. "Who else?"

"Well, I got some law enforcement . . . contacts, I guess you'd call 'em, up in Kansas City. Thought I'd see if they have any ideas about what kind of . . . side business Benning and his friends might be running down here."

She didn't like the way Chrissy's eyes narrowed; the girl's wheels were spinning. Stella didn't want to mention the mob or organized crime. She saw no point in scaring her.

Chrissy lowered her pinned patches of fabric to the table. "And what kind of business *are* they running, Stella?"

Stella bit her lip. "Well, I don't know. If I knew, I wouldn't be trying to find out, now would I?"

After a few more seconds of frank and suspicious gazing, Chrissy picked up the quilt block again and went back to work. "But you're going to tell me soon's you learn something, right?" she said.

"Mmm-hmm," Stella said, feeling worse than she usually did about lying.

Unfortunately, she didn't have a lot of success with the rest of her calls. Between the customers who straggled in, helping

Chrissy with the sewing, and not finding people at their desks or answering their cell phones, Stella hadn't made much progress at all when closing time rolled around.

She and Chrissy stopped by the FreshWay to pick up dinner fixings. When they got home, Todd was doing skateboard tricks across the street in old Rolf Bayer's driveway. Stella was surprised, since Bayer had always been hostile to everyone in the neighborhood, and seemed to reserve a special hatred for kids. He'd yelled at Noelle years ago for making chalk drawings on the sidewalk in front of his house.

"Hey," she called, walking into the street as Chrissy took the groceries into the house. "You tryin' to get Bayer to call the cops on you?"

Todd shot out into the street, leaping over the curb and landing hard, then skidded to a stop next to her. As usual, he hadn't bothered to tie his shoes; it was a wonder that the puffy, enormous things stayed on his feet.

"He told my mom he was going to sic the city on us!" he said in a tone of outrage. "Called us trash. So I told him I was gonna skate on his driveway until I broke something and then we'd sue his ass to hell."

Stella figured she knew what had Bayer's dander up—the Groffes' lawn had been neither watered nor cut in a long time, and the girls usually left their Big Wheels and Cozy Coupes in the front yard.

"Well, lemme ask you something," she said. "You ever thought about cutting that grass of yours?"

"Mower's busted," Todd muttered, toeing the ground.

"Ah," Stella said. Poor Sherilee. In her line of business, Stella occasionally forgot that getting rid of a bad man was only the first step to getting one's life back. And with Sheri-lee's schedule, she could see how lawn care might have fallen down on the priority list. "Well, look here, mine's working fine. You go and get it out of the garage. It's got gas in it. Put the clippings in the garden bin, okay? I don't want to see them left out on the lawn."

"Aw, Stella—"

"Shut up, punk, and listen. When you're done with that, come on back here and I'll loan you some sprinklers. Hoses if you need 'em, too. That lawn is officially your job, now, hear?"

Todd crossed his arms and glowered at her. "Why the fuck would I want to do any of that?"

It had been a long day, and Stella's patience was stretched thin. Without thinking she reached out for the collar of Todd's grimy T-shirt and twisted until she was practically choking him.

"Look here," she said. "You want to grow up like the dirt-bag who walked out on your mom, or you want to maybe be someone she can be halfway proud of? Huh?"

It wasn't until Todd made a strained gasping sound that Stella realized she might be squeezing a little too hard, and re-laxed her grip. Todd rubbed at his throat and glared at her.

"Besides," she said, softening, "there's twenty bucks in it for you."

"Mom won't let me take no money," Todd muttered.

"Well, that's right. She shouldn't. But I'm going to give it to you anyway. That can be our secret."

Todd stared at her a moment longer. Finally, he nodded. "I'll do it for ten," he said, and as he trudged into her garage to get the mower, skateboard tucked under his arm, Stella felt an odd little tug at her heart.

Maybe there was a chance for the kid.

Inside, she put a pot of Rice-A-Roni on and tossed some pork chops with bread crumbs and Lipton French onion soup mix, drizzled them with butter, and stuck them in the oven. Chrissy was slicing veggies for a salad and setting the table, so Stella took her cell phone out to the screen porch at the back of the house and dialed Noelle's number.

"Hi. You've reached Noelle! Gerald and I aren't here right now . . ."

Stella's throat tightened at the sound of her daughter's voice. She called a few times a week, always when she knew Noelle would be at work, which wasn't hard to do, because Noelle worked long hours at the beauty shop.

This Gerald thing on the machine was new. But it wasn't a surprise.

Stella knew a fair amount about Gerald already. An old client who lived in Coffey e-mailed Stella to let her know when Gerald and Noelle started keeping company. Within two weeks of their first date, Stella had his priors memorized. Could draw his family chart from memory, the whole unremarkable clan over in Arkansas. Knew the details of the warrant he was avoiding across the state line, for putting his old fiancée in the hospital.

Stella still didn't understand what it was that made a girl who grew up in a house filled with anger and violence seek out the same. Even if Ollie never smacked Noelle, she was barely six the first time she saw him punch her mother—and Ollie doled out a steady stream of verbal abuse to both of them. Why hadn't

Noelle arrived at adulthood, looked around, and said to herself, "Oh goody, look at all these perfectly nice, ordinary men—they're not one bit like Dad"?

But Gerald wasn't the first man her daughter had dated who treated her badly.

He was the second.

Unfortunately, Stella had dealt with the first one so decisively that he lived in Alaska now, not daring to show his face in the continental U.S. Stella didn't regret it—not even when Noelle called her up sobbing and cursing and promising never to speak to her again for the rest of her life.

No, she only began to regret it when Noelle went out and found herself someone worse.

Stella dialed her daughter's number again and listened to Noelle's voice, that sweet voice that had called her "mama," had shrieked with laughter during tickle fights, had sung in every concert the Prosper High School chorus put on.

"Oh, sugar, why do you want to do this to yourself?" Stella whispered, then hung up when the phone beeped.

She slipped the phone back into her pocket and rocked back and forth on the glider. She was keeping a close watch. If things got to where she needed to intercede with Gerald, she would. But she'd learned a lesson, and the fact that it broke her heart didn't make it any less important that she stay a little further out of her daughter's life than she wanted.

Next time, there was nothing to stop Noelle from moving even further away. And though Stella doubted there was anyone better at finding people who wanted not to be found, she was terrified of pushing Noelle further out of her life than she already was.

After the dinner was done and the dishes washed, Chrissy settled in to watch *Talladega Nights* on pay-per-view, and Stella went to check her e-mail. She planned to make an early night of it. Tomorrow, when she had a little more information, she'd put together a plan. Head up to Kansas City, if that's what it took.

When the phone rang she picked it up right away. No sense taking Chrissy away from her movie. Lots of folks used TV as an electronic babysitter for their kids; Stella was finding it convenient for keeping Chrissy's mind off trying to get involved in the case.

"Hello?"

"You lookin' for Roy Dean," a voice said on the other end. A weird voice, tinny and deep, as if its owner was speaking through layers of Reynolds Wrap.

"Might be," Stella said slowly, trying to place the voice and having no luck.

"I got some information could help you find him."

"Is that right? What sort of information?"

There was a pause, and Stella could hear breathing.

"I don't want to say, over the phone."

"Whyever the hell not?"

"Line might not be secure."

Stella sighed heavily. "What, you think the FBI came in while I was at work and bugged my place? Wait—fine, fine, whatever. You want to meet somewhere?"

"Yeah. And I was thinkin' you could make it worth my trouble. You know."

Stella was mystified: could it be a friend of Roy Dean's? Someone he'd blabbed to at a bar? One of Benning's employees? Benning himself?

"What did you have in mind?" she asked, trying to sound puzzled.

"A hundred ought to do it."

"A *hundred*?"

"That's what I said."

"That's—oh, whatever, fine. Where?"

"Bench on the southeast corner of the pond next to the county golf course. Be there in an hour."

Stella could picture the muddy little pond, a ball-catcher at the bottom of a hill. She didn't remember a bench, but the county was messing around with the community park and golf course these days, ripping out the landscaping they'd installed in the sixties and seventies and updating it. Bright tubular plastic equipment replaced the swings she'd pushed Noelle in. A mulched plot of azalea bushes grew near the park entrance where there had been an overgrown bank of arborvitae. Worst of all, "exercise stations" had sprouted along the brick walk that used to be a simple muddy track around the pond.

"I'll find it," Stella grumbled, hanging up.

She changed into some stretchy black yoga pants and fastened on her holster, a quick-draw abdomen model made of black nylon with Velcro in the back, and tucked the Raven into it. She shrugged on a tank top and slipped a light jacket over it. It was too hot by half to be dressing like that, but Stella didn't intend to meet up with unknown would-be conspirators without some sort of insurance hidden on her.

As she was corralling her hair into a big plastic barrette, the phone in her bedroom rang. She picked it up, pretending not to notice the gosh-wonder-if-it-could-be-Goat thrill that zipped around her insides.

"Hello?"

There was only the sound of breathing—rather labored breathing—before a young woman's voice finally said, "Is this Chrissy? Or the other one?"

"Uh, this is Stella Hardesty. Who's this?"

"It don't matter who I am. Kin I please speak with Chrissy?"

Stella considered. It wasn't likely to be one of the other Lardner girls—presumably they knew their sister's voice. Ditto any close friends. Which meant that a stranger was calling for her client. A stranger who somehow knew that Chrissy was staying at Stella's place.

"Chrissy's occupied at the moment," Stella said briskly. "May I take a message?"

A bit more silence, then, "How about if I wait? Is she in the bathroom or something?"

"Actually, I'm taking all of Ms. Lardner's messages at the moment. Can you tell me the nature of your call, please?"

"It's—I'm—see here, I need to talk to Roy Dean."

That caught Stella by surprise, but she answered carefully: "Roy Dean isn't here, I'm afraid."

"Well, y'all gonna be seein' him soon?"

"We . . . may be, yes," Stella said, thinking fast. Whoever the mystery caller was, she clearly didn't know Roy Dean had disappeared. It was possible she might unwittingly spill information that would lead to him.

"Well, look. I need him to, to come over and get this, uh, this *thing* that he left here at my place."

Stella's heart sped up. The way the girl said *thing* . . . it was as if she had a secret to keep. "What sort of thing are you talking about?" she asked carefully.

Another pause. This gal required a fair amount of thinking time, Stella decided. "Something of his I don't want around here no more, that's what kind of thing. Look here, I didn't know he was married, not when we first hooked up, okay?"

"Um . . . okay, sure. Can you at least tell me when he dropped the thing off?"

"A few days ago. But look. He said he'd be back for it and he ain't been. I can't keep it around here, you know? I don't want to be responsible."

Tucker—it had to be Tucker. Roy Dean had dropped the baby off with this girl—his girlfriend, from the sounds of it—maybe even the one he'd been pestering at the speedway. And then, for whatever reasons—reasons having to do with Benning and the Kansas City mafia, maybe, or more likely something a lot more simple, like he got drunk or high or otherwise distracted—he hadn't been back for the boy.

"Look here," Stella said in as kind a voice as she could muster. "Is this thing . . . being well looked after?"

"Huh? Yeah, yeah, it's fine. Look, tell Roy Dean to come get it tomorrow at noon. I'll come home on my lunch hour, and he better be there."

"Sure. Just give me the address."

"He *has* the address," the girl spat, with a full measure of disdain. "He's been here plenty."

"Oh. Well, could I at least have a name?"

"He'll know, okay? He'll know damn well who it is—just tell him Darla said he better be here."

Click.

Stella slowly lowered the receiver back to the cradle on her nightstand. She finished with her hair and went out to the living room, hesitating in front of the TV and wondering what to tell Chrissy. On screen, Will Ferrell was saying the Baby Jesus prayer. Somehow it seemed fitting.

"Chrissy . . . sweet pea . . . you happen to know a gal named Darla? Might have been keeping company with Roy Dean?"

Chrissy shook her head, glancing away from the television. "No, but I feel sorry for her if she has been."

"Yeah. It's just . . ." Stella considered describing the conversation she'd just had, but without knowing who and where the girl was, there was nothing they could do for now, other than get Chrissy completely riled up—just when Stella had finally gotten her all settled down. "Well, nothing that won't keep until tomorrow."

At least, until noon. Somehow, between now and then, Stella had to find Darla. Which shouldn't be too impossible, in a town the size of Prosper. Though if Roy Dean had taken his lovin' out of town, she could quickly have a monster search on her hands.

Stella sighed. One damn problem at a time. Right now she had a date with a park bench.

"Hey darlin', I got to run out for a bit," she said.

"You meeting up with the sheriff?" Chrissy asked, sitting up straight. She had changed into what Stella figured passed for pajamas: a pink T-shirt with a kitten screen-printed on the front and the words *Sweet Pussy*.

"Why would you think that?"

"Well, just 'cause of him calling earlier. I figured maybe you called him back and he talked you into a date."

"Oh . . ." Stella was about to dismiss Chrissy's guess, but the truth was she didn't have any better excuses. "Going out for

Pringles" would work, but it might not give her enough time. "Yes, you got me, girl," she said. "Ought to make you into a detective or something."

That got her a wide grin. "You think?"

Stella took care to lock the door as she left.

On the way to the golf course, she went back over what her caller had said. The thing about the hundred bucks was a joke. Stella had about fifty-five dollars in her purse, what was left from her once-a-week ATM visit. Taking out another hundred would put her a little too close to overdraft territory for comfort.

Stella had some money put away. Not a whole lot, but enough, if she was careful, to get by on as long as the store continued to bring in its usual unspectacular haul every month.

Because of the circumstances of Ollie's death, insurance hadn't paid out a penny. Luckily, when Stella's mother passed, there had been enough to pay off the mortgage and the car loan and set some aside. After Ollie died, Stella used a chunk to employ herself a fancy financial adviser up in Independence. The man taught her a few things Ollie'd never seen fit to explain, and recommended a few books. Now Stella knew enough to scrape by.

The idea, of course, was to supplement her income with her little side business. And sometimes that actually happened. The bonus the Kansas coffee importer's wife had given her, for instance, had paid for the new dishwasher and gas range. But many of her clients had to work out payment plans, and Stella never had the heart to turn anyone away for lack of creative financing.

She had one gal who settled her account by making drapes

for every room in Stella's house. That one was worth it: seeing the ex-girlfriend of the chief of police of a small town near the Iowa border—a woman who'd once believed that no one could help defend her from the most powerful man in town—up on a ladder installing the curtains, whistling and shimmying to an old Pointer Sisters song, was a rare privilege.

She had a couple women who sent her plain envelopes of cash every month. Sometimes it was a few twenties, sometimes more. Occasionally less.

With Chrissy, Stella hadn't even bothered bringing up the subject of a payment plan beyond the fistful of rolled fives, tens, and twenties the girl handed over at her initial consultation. Chrissy already had too much on her mind. No matter; they'd work it out eventually.

Stella pulled into the access road that ran along the park. Bright streetlights had been installed in the parking lot, an improvement she welcomed. As she parked, she could make out a figure sitting exactly where he'd promised to be, on a bench they'd sunk in concrete across the pond. He was a heavyset man, and sat with his arms stretched out casually along the back of the bench, legs crossed.

Had it not been dark out, he could have been there to feed the ducks.

Stella patted the outline of her gun and slipped her car keys into her pocket. As she made her way around the pond, following the curvy outline of the fancy schmancy brick walk, she was relieved that the man made no move toward his pockets. When she got within twenty feet, she could see his eyes shining in the moonlight.

"Hello," she called. "Here I am, right on time."

"I appreciate that. Can't stand a tardy bitch, myself," the man said, and chuckled. His voice was slightly high-pitched and had a flat, nasal quality, and he seemed to find himself plenty amusing, which irritated Stella.

"So what is it you have to tell me?" she asked.

She heard the slightest shuffle behind her, coming from the left side of the path, away from the pond—a leaf against a rock, or maybe trash blowing—and turned to look.

At that moment something came at her from the right: a low, broad dark shape moving fast thudded into her hip and knocked her to the ground. Stella reached for the Raven, but before she could get to it her arms were yanked hard from behind. There were two of them—plus the man on the bench, who was getting up slowly, like he had all the time in the world. *Fuck me,* Stella thought, just like a damn greenhorn, not even checking her periphery first.

"Check this out," she heard a voice say. She felt hands roving her body as the other guy held her, kicking and struggling, in place. The man searching her wore a stocking cap with eye-holes, pulled low on his face. His hands found her holster; in the next second it was yanked from her waist. For a second she was sure she was about to be shot with her own gun, a feeling that intensified when she felt its barrel pressed against the hollow behind her right ear. She scrunched up her whole face and waited for the shot.

In what she figured was her final half second on earth, Stella marveled at a new revelation: waiting to get shot was different from waiting for a man to punch you on a jaw that was still healing from the last time, or hit you on the temple with a beer bottle, or knee you in the gut.

Or maybe it was Stella herself who was different, who had changed since the last time she'd been victim to the violent reckoning that Ollie routinely dished out. Three years, sixteen days, in fact—that counter had been put in motion when Ollie slumped to the floor and bled out, a counter that would never be turned off again.

Three years, sixteen days of freedom. Of calling her own shots.

And what she felt now wasn't anything like she used to feel. It wasn't dull dread, a sense of the inevitable, a wish that he'd just get on with it, even a longing for the relief that would come from being knocked out.

What Stella Hardesty felt, with the barrel of her own gun jabbed a few inches from her brain, was mighty pissed off. To her surprise, it suddenly mattered a great deal to her that she not go down for the last time here, by the little mud pond on the edge of town, at the hands of two men she didn't even know.

"You *cocksuckers!*" she screamed and tried to wrench her arms away from the man holding them behind her back. She managed to work one leg free and kicked with everything she had, connecting a solid hit to the balls of the guy in front of her.

She had the satisfaction of seeing him double over and start to vomit before she took a hit to the face that sent her sprawling.

And a second one that sent her out.

FIVE

· · · · · · · · · ·

Stella could open only one eye. She could see enough to know she was in a hospital room, but the details were flickery and vague. It was her right eye that still seemed to be working, and for a moment she thought that was a good thing, her being right-handed and all. Then she realized that made no sense at all.

Her next thought was that she must have had a stroke that not only left half of her body incapacitated but also played havoc with her reasoning. Great, she thought, not just the lurching and the drooling, but embarrassing conversational gaffes, too?

And then it occurred to her that such a state wasn't all that different from lots of the customers down at BJ's as the evening wore on, and she felt a little more cheerful, despite a splitting pain that seemed to bisect her head as though someone had stuck a shiv in one ear and shoved until they saw the point coming out the other.

Might have to blow Big Johnson, she thought, just to celebrate if and when she got back on her feet again—and to cement her new status as a regular in his joint, since she probably wouldn't be fit to drink anywhere else.

"That so."

The sound of Goat's voice—deep, rumbly, and close—gave Stella a shock that started in the gut and blasted out, causing her arms and legs to spasm and her reluctant left eye to gap open just a little. So, she *could* see out of both her eyes. And what she was looking at was Goat Jones's broad, tanned face leaning in and staring at her with what appeared to be equal parts concern and amusement.

She could smell him, too, his woodsy scent that had notes of laundry softener and coffee and a faint hint of man, just sheer sweaty testosterone-y man. That final bit gave her a different sort of tremor that let her know that another quadrant of her anatomy had also pulled through.

"Goat," she said, licking her lips, which felt sticky and crusty. It occurred to her that it was unlikely that anyone had bothered to brush her teeth, and Goat was leaning close enough she was going to have trouble talking to him and sparing him the effects of her breath at the same time. "You got any gum?"

He stared at her hard, then split into a grin. "Gum? You get the shit kicked outta you, get left to marinate in the golf pond, dragged out by a couple of stoned teenagers, and all you can think to ask for is gum?"

Ah . . . that. Goat's words filled in the details on the sketchy framework of last night's history. She'd remembered getting into a jam . . . oh, yeah, and there was the thing with her gun, too—and then—

The entire sequence came back to her, right up to landing that sweet kick to the asshole's gonads. Bet *he* was a little worse for wear today. Probably lying on a couch with a bag of frozen peas duct-taped in his skivvies.

That made her feel a little better.

"What's so funny, Dusty? You still thinking about goin' down on Big Johnson?"

Stella felt her one good eye go wide. Shit. She'd said it out loud. "I didn't say that," she protested. "What are you talking about?"

"Yup, just a minute ago you were coming out of la la land. All these drugs they got in you for the stitchin' up and what-not must be wearing off. And you were saying—"

"I said I got to *show* Big Johnson," Stella said, feeling her face grow hot. She could also feel little itchy pinpricks of sensation, and she put her fingertips to her cheek. Felt stitches. Well, damn. Traced them from close to the bridge of her nose down to the back of her jaw on the left. And there was some sort of bandage-and-tape thing going on up on top of her skull, too. She continued her exploration and found a little nest of stitches buried in a shaved patch on the other side of her head, the skin there raised up in a sizable goose egg.

"Yeah? What-all you plan to show him?"

"Obviously not my beauty pageant sash," Stella said, sighing. "How bad off am I?"

Goat looked at her with one corner of his mouth quirked down and the other up; like his eyebrows, his mouth appeared to have a mind of its own when it came to expressing mixed feelings.

"Well . . . ," he said slowly. "Considering they hit you hard enough to put you out for a few hours, I guess I've seen plenty worse. I mean, not on a girl . . . I mean, a woman . . .

or anything . . . not that you look any *worse* than a guy who's had the crap kicked out of him—"

"Jesus, Goat, shut the fuck up and get me a mirror."

Goat folded his arms across his chest and stared at her with a squinty expression. "You sure that's a good idea? You know, you're just damn lucky you're not in worse shape. Dr. Guevera says you're in a lot better health than she expected. Heart like a teenager."

Great. *Better than expected* . . . it wasn't exactly a ringing endorsement for her appearance. It was nice to be judged healthy, but Stella already knew she was in basically superb shape—her job required it. Under her curves were muscles she never knew existed until a few years ago. There was a reason she spent an hour every day on the stupid Bowflex and ran her ass off a few times a week. "Really? What kind of health did she expect me to be in?"

"Oh, come on, Dusty, don't get all prickly. I'm sure she just meant—well hell, you know, we're not spring chickens here, me and you. Be happy, you're on top of the curve. Besides, you look fine to me. You always do." He looked away, reddening. "How about we talk about what you were doing down at the golf course, instead? And who your little playmates were, that decided to show you such a nice time."

Stella rolled her eyes, which turned out to be a bad decision, since it made the ache in her head turn into more of a symphony of pain. "How should *I* know who they were?" she demanded. "It's not like they wrote their names in my yearbook before they took off."

"Well, let's back up a little then. What did you do after we talked yesterday? What kind of rocks have you been turning over, looking for beetles?"

Stella was sorely tempted to tell Goat everything that had happened: breaking into Pitt Akers's apartment, with all that extra cat food. The trip to see Benning, his threats, spotting the shed at the back of the lot, the evidence of his living-it-up lifestyle. The call from Darla and Stella's suspicion that Tucker might be marking time in nothing worse than a pissed-off girlfriend's house—in which case she'd stirred up the mob pot for nothing and bought herself a mess of trouble in the bargain.

There was something about having the tar beat out of you that made a big strong man with a badge and a gun seem strangely comforting.

But the risks were too great. So far she'd seen no trace of Tucker at all, and she had to get more leverage before she could take a chance on pushing Benning any harder.

Not to mention the stakes being raised by his thugs. It had to be the guys Arthur Junior had seen in the shed that day. Stella wished she'd gotten a look at them, but the only one she'd have a chance of even recognizing again was the man on the bench. Stella would lay odds that was Funzi himself, since he seemed to be older than the other two, and a little thicker, and probably didn't move quite as fast. Plus, he looked pretty comfortable directing the action while sitting on his ass.

If Stella told Goat everything now, he would have to act. But now that she knew how far Funzi and company were prepared to go, she was more frightened than ever of what they might do with Tucker, if for some reason the boy had ended up in their clutches. If they got wind of an AMBER Alert or a cross-county search or something, Stella didn't doubt they would make the boy disappear forever.

She glanced at the clock on the wall and was reassured to see that it was only a little after nine o'clock. There was still time to keep her date with Darla—Roy Dean's date, actually—if she could just find out who and where Darla was. Tucker had to be there. He *had* to.

"Well, let's see," Stella said. She'd play along now, then try to get rid of Goat so she could figure out her next move. "Chrissy and I had lunch over at Roseann's, and then we minded the shop and sewed all afternoon. We're making a quilt for little Tucker."

"That so? You conveniently left out the part where you went to the beauty parlor first."

"Where I did *what*?"

"Went to the beauty parlor. For a facial and a full-leg wax. Your social secretary told me."

"My what? You mean Chrissy? When did you—"

"Hell, Stella, when you didn't come home by midnight that gal went through your address book and called me on my cell phone, got me out of bed. Had me out driving around all night until I got the call that they hauled you out of the pond and brought you here."

"You . . . were looking for me?"

Stella tried to keep a dopey little grin from settling on her face, but the thought of Goat driving around town, *worried* about her, made her feel warm and fuzzy on the inside.

"Well Christ, it was easier than listening to that young lady carryin' on. She's out in the waiting room, you know. Been there ever since they brought you in, sleeping in a chair, far as I can tell."

"She is?"

"Yup, and as soon as I'm done with you, you can visit with her. But I'm in here on police business, and so far you haven't been giving me much, so I suggest we ramp up the confessin' so we can both get on with things. I'll take up where you left off, and you can just lie here and get better."

Yeah, right, like that was going to happen. Stella intended to get herself out of the bed and back into the action as soon as it was humanly possible—but there was no sense advertising the fact. "Well, you got the story from Chrissy, you know where I was all day. Last night I got a call, around ten or so, from someone saying that he had information about Roy Dean and would I come meet him out at the golf course."

"So you just went, eh? Didn't think about maybe meeting him in, I don't know, a public place? Maybe giving me a call first?" Goat leaned forward aggressively and glared at her, and Stella thought, *Oh yeah, here it comes.* Leave men out of the action and they can't stand it. They just have to be the ones who do the stomping around and spitting.

"Well, how was I supposed to know what they were gonna do?" she demanded. "All I've done so far is give the girl a place to stay. I don't know why anyone would get all het up over that."

"Yeah. And you didn't bother to take anything along to protect yourself? I don't know, Dusty—in the past, you've proven yourself to be a resourceful woman in that regard."

Any levity in Goat's expression was gone now, and Stella felt her throat go dry as she let his words sink in. Ollie—he was talking about Ollie.

"Did you take some sort of weapon with you?" he demanded,

his voice low. "'Cause they didn't find anything when the EMTs went out to get you. Come on, Dusty, this isn't about me trying to get your permit in order or give you a time-out for nonregistration. I need to know what you had on you."

"I—nothing. I have pepper spray in my purse, but I left it in the car," Stella said. Then she told a bigger lie. "I don't even know how to shoot."

Goat worked his lips, evidently trying to figure out a response, but ended up saying nothing. Stella held her breath until he eased back a little.

"So, you're still sticking to just hand tools," he said, irritation evident in the creases between his brows. "Maybe you ought to carry around a screwdriver or a hammer with you, at least. Maybe you could have pounded a nail into one of those guys."

Stung, Stella said nothing at all.

She couldn't believe Goat would make such a casual reference to the wrench she'd used to kill Ollie—even though she knew everyone in town talked about it. Made jokes, even. She'd bet that half a dozen housewives watched their husband under the sink tightening up a pipe seal and thought about the wrench he held in his hand, wondering what it had felt like when Stella, not even fully aware of what she intended to do, brought it crashing down across her husband's forehead.

She blinked hard. That was a memory she had sealed up under the tightest security.

For the longest time, she couldn't remember any part of it. After the funeral, she'd come home, and other than letting the ladies from church help her box up Ollie's things for charity, she'd just gone about her days on autopilot. When she thought about that day, she remembered Sheriff Knoll taking her gently by the arm and helping her up, and she remembered looking down at Ollie, slumped on the floor, and thinking that it wouldn't do for him to ignore their company that way.

Later—much later—little bits and pieces would come to her at the oddest times. Sitting in a hot bath the following winter, she remembered closing her hand on the wrench, picking it up from the top of the stove where Ollie left it after tightening up a loose bolt on the range hood. A few weeks after that, she was cracking eggs for an omelette and she remembered the peculiar sound he made as he crumpled to the floor, a whispered, non-sensical protestation.

Eventually, she remembered it all. Remembered it, and made her peace with it. But she still kept it tightly hidden in a corner of her mind. It shouldn't be coming out like this—not while she was in this vulnerable state, lying here in a thin hospital nightgown with her face slashed and resewn, while the man she longed for tried to drag out her secrets.

She felt the barriers go up, the invisible ones, the walls that would keep Goat and everyone else as far away from her as she needed them to be. Chalk it up to emotional exhaustion, but she didn't have the energy to juggle her conflicting desires. It was time to compartmentalize. There were evildoers walking the earth who badly needed to be dealt some justice, and Stella knew she was the only one who could keep dealing it until they got Chrissy's boy back.

"What are you going to do now?" she asked, letting her eyelids slide down, setting her lower lip aquiver.

"I've been out to talk to Roy Dean's parents," he said. "They seem to think their son's just taken the boy for a little father-son time. You know, camping, fishing, like that."

"Funny," Stella said, frowning as much as her stitches allowed. "He never struck me as the type."

"Well, they say their boy's quite the outdoorsman. They're getting me directions to a little cabin he sometimes stays in, down near the lake."

Had to be the trailer, Stella thought. "What else you got?"

"I'm planning to call on some people Roy Dean's evidently been doing business with," he said. "Evidently he's been dealing in auto scrap. Plus I've got Mike and Ian out talking to Roy Dean's neighbors, his friends, his parents. We're on the lookout for his car, but so far nothing. We're looking into phone records. You know—all the usual."

Stella nodded. Just what she expected. "You must be exhausted," she said, turning up the sweet in her voice. "Running around all night. I'm so sorry to have caused you all this trouble. I guess you best get home and get a little sleep before you start your day."

Goat frowned. "Only one needing to rest here is you. I spoke to Dr. Guevera, by the way, Stella, and she says she's keeping you another night to keep an eye on your head. They don't take these concussions lightly."

Stella nodded, keeping her expression as neutral as she could.

Dumbasses—didn't they realize she'd taken her own concussions plenty seriously, waking up on the kitchen floor or sprawled across her bed, blood congealing from where Ollie'd split her lip or busted her ear, wondering if this would be the time she couldn't avoid the hospital? She'd been lucky that way, if you could call it luck—it had seemed like luck at the time.

Because Ollie had never actually broken anything. She

never had to go to the emergency room and make up excuses for why her arm or shin was bent at a strange angle. She never had to pretend to have fallen down the stairs or tripped over a laundry basket.

No, she dealt with all her injuries the old-fashioned way— at home, with a bottle of rubbing alcohol and a stack of bandages and a hell of a lot of CoverGirl concealer.

So one more concussion didn't scare her all that bad, thank you very much.

But there wasn't any reason to share that information with Goat. "Yes, I suppose you're right," she said meekly. "I'm actually feeling pretty tired myself, to be honest. Maybe I'll see if they'll give me a few more of those Tylenol, and take a nap."

"That sounds like a good plan. I'll tell Chrissy to come on back on my way out, so you all can have a short visit." Goat stood, then hesitated, gazing down at her. "I'll call you later in the day, let you know what I come up with. I don't want you worrying. We're going to find that little boy."

"I don't doubt it," Stella said.

Goat stared at her a moment longer, and then, moving so fast she couldn't even jerk out of the way, he slid one big callused hand under the thin blankets and ran his hand up her leg, letting his touch linger somewhere north of her knee.

"Tell you what, Dusty, I think you best get your money back for that wax job. You're about as hairy as a polecat."

Chrissy took one look at Stella and dropped her purse on the floor. Her hands flew up to her face, and she let out a little choked gasp.

"Oh shit, Stella, look what they *done* to you!"

So she was frightening people now. . . . Stella guessed she should be grateful that Goat had handled his horror so well.

"Just give me a mirror, will you?" she demanded, not bothering to cover her crankiness.

Chrissy nodded and blinked tears away. She picked up her purse and rummaged around in it, coming up with a plastic-handled makeup mirror, but she didn't give it to Stella right away. Instead, she sat gingerly on the side of the bed and patted Stella gently on the top of her head and then on the shoulder, so softly it practically tickled.

"I'd hug you but I'm afraid I'd just hurt you worse," she said miserably.

"Oh, come on, Chrissy, I'll be fine. You and I both know—well, we know we're tougher than people give us credit for. Right?"

Chrissy paused and mulled that over, then nodded decisively and leaned down for a big hug, smashing Stella's tender ribs and pulling at the stitches. But Stella let her, and even tried to hug back a little.

When Chrissy finally pulled away, she handed Stella her little purse mirror. It was so small that Stella couldn't see her whole face at once, and after squinting at herself for a few minutes, she figured that was probably a blessing.

She couldn't get over how darn colorful she was. Two black eyes—but the flesh was actually shades of purple and gray and a sort of green, a rainbow of bruising all around the sockets. The stitches were done with neat little knots in black suture thread, and the path they traced made a sweeping curve, so it almost looked like some kind of tattoo, like the ones made to look like barbed wire that the kids were so fond of.

The shaved part of her scalp was almost a perfect square, and Stella couldn't figure out whether that was a good thing or not. She tried pushing her hair over the patch to hide it, but the curls sprung right back the way they were, leaving the bald flesh exposed. She'd have to work at that with a little gel or something.

One thing she hadn't noticed earlier—her bottom lip was split and swollen and stuck out all puffy, like a movie-star collagen job gone terribly wrong. Jeez.

She handed the mirror back and tried for a smile, which hurt like a bitch. "Guess I'm not going to get on *American Idol* anytime soon."

Chrissy shook her head slowly. Then she took a breath and leaned in. Her eyebrows lowered and a flush of pink washed over her cheeks.

"We need to get out and get those sumbitches," she said fiercely. "Stella, if they gonna do you like this, why, I don't think they're just babysitting little Tucker."

"Oh," Stella said. "Oh. Uh . . . Chrissy, see, I haven't maybe told you every last thing I've found out."

"What—what do you mean?"

"No, no, calm down," Stella said as she saw Chrissy tense up, the tendons in her jaw standing out.

"Don't tell me to calm down, Stella, it's my—"

"No, listen. Some of it's, you know, maybe good news. I mean, not good but, er, not terrible."

"Stella, you tell me and you tell me right now." She inched

over on the mattress a bit, her hip bumping painfully against Stella's aching side.

"Well . . ." Where to start? With the most hopeful possibility, Stella guessed. "You know that Darla gal that called? She was talking about having something of Roy Dean's over at her house. Wouldn't say what it was, but the way she was carrying on, I got to thinking it might just be Tucker."

"Tucker? She's got my baby *boy* over her house?" Chrissy said, voice escalating incredulously. "What's she done with him?"

"No, now, I didn't say for *sure* he was over there, just that the way she was carrying on, saying have Roy Dean meet her there today because she didn't want the responsibility for—um, whatever it is he left there."

"Well shoot, let's go!"

"But now see, the problem is, she didn't say where she lived. Or what her last name was. I have a feeling I might have a description of her, seeing as it might be a woman somebody saw Roy Dean with the other day."

"How do we find out?"

"Hang on, sugar, let me tell you the rest first. This Darla's expecting Roy Dean at noon. She's gonna get us instead. We just got to figure out where she's at. But there's a little more I need to tell you."

"Like what?" Chrissy demanded.

"Well . . . you know how you said Pitt was visiting at your place when Roy Dean came over . . . and you went out in the back yard for that hibachi, and then he was gone when you got back in the house?"

"Yeah . . ."

"And how he thinks Tucker's his baby and all?"

"Well sure, but like I done told you, there's no way he'd take Tucker. He ain't crazy that way. He's all follow the rules and shit, he'd never—"

"Honey, I went over to his place yesterday. He wasn't there, so I broke in. Now don't get mad—"

"Mad? It's a little late for mad, isn't it, Stella? Anyway, I don't much care what you do or who you do it to if it means we get Tucker. What-all did you see?"

"Not much, really. He sure is a neat and tidy kind of fella. There wasn't a whole lot to look at. But I did see one thing that made me think he might have, um, taken a trip of some sort." She told Chrissy about the cat, the huge mounded supply of food and the full water dish.

"I always hated that cat," Chrissy wailed, as though the cat had been the one to abduct Tucker.

"Well now, we don't know if it means anything at all," Stella said hastily. "Maybe he just went, I don't know, visiting a friend, or down to Branson for a few days, or something like that."

Chrissy inhaled a big breath, let her shoulders slump, and blinked a few times. "You got any *other* ideas about who mighta took my boy? Any more bad news you ain't told me yet?" she finally asked, in a subdued voice.

Only the worst news of all. Stella considered everything she'd withheld from Chrissy so far, and came to the conclusion that she'd messed up big. Keeping everything to herself had done nothing to prepare Chrissy for this moment, when she needed to hear the entire truth.

"Yes," she said, and forced herself to look Chrissy in the

151

eye. "These guys, the ones I think beat me up, the ones Roy Dean's been working for . . . well, they're very bad men."

Chrissy sucked in breath. "How bad?"

Stella mulled over possible responses. Chrissy was not, as it had turned out, as dumb as Stella had first assumed. Not by a long shot. And now the girl had come within spitting distance of understanding the true dangers of the situation.

"Like . . . mafia bad. Drug-dealin' bad." Crazy stone killer bad, Stella thought, but didn't add.

"And these guys that done this to you last night," Chrissy demanded, "they might know where Tucker is? I mean . . . you think somehow they got Tucker or something?"

Stella resisted the urge to bite her busted lip and gave a little nod. "If it ain't Darla and it ain't Pitt that took him . . . then yes, I think there's a chance they might know something, that Roy Dean might have gone to them and, I don't know, looked for a place to stay, or, or—"

Or what? Why would Roy Dean take a baby into that mess? That was the part that made no sense at all, the part that kept Stella hopeful that answers were far more simple.

Chrissy nodded again, and Stella could tell she was thinking hard. "Did you get a good look at them?" she asked, her voice tight.

"No, dear, I'm afraid not. There was a few of them, and I was stupid. I didn't take the precautions I should have."

"Yeah, I'll say. Why didn't you tell me what you were fixing to do? Sheriff says you went over to that pond by yourself. Jiminy, Stella, I would never have let you go off on your own like that."

"Sorry," Stella managed. "Won't happen again."

152

"You bet your sweet petunia it won't," Chrissy said, and to Stella's great surprise, she leaned over and pressed the button on the bed, so the frame started to rise electronically, pitching her forward and shifting her painfully upright.

"Hey—what are you doing, girl?"

"Getting you out of here. What do you think? We got to find that Darla. Come on, we only got a couple of hours."

Stella had, as a matter of fact, been thinking along the same lines, but she hadn't quite expected to be heaved out of the bed. "Okay, but I can't just get up and walk out of here with this robe thing flapping around my bare butt."

"No, Stella, I know that. Don't be an idiot. I got you some clothes in here. I figured they might have kept your old ones, like for evidence or something. Plus I know sometimes they cut 'em off of victims."

She dug in the gym bag and pulled out a pair of cornflower blue stretch pants and a matching short-sleeved top that had a deep V neck with embroidery around the edges. As eager as she was to be on their way, Stella regarded the clothes with dread.

"Oh shit, where did you get those things?"

"In your bottom drawer. Why?"

"My sister sent them," Stella hedged—which Gracellen had, for her birthday, after Stella lied and told her she was a size ten. "They just shrunk in the dryer, is all."

"Well, we don't have time to go back," Chrissy said, "so you might as well get dressed."

She handed the stack of clothes, a fresh change of underwear on top, to Stella, and pulled a pair of sandals out of the bag.

Stella started tugging off her gown and eyed Chrissy

153

carefully. "Where were you thinking we'd be going, once you bust me out of here?"

"Well, I guess we don't have no choice but to start with what we know, now do we?"

"I can't help noticing that I'm hearing a lot of 'we' here, darlin'," Stella said. Telling the girl the truth was one thing; letting her join in the search, with all its risks and dangers, was another entirely. "Did I miss something—did you go getting your P.I. license while I was out cold?"

At that, Chrissy straightened and fixed her with a glare that practically threw sparks. "I don't really appreciate you being all sarcastic, Stella Hardesty," she said coldly. "Bad enough you didn't tell me what was really going on, Tucker being my baby and all. Like I couldn't handle it or something? Shame on you, I'm his mother. Well, cat's out of the bag now, I guess, so you ain't going to be able to get rid of me no more. We're in this together. 'Sides, last time I looked, you didn't have no license either, and plus, you done way more law-breakin' than I plan on."

Stella paused with the shapeless garment pulled down around her waist and looked Chrissy over carefully. The rebuke was the most impassioned speech she'd ever heard out of the girl, and it occurred to Stella that she might have been treating her more like a child than an adult. She chose her words very carefully.

"Chrissy, you're right. I have kept things from you, and as my client, you have a right to expect better. I promise I'll be straight with you from now on."

"And I'm coming with you," Chrissy said in the same no-nonsense tone. "We'll make a plan and then I'm coming along.

I want my baby back, and once I get him, I'll help you whup these—these—*devils*."

"I don't know if—"

"I ain't asking, Stella," Chrissy said with an edge to her voice that made Stella take notice.

Silently, she hooked her bra on and slipped into the T-shirt, tugging it over her belly, trying to stretch the fabric a little larger.

Chrissy wasn't asking. She wasn't going to be denied.

Every fiber of Stella's being resisted the idea of taking the girl along. Stella worked alone. And even more important, she didn't risk women's lives. Not anymore, not since Lorelle.

"I'm happy to have you come along to this Darla's place," she said softly. "And I don't suppose hunting down Pitt's really going to involve any special dangers. But this other bunch—they're ruthless. There are at least four armed men that we know about. Maybe more. There are two of us."

"Yeah, but we got the advantage."

"Yeah? How do you figure?"

"First of all, they ain't expecting us," Chrissy said calmly. "And second—we're moms. We're wired special to be fearless. They have no idea what kind of hell we can raise when we get provoked. Ain't that right, Stella?"

Stella opened her mouth to speak but realized she had little to add. "Well," she said, "I guess that's that. I can promise you, though, this ain't going to be any walk in the park. It's gonna be plenty dangerous and someone might end up getting hurt even worse than this."

"Stella," Chrissy scolded. "You're talking to a woman who married Roy Dean Shaw. I got myself hurt every single day. I think I can handle what a bunch of amateurs want to dish out, don't you?"

At that, Stella couldn't help but smile. "Sorry, you're right," she said. "Now get on out of my way so I can put my pants on."

With Chrissy playing lookout they were able to slip out of the hospital room and down to the elevator without anyone noticing. Stella left a note for the nurse, written on the back of the dinner menu she hadn't bothered to fill out: "Sorry, I had to go. I'll be back to settle up a.s.a.p. P.S. Don't worry, I'm feeling fine. Best regards, S. Hardesty."

On the ground floor Stella started to gain confidence. They went out the front door without attracting any attention. In the parking lot she was surprised to see her Jeep.

"Sheriff had one of his guys bring it on home from the golf course," Chrissy said. "They took the car keys out of your pocket. And I figured, with what all we got ahead of us, it might make more sense to bring your car than mine. Hope you don't mind."

"No—good thinking," Stella said. She wondered if Goat had noticed her little lockbox. There was a reason she used a combination lock on it—a key did no good. "You go ahead and drive. I'm still a little fuzzy from them happy pills they gave me."

Chrissy slid into the driver's seat and turned to Stella. "Well, I guess this is my first lesson," she said. "How do you find someone when you don't know much about 'em? You know someone down at the courthouse or something, can look up all the Darlas in the county?"

Stella snorted. She wished—that would be a handy contact to have. "No, but I got something about as good. Head us over to the Popeyes."

"Why—you got a hankerin' for biscuits or something?"

"No, you'll see."

From the way Chrissy lurched out of the parking lot, Stella figured she was still getting used to the handling. A thought flashed through her mind—Ollie would have had a fit to see Chrissy snugging the tires over the curb—and she laughed. It hurt, but it felt good, too.

"What's so funny?" Chrissy asked, cutting her a glance.

"Nothing. I just didn't expect to be chauffeured around today."

"Well, get used to it. We got to save your strength."

Stella closed her eyes and settled back and wondered what exactly Chrissy expected her to do. "They got my gun," she said after a moment.

"Oh, I got that took care of," Chrissy said. She reached behind and patted a cardboard box sitting on the backseat. "Picked up a few things from my folks' house. Go ahead, take a look."

Stella reached for the box, the type used to hold a ream of paper, and pulled it onto her lap. It was surprisingly heavy. She lifted the lid and found herself staring at an eclectic arsenal of weapons.

Lying on a pile of old rags was a grimy, blocky old steel handgun. There was also a wicked-looking big hunting knife with a hook, two smaller knives, a couple of holsters, and three boxes of cartridges, one open and half empty.

"Holy shit, Chrissy," Stella said. "Your folks some kind of

survivalists or something? Fixing to hunker down for the big standoff with the FBI?"

Chrissy's face hardened and she didn't look at Stella. "I don't appreciate that," she said after a moment. "My family ain't much, but they ain't criminals. Well, I mean they get into stuff here and there, but they ain't *that* kind of criminal—the crazy kind."

"Sorry, hon," Stella said hastily. "I didn't mean to offend you. It's just, you got to admit, this is a hell of a lot of firepower, and I wasn't exactly expecting it."

Chrissy shrugged. "Well, the gun, that's an old Soviet Makarov, my uncle Fred brought it back from Vietnam. Daddy used to let us kids shoot it sometimes when he took us out for rifle practice."

"They didn't let anyone bring these back," Stella said, picking up the handgun. It was heavier than it looked, with a star carved in the pistol grip and a simple safety catch at the rear of the slide. There were two magazines in the box, both empty.

Chrissy snorted. "You didn't know my uncle Fred. I don't think he cared much what he was *allowed* to do or not do. He s'posedly smuggled that gun back wrapped up in a hollowed-out Bible. I think Daddy just keeps it around for sentimental reasons. It ain't been fired in ages."

"Yeah—it looks it, too."

"Nothing a little solvent won't take off. That other stuff is just mostly for fun, you know, things my brothers pick up here and there and then they get tired of 'em and leave 'em lyin' around and they end up in Mom and Dad's attic."

"Your brothers have an interesting idea of fun," Stella said, putting the gun back and hefting the biggest knife in her hand.

"I wouldn't be talkin' smart, Stella," Chrissy said. "People say the same thing about you. Besides, you should see all the junk I *didn't* bring."

She lowered the knife carefully back into the box and considered Chrissy for a minute, the girl's ramrod straight posture, the firm set of her chin.

This was a different girl from the one who'd spent most of the last two days lying on Stella's couch. This new Chrissy had a hell of a lot more backbone and she sure seemed a lot less inclined to take any guff.

"I think I might need to apologize," Stella said carefully.

"Thought you already did that. When we agreed how I'm going to be your partner on the rest of this thing."

"Yeah, but—I think I need to maybe say I'm sorry for underestimating you. Chrissy, I do believe you got some iron in you."

Chrissy said nothing for a moment, keeping her eyes fixed on the road ahead, and then she nodded. "All right. I accept your apology. You know what, I didn't know I had it in me either. I kind of wonder now, what if I'd got this kind of determined back when Roy Dean was around? I mean, right now I'm so mad I feel like I could just beat the shit out of him myself."

"I imagine you could," Stella agreed softly.

Vengeance was a funny thing. You got a little taste of it, and it brought out things in you that you never knew were there. What was it they said? *Vengeance is a bitter drink.* Stella didn't much mind. She drank hers straight up, and now it looked as if she'd found herself a drinking buddy.

"Hold on to all that determination," she said. "We're gonna need it."

Chrissy coasted across two lanes without checking the rearview mirror when the Popeyes came into view, ignoring the outraged laying on of horns. Stella flinched, then forced herself to relax; risk was inherent in her business, after all, and she wasn't really in a position to micromanage at the moment.

Chrissy managed to align the Jeep more or less straight in a parking spot. When they walked in the doors of the restaurant, she took one look around and smacked herself in the forehead. "Well, dang, why didn't I think a them? Stella, you're a genius."

"Oh, now," Stella said modestly. "I've been doing this a while. You're just starting out—you'll get there."

"Yeah, but the Green Hat Ladies . . ."

Just then Novella Glazer spotted them and hollered out a greeting; her tablemates turned and followed suit. As Chrissy and Stella made their way over, purses of the large and floppy style favored by older ladies were moved out of the way, and the remains of the meal—plastic plates of chicken bones and a smattering of biscuit crumbs—were stacked and shoved into the trash.

"Oh Lord above, Stella, what happened to you?" Lola Brennan said, placing a hand over her heart and squinting up at Stella's stitched and bruised face.

"Oh, nothing much—just took a tumble in the shop. I'll be fine."

"You ought to be home in bed," Shirlette Castro scolded. "You must have good reason to be out and about. I don't guess this is a social call?"

Stella had consulted with the Green Hat Ladies before when she needed information. One of them had even been a client, but that was hush-hush; her husband had needed only a light touch to be reminded that a foul mouth and ungracious commentary were not welcome in the house, and she didn't care for anyone to know about their past troubles.

It was a funny thing about that generation, Stella reflected; they kept their own problems to themselves, but they loved to discuss everyone else's—so much so that this bunch of septua- and octogenarians gathered for an early lunch and gossip at Popeyes nearly every day.

"I believe you all know Chrissy Shaw," Stella said as they sat down. Greetings were exchanged.

"You ladies sure look nice today," Chrissy said. "I do like those hats."

The hats were bright green caps embroidered with the John Deere logo. Gracie Lewis's husband ran a feed and supply store, and the Deere folks sent a regular supply of swag his way. When his wife and her friends caught wind of the Red Hat Ladies trend, being a thrifty type, he proposed a way to save some money and stand out in the crowded field of mature ladies' clubs.

"I am surely glad you got shut of that Roy Dean," Gracie said. "If you don't mind me sayin' so."

"Oh, not at all," Chrissy said. She twisted her gloss-sticky lips into a thoughtful frown and added, "I guess I might ought to have done it awhile ago. I'm not sure where my good sense went."

The ladies made sympathetic clucking sounds. "Oh, now, we all have us a confused spell now and again," Gracie said. "'Specially when it comes to the gentlemen."

"You wouldn't be the first to pick a rotten apple off the tree," Novella added.

Stella laid out an assortment of facts about Roy Dean's wandering ways as the ladies took turns patting and cooing over Chrissy. It was probably a misunderstanding, she said, but did any of the ladies know any Darlas in the surrounding area? Especially skinny youngish ones with blond ponytails?

"Oh my yes," Lola piped up. She was a tiny thing, and her hat practically swallowed the top half of her head, nearly obscuring her eyes. "There was that one, over in Harrisonville, by the strawberry stand—"

"Ungainly thing, wasn't she?" piped up Shirlette. "Large bust, unfortunate overbite?"

"Oh mercy no, you're thinking of that other gal out that way. Took up with her aunt's boyfriend. What was her name, Dora, Doreen, something—"

"It's a shame Linda's not here," Novella said. "Her husband hails from Harrisonville—she'd know. She's down with her usual unfortunate troubles," she added in a stage whisper to Stella and Chrissy.

"Oh, for heaven's sake," Lola said. "You can say *hemorrhoid,* Novella, it ain't a bad word."

"Well," Novella said primly. "I suppose that's fine for some."

"We could call her," Shirlette said, pulling an iPhone out of her purse and peering at it over her eyeglasses. She tapped at it with her finger a few times and held up a finger.

"She's not moving too quick today," she said, "if you know what I mean. Oh, Linda? How are you, dear?"

Shirlette had the volume on the iPhone up high enough that everyone heard Linda's voice, though Stella couldn't make out what she was saying.

"Is that right? . . . Oh, I'm sorry. . . . Listen, guess who stopped by? Who? No, Stella Hardesty. And she brought that darling Chrissy Shaw, remember? One of the Lardner girls? . . . That's right, the pretty one. Anyway, do you know a Darla out Harrisonville way? Young gal, blond . . . Yes, ask him . . . ."

Shirlette drummed her fingers on the table as all six ladies listened to the sounds of conversation on the other end of the connection. "Is that like it sounds? Here, Novella, gimme a pen. . . . Yeah, go ahead, Linda . . . mmm-hmmm . . . okay, I'll tell her. No, I'll tell you later. What? . . . Look, Linda, it's *Stella* who's asking, you catch my drift? She don't have time to be waiting for this information. Yes, I'll call you back."

She dabbed at the phone and slipped it back in her purse. "Well," she said breathlessly, "there *is* a Darla over in Harrisonville, Darla Merton."

"That's right," Lola said, snapping her fingers. All the ladies leaned in, and Stella found herself following suit. "That's the one. Kind of a loose one, if I recall."

"A regular tramp is what Linda said," Shirlette agreed. "She might as well install a revolving door on her bedroom. She's out on Dixon Road past the Mobil station. You take a soft right and go over a dip and there'll be a dirt bike track on the left. She don't know the house number, but it's the yellow-brick ranch on the right—it's a duplex and she's on the right side."

"I know where that Mobil is," Chrissy said, gathering up her purse.

"Please thank Linda when you see her," Stella said. "I wish we could stay and catch up."

"But you have *important* work to do," Gracie said, winking. "You don't have to tell *us*. Well, God bless y'all. And Stella, get to healin', you hear?"

After quick good-byes, they hurried back to the Jeep, Stella moving as fast as she could.

Chrissy hurtled out of the parking lot. "It's twelve minutes to noon," she said. "We got to haul ass!"

It was pretty much a straight shot to Harrisonville down County Road 9, and Stella gripped the dashboard most of the way as Chrissy pushed the little Jeep hard. At the Mobil she barely slowed down, and Stella was surprised the wheels didn't lift up as Chrissy took the corner. The yellow-brick duplex came up fast on the right, and as she screeched to a stop the dash clock read 12:09.

"Now hold one second," Stella said, slapping a hand down on Chrissy's arm to prevent her from bolting out of the car. "You know she's expecting Roy Dean."

"I don't care if she's expecting Tim McGraw—"

"What I'm sayin' is, we can make this easier if we start out reasonable, just stay calm and cool and help her see we're offering a win-win all around here."

"And *then* I call the bitch out, if she gives me any shit."

"Well . . . okay."

Chrissy wrenched her arm away and got out of the Jeep, and Stella had to hustle to keep up across the burned-out lawn and onto a cracked concrete porch.

Chrissy laid into the door, pounding with a clenched fist. When it suddenly burst open, a large man popped into view and Chrissy went flying inexplicably floor-wards. Only when she was laid out on the carpet with the large man sitting on her chest did Stella see the second man, more of a kid, really, who had taken Chrissy down by throwing himself at her legs and yanking them out from under her.

"Ow," Chrissy said. "Git off me."

"Shit, Dad, that's a *girl*," the younger man said, scuttling away crab-style before jumping to his feet.

The first attacker had apparently come to pretty much the same conclusion because he lumbered off Chrissy. "Hell," he said, sounding more annoyed than sorry.

Stella offered Chrissy a hand and hauled her up, the effort ratcheting up the ache through her ribs. "You okay?" she asked.

Chrissy glared at the two men who, now that they were standing sheepishly side by side, could be seen to be clearly related, with the same blockish heads and thin lips and fleshy eyelids. She rubbed at the small of her back and cricked her head one way and then the other. "I'll live," she said sourly, before turning on her attackers. "Where's my baby? Where you got Tucker?"

The men looked at each other.

"Huh?" asked the younger one.

"Look here," the older one said. "You kind of got in the way of a operation in progress. There's someone coming along any minute now that needs a major attitude adjustment, so if you don't mind, we need to get ready for him."

"I think that's my ex you're talkin' about," Chrissy said. "Roy Dean. He ain't comin'."

"He sent you in his place?" the young one said, clearly agitated at the notion. He looked like a man who had his heart set on delivering a beating.

"No, he did not. He's done disappeared. Look, all's I want is my boy, and then I'll go. Where's Darla?"

"That ain't any of your business," the older one said, stepping forward angrily.

"I think it is." Stella kept her voice calm, but she drew up to her full height and glared at him. "Are you her father?"

He hesitated only for a second before saying, "Yes I am. Bill Merton."

He turned to Chrissy and added, "Your ex has been treatin' my girl pretty poor—he needs his ass kicked."

Chrissy sighed. "I don't doubt it, and I don't much care what you do to him. But way I heard it is he mighta dropped off my little boy here and left him."

The men glanced at each other, clearly mystified. "I don't know anything about no baby," Junior said.

"Call your sister," the elder Merton demanded.

Junior pulled a phone out of his pocket and dialed.

"I'm going to go look around," Chrissy muttered, her disappointment clear from the slumping of her shoulders.

Merton started to object.

"Let her go," Stella snapped. "She won't hurt nothing."

As Chrissy made her way down the darkened, cat-smelling hall of the house, Stella listened impatiently to half a phone call for the second time in an hour.

"Darla," the boy barked into the phone. "Roy Dean leave some kinda *baby* with you? . . . No, he ain't been by yet. There's these two women—I *said* he ain't come by, you deaf or something? What's her name?"

He directed the latter at Stella, jerking a thumb down the hall where Chrissy could be heard opening and closing doors.

"That's Chrissy Shaw, Roy Dean's ex," Stella said.

"Chrissy Shaw, Roy Dean's ex," the boy repeated into the phone. "Her little boy's gone missing, and she thinks Roy Dean had 'im. . . . You're sure? . . . Hell, I don't know, I'm just askin'. Well, don't get mad at *me,* I didn't do nothing! . . . Darla . . . Darla, I'm giving Dad the phone."

He handed the phone to his father. "*You* talk to her. She's goin' all PMS on me."

"Darla Jane," Merton said in a voice that didn't invite argument. "You settle down now, girl. Roy Dean apparently ain't comin'. . . . No, I don't believe they found him to tell him the message. Now you come on home, and we'll figure out what to do. Mmm-hmmm. That's right . . . love you."

He handed the phone back to his son as Chrissy came shuffling back into the room looking like she wanted to hit somebody herself. "Tucker ain't here."

"Look," Merton said. "I'm sorry we took you down like that. Just, we were expecting that no-good Roy Dean. He's been beatin' up on my daughter. Which I don't take kindly to."

"I don't guess I blame you," Chrissy said. "Though you could have looked out the front window or something and seen I wasn't him."

"We *did* look," Junior protested. "We saw your car pull in. But then we had to get in ready position."

Amateurs, Stella thought. She'd lain in wait dozens of times, in alleys, behind bushes, in cars, outside office buildings—even in a men's room once or twice—and never had she taken down the wrong guy.

But that's what made her the professional that she was. Fastidious planning, careful preparation, flawless execution—when you made a career out of delivering justice, there was no room for error.

She knew there were lots of folks who'd figure that, working outside the law, Stella might have flexible standards. And it was true, in some ways—but not when it came to getting the job done. She didn't tolerate near misses or botched reconnaissance or loose ends. It made the job harder—a lot harder—but no one ever changed the world by taking the easy way out.

"So this *thing* that Roy Dean was supposed to have left here," she said. "Was that all just a trick?"

The elder Merton snorted. "There's a box of his clothes and shit out in the garage, but I expect what he's missing most is them illegal drugs he left in my daughter's home."

He dragged out the syllables in "ill-legal" to show his distaste, even as his son rolled his eyes heavenward in a grand show of impatience. "Ain't but a couple a nasty smoked-down blunts, Dad."

"And that mess of *para-pher-nalia,*" Merton huffed, glaring at his son and Chrissy in turn, as though he suspected them of being in cahoots. "Them papers and clippers and I'm sure I don't know what all else. *My* daughter ain't got no use for that sort of thing."

"Don't look at me. *I* don't want none of it," Chrissy said.

"Listen up, sugar," Stella said. "Tucker isn't here. These men don't know where he is, and it sounds like Darla doesn't know either. I'm afraid this might just be a dead end."

Chrissy nodded, frowning.

"All right," she said, never taking her eyes off the Merton men. "We're going to leave now. But if you find out anything—

and I do mean anything—about my little boy, you call me right away. 'Cause if you don't, I *will* find out and I *will* hunt you down. Now get me something to write on."

As Chrissy wrote their cell phone numbers on the back of a takeout menu, underlining the digits three times and circling them, Stella noted that any traces of the earlier Chrissy—the one who battled her fears with nothing stronger than Oreo cookies—were long gone.

With two avenues left to explore—Pitt and the hornet's nest of corruption brewing in the northeast end of town—Stella made an executive decision as they got back in the Jeep and Chrissy pulled away from the curb at what was, for her, a sedate pace.

"Sweet pea, I think it might be time to let the law do its thing," she said. "If Pitt's got Tucker, the longer we wait, the further he could be taking him."

"You're saying Pitt wants to keep Tucker for himself, like that?"

"Well . . . I'm just saying, we got to consider all the scenarios here. That's one of them."

Chrissy frowned doubtfully. "I seen them tapes. What was that, England or something? Where they got that little girl in the grocery store and snipped off all her hair in the bathroom and put her in boy clothes. But Stella, that's *over there.* Pitt wouldn't ever do like that."

"How can you be sure, Chrissy?"

"Well, I *know* him, is all. He's tryin' to *court* me to death."

Stella tried to figure out a polite way to ask how sneaking

over for noontime quickies counted as courting, or if there were some other romantic behaviors she wasn't aware of. "But let's say . . . I mean, here's Pitt, wanting you to, ah, to date him again. And on the other hand, there's a baby he thinks is his, and we know how that can get a man's spurs up, right? So if you had to guess, sugar, and meaning no disrespect, which would you say is *front and center* in Pitt's mind? You or Tucker?"

Chrissy slowed to a few miles an hour to avoid a yellow dog lying in the street, snoozing in the afternoon sun. "He wants the whole package, Stella. Me 'n Tucker and the white picket fence shit. I'd've been tempted too 'cause I *am* fond of that man, but I just know myself a little too well, you see what I mean?"

"Uh, not exactly . . ."

"Well, just that you know how some men scratch your itch a little but they still leave you feeling restless. And then there's the ones that do it for you and then some, you know? Like a little bit a what they got goes a long way, they just kind of shiver you all over. Inside, outside, and twice on Sundays . . . see? Pitt's the first kind of man, and that's how I ended up steppin' out on him when we was married, and I just know I'd do it again." She shrugged. "I guess that's the gift of being in your late twenties, is you get mature. You *know* yourself."

"Hell, if you've managed that already, you must be some kind of genius," Stella exclaimed. "It took me until I was almost fifty."

"Well . . . you're smart in *other* ways," Chrissy said kindly, driving lazily across the center line as she turned to give Stella a reassuring pat on the knee. Chrissy, who'd barely let the needle drop below eighty on the way over, was negotiating the streets of Harrisonville like a blind old lady.

"But how do you explain him leaving town then?"

"What you said—he could be visiting someone or catching a show in Branson or something. Course, that was back when you were still shuttin' me out of this here investigation, so I don't guess you even believed them poor excuses when you said 'em."

Ouch. The girl had a point, and Stella swallowed hard, guilt weighing heavy on her. "There still might be a logical reason . . ."

"Tell you what, let's just save that for now. What I'm worried about is, you said if the law gets on this and word gets back to them Kansas City gangsters and Roy Dean *is* involved with all that, then it could be even more dangerous for Tucker if he's with Roy Dean."

"Well . . ." There was an uncomfortable amount of truth in what Chrissy said. Stella still couldn't piece together a logical reason why Roy Dean would have taken Tucker, but if he'd done something stupid and pissed off the mafia, it wouldn't matter if he'd taken the Hope Diamond or a can of pork and beans into their midst: either way, he wasn't likely to come out again. And if *that* was the case, their only hope of getting the boy was to somehow get inside their inner circle and take him back themselves. "I guess . . . if you're sure about this . . . me and you are going to have to go turn over some rocks."

"What sort of rocks?"

"Ugly, nasty ones. The rocks rolling around at Benning's. Only look here, Chrissy. I think there's every chance in the world I've poked a mad dog in the eye that don't have anything to do with Tucker. I mean, even if Roy Dean took him through there on his way out of town, there's no reason those men would want anything to do with a little boy."

"Yeah . . . I guess. But I know Roy Dean. He wouldn't be able to stay away from a bunch of losers like that. Prob'ly made him feel all important. Mr. *Big* Man."

Without warning, she hit the gas, and they screeched forward down the couple of blocks leading back to the state road. A man working the front of his lawn with an edger jumped out of the way just in time as she barreled past him.

"Where are we going, exactly?" Stella asked as Chrissy turned the wrong way down 9.

"Just a quick stop at Wal-Mart. We're gonna need some supplies if we're going to bust into that place."

"But—but Wal-Mart's the other way."

"Not that Wal-Mart. We're going to the other one, over in Casey."

Stella's head throbbed, and she gently massaged her temples, avoiding the bruised and stitched areas of her face as well as she could.

"I almost hate to ask, but what are we shopping for exactly?"

Chrissy glanced over at Stella, an all-business expression on her face. "Clothes for sneaking around in. I figure we got to get back over to Benning's tonight, after dark, and look around. Best we wear black so we don't stand out. Or camo, maybe. They make practically everything in camo these days, you know."

"Oh." Stella had to hand it to Chrissy for jumping right in to the details, which were still fuzzy in Stella's own mind. Of course, Chrissy had the advantage of not having a concussion. "So . . . we'll head out there tonight."

"Yeah, well, we need to go when they're closed, right? I mean, it's not like they're going to be happy to see you again, 'specially since it's probably them as beat you up. You think we ought to get some of those night vision glasses?"

"I don't know. . . . I think they're pretty expensive."

"Yeah. Thanks to our stupid government," Chrissy said, disgusted. "They pay six hundred dollars for a toilet seat, they probably want, like, a thousand bucks for those glasses."

Stella was lost. "How does the government figure into what Wal-Mart charges?"

"Oh come on, Stella, don't be naïve. The government doesn't want us to defend ourselves. Or bear arms or anything like that. They put a special tax on things that it's our constitutional right to buy, and then the money goes straight into their pockets. Or they use it for all those programs where they spy on what's in your trash and read your mail. It's true—I saw a special on it."

"Uh, yeah." Stella decided not to argue; she was still a little light-headed. "That's too bad. I do have a good flashlight, though."

"Good, 'cause we don't want to buy too much. Because the checker might notice. I was kind of thinking we want to draw as little attention as we can to ourselves here. That's why we're driving over to the Wal-Mart in Casey, you know?"

"Good thinking, sugar," Stella said. "Plus, there's an Arby's near there, isn't there?"

Chrissy perked up and nodded. "Yes, I think there is. I sure love that roast beef, don't you? The way they slice it up so nice and thin? My sister Sue won't eat it because she says it's all parts mashed up fine and then re-formed, but I say, why, that's the same as Spam, ain't it? And everybody likes Spam."

"That they do," Stella said, smiling despite the pain in her busted lip. "That they do."

Stella figured she needed to go long on iron and protein, so she had a Super Roast Beef sandwich. It was time to quit messing around and treat the situation like what it was: serious.

Within the hour they were back in Stella's kitchen. Stella laid old towels on the kitchen table and got down her shoebox of gun-cleaning supplies from a cabinet over the refrigerator. She had brought the Ruger in from the Jeep; it was already clean, but it felt good to break it down and go through the motions.

Across the table, Chrissy carefully disassembled the Makarov, laying the filthy parts out in a neat row. She picked up the cleaning rod and the solvent and went to work on the receiver, humming softly.

"Jesus, Chrissy, anybody ever clean their firearms over at your house?"

"Sure they do, the ones they use. But I didn't want to take Daddy's everyday guns, you know? On account of he might need 'em and all."

Stella, wondering what constituted the need for an everyday handgun, remembered her pledge to be more respectful of the girl and kept her mouth shut.

"You clean guns much?" she asked instead.

"Of course," Chrissy said, rolling her eyes. "Daddy made

all us girls learn to take care of the rifles before he let us shoot squirrels. We had a couple of Marlins and they never had a speck on 'em. We used to have contests to see who could get them took apart and put back together the quickest."

That was quite a vision; Stella imagined the little tykes lined up at the supper table waiting their turn at the guns, a row of Lardner girls with blond pigtails and rosy cheeks.

"Well then, I guess I'll let you clean that thing up. After that we're gonna go out and shoot a few cans. Sound all right?"

"Yeah."

For a while they worked in silence. Stella went over the Ruger with a tiny utility brush and then polished it with a silicone cloth.

"Stella?" Chrissy said after a while.

"Mmm-hmm?"

"You got anything to snack on? I have to tell you, I'm just a little bit nervous. And when I get nervous I get hungry, you know?"

Stella knew. She was the same way. She also got hungry when she was worried or pissed off about something or bored. She smiled. "How about I make us some popcorn?"

"Oh, that'd be perfect."

Stella got out her mother's old soup pot. Added the oil and a good layer of kernels. Put a stick of butter in the microwave to melt and shook the pot when the corn started popping inside.

She tossed the popcorn with the butter and a few good shakes of salt and set the bowl in the middle of the table. As the two of them sat munching on the popcorn and sipping ginger ale and cleaning the guns, Stella noticed she was feeling something that she hadn't felt for a long time.

The scent of gun oil mingled with the buttery popcorn aroma, and the silence between her and Chrissy was companionable. Stella closed her eyes for a moment and remembered other times she'd sat around this very same table.

It had been her parents' kitchen table. On Sundays, Stella liked to sit with her dad while he shined his shoes before church, handing him the rags and the tins of polish and the big brush, happy to be his assistant in such an important chore.

Later, her parents got a new table and gave the old one to Stella and Ollie. Noelle used to sit at the table for her after-school snack, coloring with her crayons, her little legs swinging, not long enough to touch the floor.

When Noelle was in high school, Stella waited up for her to come back from dates with Schooner, the high school boyfriend Stella wished she'd held on to, the one Noelle liked before she developed a taste for losers. They would sit at the table and sip tea and Noelle would describe every little detail of the pizza they'd shared or the movie they saw and Stella would listen and try to hold on to every moment, knowing her baby was growing up.

Now she was at this same table with Chrissy, and as much as she missed her own daughter, she was happy to have the girl's company.

The thought that she was dragging Chrissy into the midst of a bunch of crazed, armed criminals hit her in the gut— followed fast by a memory of Lorelle. Or rather, of Lorelle's feet, white and bloodless and puckered from all that time in the water, floating just below the murky surface in the rain barrel.

"You know," she said, voice shaky, as Chrissy scoured out

the spare magazine with a cotton patch. "You don't have to come along tonight. I can do this by myself."

Chrissy snorted. "Like hell. I'm not staying here."

"It's just—you know. There's a chance things could blow up. You should think about what you're getting into."

"I guess I know enough. Roy Dean's done something stupider than I ever thought he could. Got himself involved with guys mean enough that they'll beat up an old lady. Oh, I mean, not *old* old, but . . . you know."

"Jeez, Chrissy, I'm *fifty,* not eighty."

"You *are?*" Chrissy whistled, and Stella felt a little better. "No kidding. My mom's like forty-eight and you're in way better shape than her. She can't probably even run two blocks without sitting down to rest."

"Well . . . thanks." Stella brightened a little. The first time she'd gone jogging, in an old pair of Keds and baggy leggings, she'd made it halfway around the block before she had to stop and walk home, wheezing the entire way. Now she was up to ten-mile runs through town and out dusty farm roads. She might not look it, but she was in the best shape of her life, which was a good thing, since she was planning to take on a bunch of guys who were a lot more fresh-minted.

"Yeah, so, what do you think it is anyway? Drugs? Prob'ly drugs; seems like that's what people get craziest over."

Stella considered whether she ought to tell Chrissy everything she knew. She owed it to the girl, really; it wasn't right to leave her in the dark.

"Listen, honey. When I went over to talk to Benning yesterday, I had a little more than a feeling about what-all he was up to. See, the night before . . . when I said I was going to Lovie Lee's divorce party?"

"You didn't," Chrissy said. "I should have figured."

Stella told Chrissy what Arthur Junior had said about the car theft. Chrissy, who had finished cleaning and wiping off all the gun parts and was working on putting them back together, stopped working and listened with her head shaking slowly back and forth.

"Figures, don't it? Do you know Roy Dean still had all his Matchbox cars in this big old paint bucket in the garage? Threw out my box of bridesmaid dresses because he said we didn't have room, but we got to keep those stupid cars."

"Boys will be boys, I guess," Stella shrugged.

"Boys will be assholes, more like," Chrissy said. She held up the reassembled gun and turned it this way and that, gleaming under the kitchen light.

"Okay, Stella," she said. "I'm locked and loaded. Show me something I can shoot the shit out of."

SIX

. . . .

Stella was relieved to discover that not only did Chrissy know how to handle the Makarov, she wasn't a bad shot.

They drove out to the back side of an old peach orchard, the trees so ancient and gnarled they didn't give up much fruit anymore, and set up a row of Fresca cans on a folding table she brought from home. Then they started shooting. When Chrissy missed, it wasn't by much.

The Ruger felt good in Stella's hand. It had been her father's personal firearm, and aside from target shooting, it had spent most of its days locked in Buster Collier's gun cabinet along with his hunting rifles. Stella had always thought it was pretty, with its ivory grip. On the rare occasions that her father let her hold it, he'd cupped her hand in his bigger, stronger ones and made sure her fingers didn't go anywhere near the trigger, even with the cylinder empty and the safety on.

Buster had died of a heart attack when he was still in his forties. He'd walked her down the aisle, but he hadn't lived to see what a monster Ollie turned out to be. Maybe it was better that way. Buster might have killed Ollie himself, and Stella doubted whether the law would have been as lenient with him as it had been with her.

Picking off Fresca cans with her father's gun, Stella wondered what he would have thought of the career she'd stumbled into. She was certain both her parents would have understood about Ollie. And they'd always preached a duty to lend a hand to those in need. Surely no one was more in need than Stella's clients, the ones society couldn't—or wouldn't—protect, the ones who resorted to begging and promising and praying as their only weapons against the horror in their own homes.

When Stella started helping these women, she remembered how her father dressed so carefully each morning, putting on the Missouri Highway Patrol uniform shirts her mother pressed and starched, the heavy belt that contained the radio and the summons book, and finally, the gun. Buster had only drawn it twice in the line of duty, and he hadn't fired either time. But it was a powerful symbol of order for Stella.

That gun went back to the Highway Patrol. But the Ruger was hers now. The ivory was slick-cool in her hand. She kept her arm firm against the recoil, sighted carefully, and fired over and over. The smell of the guns firing was acrid on the air, burning her nostrils, but she breathed it in hungrily anyway. Target practice had a calming effect on her, and she did it regularly, even if she'd never fired a gun into a man's flesh and hoped she'd never have to.

She and Chrissy settled into a rhythm, without speaking, taking turns sighting down the cans and blowing them off the table, stopping to reload now and then or to stack the cans back on the table.

When the cans were nothing but shredded scraps of metal, Stella and Chrissy gathered them up in a plastic trash bag Stella had brought from home.

"Guess you'll do," she told Chrissy, grinning.

"You ain't too bad either."

For an instant they just looked at each other. Stella was praying they wouldn't have to shoot, when it came down to it. She figured Chrissy was doing the same.

At home Stella defrosted a couple of rib eyes and microwaved some potatoes. They ate on TV trays out on the back porch, saying little as evening settled down and the sky turned pink and red.

"You probably shot people before," Chrissy said as they dug into bowls of rainbow sherbet with Cool Whip and Nilla wafers crumbled on top.

Stella was silent for a while before answering. "Honey, I haven't."

"Oh." Chrissy licked Cool Whip off her spoon, a bit of the white stuff perched on her upper lip. "'Cause, what they say and all, I just thought . . . and I wouldn't think no less of you, either."

"Well, thank you. That means a lot to me. But . . . killing a man. I mean, it changes you." She paused—that was the first time she'd actually admitted to anyone what she'd done to Ollie. For a second she wished she could take the words back, but it seemed important for Chrissy to know. "It's a one-way street. You come out harder. And maybe stronger. But I hate to think what would happen to a person if they made it a regular habit. I sure don't want to find out. Especially when— so far, anyway—it seems like there's other ways to handle men that need . . . handled."

Chrissy nodded. "I imagine I understand. I mean, if we ever do find Roy Dean, I don't need him dead, just—just really far away from me, and maybe hurtin' a little bit, too. Or a lot, even."

That wasn't a bad summary of what Stella promised to deliver when she took on a new client. She was relieved that the girl got it; she didn't need a loose cannon for a partner.

She examined Chrissy carefully. She had pulled her hair back with a pair of orange plastic barrettes that featured butterflies with sparkly wings. Her eyelids were dusted with gold eye shadow. She was wearing a scoop neck top that showed a bit of her creamy, youthful cleavage—and the edge of a fading ghost of a bruise.

Chrissy's eyes didn't look vulnerable, but they didn't look bloodthirsty either. They looked alert and hard and determined.

"Tucker don't have nobody else," she said. "Sometimes I wish I'd tried a little harder to find out who his daddy was. You know? I mean, back then I thought I could do everything myself, and mostly I have, but right now it sure would be nice if there was some man out there who loved Tucker as much as I do. Who was willing to do anything for him."

"I know, darlin'." Stella did, too. She remembered sitting in church years ago, watching other men with little ones on their laps or a hand on their son's shoulder, and cursing herself for not picking out a better father for Noelle. "But there's nothing a man can do here in this situation that you can't do. You and me."

Stella prayed that was true.

Thought of Goat, of his broad shoulders and strong arms and determined jaw and—she couldn't help it—of that heavy belt with his service revolver and cuffs, and was sorely tempted to call him. But Goat couldn't go in the way they needed to, which was to say, sneaky and immediate.

"Honey," Stella said. "We're going to use whatever tricks we need to until we find Tucker. Even, you know, unlawful-type tricks."

"Yeah, I know."

"I just didn't want you to think that I was worried about getting caught or something. I don't mind that. I mean, I'd mind, I guess, going to jail and all that, but Tucker comes first."

That made Chrissy smile. "Yeah, right. You'd probably love getting arrested. 'Cause then Sheriff Jones would have to frisk you and all. Prob'ly strip-search you."

"Chrissy!" Stella exclaimed, shocked.

"Well, come on, you're all googly when he's around. It's, like, obvious."

"I am no such thing!" Stella could feel the blush creeping up her face.

"Oh, please, Stella, when he's around your voice goes up and you twist your hair and all that. You might as well hang a sign around your neck says 'do me now.' Hey, it ain't a bad thing, is it? I mean, you got to signal to the man you're interested somehow, don't you? I guess you could come right out and ask him out, but you probably want him to ask you first or something like that, right?"

"I can't—I wouldn't—Chrissy, he's a *law* man, for crying out loud. I'm . . . not."

"My ma's a Baptist and my dad won't go in a church," Chrissy said. "She likes spicy food and he don't. She's itching to go on one of those RV trips and he wants to go to Branson. But they get on good. Conflict's like the center of every good relationship, you know?"

"I'm not talking about *conflict* here, I'm—listen, can we drop this subject? We got to get ready, don't we?"

Chrissy shrugged and gathered up the plates and glasses, but she had a smirky little expression that didn't fade even as they worked side by side in the kitchen cleaning up.

Stella retired to her room to prepare for the rest of the evening. The stitches in her face itched fiercely, and any lingering effects of the pain medication had long since dissipated. She dabbed around the edges with the Betadine swabs they gave her at the hospital, and smoothed on a little antibiotic ointment. At first she tried to apply it just to the worst spots, but eventually she gave up, squeezed out a glob and rubbed it all over her face, then frowned at the result: now she was puffy, bruised, scabbed, *and* cursed with excess shine. She considered dabbing on a little concealer and then realized how ridiculous the idea was: pretty didn't really play into her agenda.

Which led her to go over the plan. Essentially, there wasn't one, other than to get close enough to Benning and Funzi and the others to find out what they were up to. Yeah. Maybe they'd be sitting in a kiddie pool unarmed, drinking root beer and talking about where they'd stashed Tucker and the best way for someone to sneak up and take him back.

Stella snorted with disgust as she pulled her hair back and secured it in a short ponytail with an elastic. It was far more likely that she and Chrissy were going to have to beat the information out of one of them. With any luck they'd be able to separate one of the losers from the rest, and somehow make him tell them everything, all without causing the others to wonder where their friend had got off to.

And that's if Funzi and his associates were even at Benning's. Maybe it was bowling night, or maybe they'd got tired of the local color and gone back up to Kansas City. They could try to get something out of Benning and his skinny-ass girlfriend, if that was the case, but if Roy Dean had somehow ended up bringing Tucker into the mess, and now the goons were gone, Tucker was probably gone with them. Stella didn't like thinking about that one bit.

No, it would be better if it was another boys' night at the playhouse.

She pulled on the pair of loose camo pants and black T-shirt they'd bought at the Wal-Mart, and laced up her hiking boots. She surveyed herself in the mirror: with her hair up and her mangled face, she looked like a kid who couldn't decide what to be for Halloween, Rambo or Frankenstein.

Disgusted, she went to the garage and loaded up her backpack with supplies. In addition to a pair of powerful LED flashlights she packed a coil of nylon rope, a utility knife, a compact set of bolt cutters, pliers, her cell phone, and bottled water.

Chrissy was in the kitchen with the box she'd brought from home, strapping a shoulder holster over her own black T-shirt. It crossed in the back and bisected her generous bosom in the front. She picked up the Makarov, gave it a fond little dusting with her fingertips, and slipped it in the leather holder.

She'd tucked her camo pant legs into pink high-top Converse sneakers. Stella couldn't help grinning at the sight of her; with her ample curves and blond ringlets spilling from her baseball hat, she looked like a demolition cherub.

Stella put on her own abdomen holster and patted the Ruger. After shooting it earlier, it had become comfortable in her hands, and she liked the feel of it close by.

"You take the big knife," she told Chrissy, rummaging in the box for an ankle holster. She found one, a Velcro and nylon model that fit the knife as though it had been made for it.

"What about you?"

Stella thought for a moment. The other knives that Chrissy brought were small and wouldn't have much stopping power, and there didn't seem to be much point to bringing them, especially as she'd packed her utility knife.

Stella had a sudden thought and went to Noelle's old room, where she stored all her sewing supplies. Since she started her second business, her sewing machine had been gathering dust, but her best Gingher scissors were in the tool caddy where she left them. They were weighty in her hand, a good pair of nine-inch trimmers.

On a whim she grabbed her rotary cutter, too. She made sure the safety was on and slipped it into her pocket.

Back in the kitchen, she found another ankle holster, an old leather one with buckles, which she fitted carefully to her leg. The scissors fit well in the sheath, their handles sticking up in easy reach.

Stella got a couple of Advil, considered them for a moment,

and added two more, gulping them down with a glass of ginger ale.

"Bad?" Chrissy asked, watching her.

Stella shrugged. "I don't feel the best I ever have," she admitted, "but the smartin's gone down, mostly."

"You look good," Chrissy said.

"You got to be kidding."

"No. I ain't. You look like trouble with a capital T."

Stella wiped her mouth on her arm and burped. "Well then, I guess I can't ask for much more, right? Let's get this show on the road."

She was reaching for her backpack when the doorbell sounded. Stella froze and glanced at Chrissy, who was smoothing down her T-shirt under the cross-body holster.

"Shit," she said. "Who the hell—"

"You got to answer it, Stella," Chrissy said urgently. "You don't want folks wondering where you are. Plus, it could be the sheriff."

Stella grabbed an apron off a hook on the wall and tossed it to Chrissy. It read "Your Opinion Wasn't in the Recipe" and had been a gift from a client who'd bought herself a matching one once her husband had learned the hard way not to criticize.

As Chrissy hastily tied on the bright red apron, Stella tugged her pants legs over her ankle holster as well as she could and yanked her T-shirt low to cover the bulge across her stomach. They looked each other over and Chrissy gave Stella a thumbs-up.

Stella took a deep breath, went to the door, and peered through the peephole. A not tall, spare-built man in a shiny blue sport coat and too-long brown pants stood in the doorway, grinning nervously. His yellowish hair had been recently slicked down but was already popping up from the attempted part. He wasn't a whole lot to look at—neither handsome nor the least bit intimidating. Stella swung the door open and glared. "Yeah?"

"Hello," he said a little breathlessly. "You must be Stella Hardesty. Pleased to make your acquaintance. These are for you."

From behind his back he produced a small bunch of flowers, pink mums with a healthy puff of baby's breath, and thrust them at her. Stella took them, too surprised to object, and was starting to express her cautious gratitude when he craned his neck around her and peered into the house.

"There you are!" he bellowed, spotting Chrissy. "Oh Good Lord in Heaven, there you are!"

As he made to sprint past Stella, her instincts kicked in and she stuck a foot out. He tripped, shiny brown shoes colliding with her hiking boots so that he splatted with considerable force, flying flat out into the small foyer on Stella's throw rug.

He made an *oof* sound and a small box that he had been holding went flying. Stella drew her gun and had it on him in a split second, and was standing over him in an uwavering spread, the adrenaline from the afternoon coursing through her veins. Just as she was about to scream something harsh and threatening, Chrissy knelt down in front of him on her hands and knees and shook her head.

"Pitt Akers," she said, "What *have* you done?"

What the young man had *not* done, as it turned out, was to have kidnapped Tucker. Nor had he developed much more

188

hard-boiled courage in the intervening days since he'd last hid in a guest-room closet.

It was the latter that made Stella so certain of the former. After she'd interrogated Pitt for a mere five minutes or so it seemed pretty clear that his story was, in fact, the truth. When he heard—through the closet door behind which he'd barred himself—Roy Dean demanding his hibachi back, he was finally convinced that Chrissy's relationship with Roy Dean was well and truly over. He'd gone hastily back home to pack a few things and then jumped in his car for a road trip back to his family home in Sikeston, several hours away, where he got the engagement ring she'd returned to him after their marriage ended, and which had been stored in a wad of tissue in a matchbox in his mother's sewing caddy. He then shared the joyous news of his impending reunion with Chrissy, first with his parents over a pot roast dinner, and then with a few childhood friends. This second celebration turned into the sort of evening out at the roadhouse that tacked an extra day onto the trip for recovery purposes, but by this afternoon Pitt felt lively enough to make the drive home, where he took care of the litter box and showered and dressed in his finest duds and came over to re-propose.

It was, Stella supposed, to Chrissy's credit that she emerged dry-eyed but kindly from the brief, private discussion she and Pitt had in the guest room—and to Pitt's that he left without an argument, though they could hear his hiccup-sobs starting up as he cleared the door on the way back to his car.

Chrissy turned to Stella the minute he was gone. "For the love of Pete," she sighed, "I ain't got time to wipe up any more broken hearts here. Let's rock and roll."

They stowed their gear in the Jeep and hit the road. Stella, feeling a little better since the Advil had kicked in, took the wheel and set her pace just a little above the speed limit. When they got close to Benning's, Stella cut the headlights and crept along at five miles an hour. Once she could see the lights of the compound up ahead, she pulled across the road and drove onto a pull-in between two fields. The dirt ruts were nearly as weedy as the fields, but none of the vegetation was much over ankle high, and the silhouette of the Jeep would be pretty obvious from the road if anyone shone a light in their direction, but there wasn't much to be done about that.

At least there was little moonlight tonight. It was a thin sliver of a crescent moon, and clouds scudded past it, throwing the landscape into near-total darkness.

Stella took the flashlights out of her backpack and handed one to Chrissy. "Shine just right in front of you, not ahead," she warned. "And let's keep 'em off as much as we can."

They walked the field, stepping over the clumps of weeds, crunching dirt clods, and trying not to twist their ankles, staying silent. When they came almost abreast of Benning's across the road, Stella spotted a figure on the other side of the gate, illuminated clearly by the sodium lights up on poles behind the trailer and around the sheds and between the rows of ruined cars. Two, three—she counted four lights, plus what looked like more back toward the large shed she'd spotted the other day. The light was glaring and eerily yellow; what she could see of the guard's skin appeared unnaturally pale and waxy.

He looked young and bored, a buzz-cut, muscular guy with what looked to be a semiauto rifle across his lap, his hand resting lightly on the stock. He sat on a camp chair with his legs splayed wide, tapping his foot and nodding to a beat Stella could feel reverberating through the ground more than she could hear it coming from the boom box at his feet.

She held up her palm and Chrissy stopped behind her. Stella touched her arm and pointed off in the direction away from the road, and dropped down on her hands and knees. Chrissy followed suit.

"I think we better crawl," Stella whispered. "I don't know what kind of shadow we'd cast if he looks this way."

Chrissy murmured her agreement and before Stella could stop her, she slithered ahead on her chest with surprising strength. Stella did her best to follow suit, though when a weed stalk poked her torn and stitched cheek it was all she could do to keep from yelping with pain. In a few dozen yards she was breathing hard, and she was glad she'd ratcheted up her fitness program in January. Her old self wouldn't have made it ten yards.

After what seemed like an hour they were a good distance past the gate, and Stella signaled for Chrissy to stand up. They walked the rest of the way to the corner of the Benning property, where the chain-link fence made a right angle.

"Here, let me," Chrissy said, unzipping Stella's backpack and taking out the bolt cutters.

She went to work on the fence with surprising efficiency, snipping the wire one section at a time. Stella slid the backpack off, took out the pliers, and used them to pull the fencing back as Chrissy cut. It didn't take long to get a three-foot hole cleared.

They stopped to rest for a minute, drinking from the water

bottles. Stella put the tools back in the pack and shouldered it again.

"Ready?" Stella asked.

"Guess so."

Stella ducked down, making it through without even snagging her shirt. As she turned back to check on Chrissy she caught a blur of movement out of the corner of her eye and suddenly the two huge dogs from the other afternoon came hurtling toward her, teeth snapping in the pale moonlight. When they were twenty feet away one of them started an eerie howl and the other immediately joined in, barking viciously.

"Fuck!" Stella muttered, hoisting her flashlight and preparing to club it down on whichever dog reached her first.

Two shots cracked out and the dogs stopped in midstride and went spinning sideways, legs splayed and pinwheeling. The one that was barking switched midyowl to a high-pitched keening cry, and there was one more crack and it fell silent in the dirt, a shuddering pile of fur.

The dogs were still ten feet away.

Stella turned to Chrissy in amazement. She was standing in a perfect shooter's stance, the Makarov still clutched in her grip and pointed toward the dogs. But as Stella tried to put together a coherent comment, Chrissy began to shake, the tremor starting in her hands and shivering its way back through the rest of her body.

Stella put a hand on her shoulder, and she could hear Chrissy take a big gulp of air.

"Nailed 'em, girl," Stella said. "I didn't even have time to draw."

"I—they're faster than squirrels."

"I guess they are, huh. You did good, sugar."

Chrissy slowly lowered her gun arm, but she didn't rehol-ster. Stella didn't blame her. She reached for the Ruger.

"I think we're getting some company," Chrissy whispered.

Coming from the same direction as the dogs, the guard had left his chair and was walking slowly toward them, sweeping the beam of his own flashlight to the left and right. The arc would illuminate them in ten or twelve more steps.

"*Move*," Stella blurted, and she ducked and ran to the dead dogs. She grabbed a hind leg and pulled as hard as she could. The thing was huge and surprisingly hard to pull as dead weight, but adrenaline socked in and powered her along. Chrissy grabbed the second dog, and they staggered toward a stand of trees and scrub. When they reached the bushes, Stella yanked Chrissy's arm and they hit the ground and listened to the guard whistling and calling to the dogs while they tried to catch their breath.

"He's not going to stop looking until he finds the dogs," Chrissy whispered.

"He's going to holler back to the rest of them when he fig-ures out something went wrong," Stella said. "Right now he might still think it was a rabbit or something, but—"

"Shit. What're we gonna do?"

Stella could feel her heart pounding in her chest. What, indeed? This was far from her standard operating procedure. Her brand of ruthless usually involved an element of surprise, and an unsuspecting and unarmed target. It didn't really take a whole lot of muscle to catch losers off guard and threaten to shoot their dicks off.

But in this dark junkyard corner, her options were shutting

down fast. Unless the guard was a certified idiot, he had to figure that the dogs had run into trouble. And if he swung the light just a little wider, he'd see the hole in the fence.

In the moonlight she could make out the rifle in his arms, cradled like a baby—and a lot more tensed muscle than she'd noticed earlier when the guy had been sitting. His T-shirt, with the sleeves ripped off, revealed bulky biceps and ripped forearms. He moved with the grace of a well-oiled young machine.

She wasn't sure that the two of them stood a chance against him, and the minute he got his buddies involved, she and Chrissy were screwed for certain.

There really wasn't any choice—she had to take him down. But even if she managed to surprise him, the odds weren't great that she could overpower him—unless she somehow managed to end up sitting on him, in which case he probably would have a struggle just to breathe.

She was going to have to shoot him, and she regretted it, because hurting men was something she reserved for woman-haters, and this guy didn't look old enough to have even developed much of a grudge against the fair sex.

Stella bit the inside of her lip, took a deep breath, and rolled up onto her knee. "Help me, Big Guy," she prayed and then took her best shot.

Immediately the man fell down. Sideways, clutching his leg. Stella grabbed Chrissy's arm and they lurched forward, running to where he lay on the ground, moaning and cursing. She kept the Ruger trained on him, but he'd dropped his own gun and was clutching his leg below the knee. Stella used her momentum to hit him head-on, and they tumbled together and rolled; when they came to a stop Chrissy was standing above them, pointing her gun down at the guy's face, her look pure, fierce concentration, as though she was trying to figure out the puzzle on *Wheel of Fortune*.

"I'll shoot your durn head off," Chrissy said. "You say so much as one thing I swear to holy God you're gonna have a hole where your face was."

Now that they were closer, the guard looked even younger. Sixteen, seventeen, with a smooth face that didn't look like it needed shaving too often, popping out in sweat. It was clear that he was in pain, his eyes bugging out of his head, his mouth working in fear.

Stella crawled away from him and stood up. She slid her backpack off and got out the coil of rope. "I did you a favor shootin' you where I did," she said. "I could've capped your knee. Know what happens then?"

The boy shook his head, fast.

"You don't ever walk too good, that's what. With this hole here, you got a good shot at healing up right. You play basket-ball?"

The boy looked around wildly for a moment, then gave a half nod. Stella yanked his arms hard behind him while Chrissy took out the buck knife and cut off a length of the rope and handed it to her. While Stella secured the binding, Chrissy cut a second length of rope and went to work tying off his leg above the bullet entry. It was a big, messy hole, but it seemed to have missed the bone. If Chrissy was put off by the blood it didn't show.

"Well, that's too bad; basketball's a shitty sport. Still, you'll get a chance to keep playing it if you do what I tell you."

The boy shook his head, determination showing through his pain. "Fuck off."

Stella raised her eyebrows. "Is that 'fuck off, I enjoy getting shot and I hope you'll do it again,' or 'fuck off, I'm out of my mind with pain and don't know what I'm saying?'"

The boy just frowned and stared at the ground.

Chrissy kicked him, hard, below the hole in his leg. He made a sound that wasn't like anything Stella had heard from a human before.

"How do you like that, dirtbag?" Chrissy said, winding up to do it again.

"Hang on there, sweetie," Stella said, laying a hand on her shoulder. She crouched down to look the boy in the eye.

"Now I understand you got your reasons for not wanting to talk to me," she told him. "If my boss was some kind of king-pin or what have you, I guess I'd be worried myself. I wouldn't be in any hurry to spill the beans. In fact, you're probably sitting there thinking your odds with us are better than with the rest of those clowns. Am I right?"

The boy didn't say anything, but he gave the muscles around his mouth a workout.

"So that makes it our job to convince you that isn't the case. You look at me, you probably see a wrinkly middle-aged woman your mom's age. You think—"

She paused. At the mention of his mom, there had been something—a little blip of emotion that flashed across his eyes. Stella reconsidered her approach.

"Were you one of the ones that nailed me the other night?" Stella kept her voice pleasant as she fixed the knots in place.

When he didn't answer, she gave Chrissy a tiny nod, and

the girl toed his leg again. Not as hard, but enough to make him grunt with pain. Sweat beads had popped up along his forehead. He worked his lips a bit and then muttered, "No."

"What's your name?"

"Patrick."

"How old are you?"

"Seventeen." His voice hitched, ending in a bit of a squeak. Hell, bound up like that he looked about as threatening as a teddy bear. "What'd you do to the dogs?"

"Killed 'em," Chrissy said. "Shot 'em, and it didn't bother me a bit. I think I might have got me a taste for shooting things."

Stella glanced up at the cold steel in Chrissy's voice.

"I am looking for a little boy," Chrissy continued. "My son is missing. He is eighteen months old. I want him back. It's not right, him being away from his mother. Now, do you know anything about him?"

Patrick squeezed his eyes shut and grimaced from the pain.

"You know mothers," Stella said conversationally. "Chrissy here's actually a nice lady most of the time. Wouldn't swat a fly. But get between her and her boy and . . . whoo, I tell ya, I'm not sure I like your odds. I bet your mama's the same way. I bet if she knew who you were working for, she'd probably hightail it out here and take old Funzi's head off. Am I right?"

Genuine anguish seeped into the boy's eyes. "You're wrong. It's a family thing. We're related. Funzi's her cousin. Look, my dad took off when I was little, okay? I got three little sisters. Funzi's just helping us out."

Stella prodded him again, a little harder. The wound, which was down to a trickle of blood, gave up a small gush. "You think your mama would appreciate *this* kind of help? Huh? Do you?"

Though Patrick's face had gone chalk white, he kept to his stony silence.

"You're telling me your mama handed you over to Funzi? Told him, forget finishing high school, forget college, I prefer you take my boy and teach him how to maim and kill, please?"

"I can't cross him. I don't care what you say." The boy's breath was ragged. "He'll kill me. He'll kill me *slow*."

Man, it was worse than Stella thought. If Funzi'd got the kid running this scared, he must be the genuine, ruthless, bloody-handed mob article. She wasn't sure how to convince the boy she was every bit as much of a badass threat as Funzi.

Because, in the end, she wasn't. There was no way she was going to kill this man-child with peach fuzz growing on his upper lip.

As Stella hesitated, Chrissy shouldered her out of the way and leaned in hard on Patrick, her face just inches from his. "I don't know if your mama's a nice lady or not. I don't know her, period. That's why I can drive over there and start hurting her bad. If I *knew* her. I might have second thoughts, but I'm not even going to give her time to offer me a glass of tea. First thing I'm going to do is shoot her just like Stella done you, see? Except she don't have anything useful to tell me, so I don't know if I'll really take the time to tie her off so she don't bleed out. Aw, hell, I know it'll take a long time to lose enough blood from a hole here—"she jabbed Patrick hard in the skin an inch from the bullet's entry—"so I might just have to aim a little higher. There's some artery in the thigh I guess pumps a lot of blood, the, what do you call it—"

"Femoral," Stella said softly.

"Femoral, yeah," Chrissy said. Then she drew back slowly, never taking her eyes off the boy's face.

He gulped. Hard. And Stella knew they had him.

"I'll tell you what I know," he wheezed. "You stay the hell away from my mom. Funzi's got your kid. For his wife."

There was a moment of shocked silence.

"What are you talking about?" Chrissy demanded.

"Roy Dean gave him to Funzi, okay? He and his wife couldn't have kids. Been trying forever. Roy Dean said you wouldn't care."

Chrissy's eyes narrowed. "He said *what?*" she demanded, and Stella grabbed her arm before she could do the boy any more damage.

"He said you never did want that kid in the first place." The boy squeezed his eyes shut tight, a sheen of perspiration dampening his forehead. "Said he was an accident and all. He like . . . said you wanted to give him up for adoption . . . that he was doing you a favor."

Stella could feel Chrissy start to shake and clamped her hand down harder. "Easy there, girl," she murmured. "Easy. Whatever's happened, it ain't this boy's fault."

Chrissy shone her flashlight directly in Patrick's eyes, causing him to squeeze them shut. "Where'd Funzi take my Tucker?"

"I don't know, okay, I don't know! Probably the lake house, Mrs. Angelini spends most of the summer there."

"What lake house?"

"They got a place in that new development down by Camden Beach, you know? About thirty-five miles from here."

"Tucker's with Funzi's wife? You're sure?" Stella asked,

thinking fast. If Patrick was telling the truth, and Funzi and his wife planned to keep the boy, it could be a stroke of luck. The woman was bound to treat him well, especially if she had started to think of him as her own.

"They—they treatin' him good?" Chrissy said, echoing her thoughts. Her voice was thin and wavery.

"How the hell am I supposed to know? They plan on raising him—you get it? Like you know, their *own son*."

"Ain't they ever heard of *adoption*?" Chrissy said.

Patrick's expression shifted for the first time from straight fear to surprise. "Who's gonna let *them* adopt? Don't you know who Funzi *is*? They got the whole organized crime unit up in Kansas City trying to crawl up his ass."

Stella sighed. "So that whole thing's true? Y'all really are mob?"

Patrick said nothing, and a single tear squeezed out of one eye and bounced down his cheek. Chrissy kicked at his bad leg, not hard this time, and Patrick's eyelids fluttered like he was going to pass out.

"Come on, boy," Stella said, not unkindly. "Don't make this so hard on yourself."

"Our family's been connected forever," Patrick said through clenched teeth. "Beez and Gus, they're like his nephews or something. They been with Funzi a long time."

"*They're* the guys that nailed me," Stella said. "Is that it? Everyone who's down here?"

"Them . . . and Reggie Rollieri."

"What's he do?"

"He covers the casinos for Funzi. And he runs a book down along the shore. He's only around a couple weeks a month."

"So Funzi, Reggie, the two goons, and Roy Dean—that's five, plus Benning is six. And counting you, seven."

Patrick screwed up his face and drew a breath. "So you gonna kill me now?"

"Me? Nah," Stella said. "Though Chrissy here might. She's turning out to be a little itchy on the trigger."

"They say you kill just about everyone who pisses you off," Patrick mumbled.

"Who says?"

"Funzi. Benning. All of 'em."

Interesting. So they'd asked around. Stella couldn't decide if that was a good thing or not. On the one hand, it was flattering to know that her reputation as a cold-hearted killer was thriving. It was probably the reason they had junior here down at the gate on guard duty, though they probably didn't think Stella was a true threat or they wouldn't have given the job to such a greenhorn.

"Well, I don't. I haven't made up my mind on you yet, but you help me out here, maybe we can work it out so you can spend next summer working at Burger King like a regular kid, okay?"

He shook his head. "I'll be dead in a week after they find out what I told you."

"Only if they're still around to come find you. Here's what we're gonna do," she said briskly. "I'm going to ask you some questions and you're going to answer them. Fast, and you're not going to leave anything out. Then I'm going to take you to a . . . friend for safekeeping. Just until we get this mess straightened out. What happens to you, that depends on how you handle yourself now. Hear?"

A single nod.

"Okay, Chrissy. Help me drag him over there."

Chrissy and Stella hooked his shoulders and dragged. Patrick moaned as they bumped over the ground, but they got him propped up against a tree close to the fence. Stella checked his leg; it could definitely use a cleaning and dressing, but it didn't look like he was going to bleed out tonight. Satisfied, she sat down cross-legged in front of him and motioned to Chrissy to join her. Sitting side by side, with the flashlight on its head making a circle of light on the ground between them and Patrick, reminded Stella of long-ago Girl Scout campfires.

"Where's Roy Dean?"

Patrick snuck a nervous glance at Chrissy.

"Remember what I said," Stella reminded him. "The whole truth. And fast. I'm feeling impatient."

"He's . . . uh, dead."

Chrissy, sitting next to her, didn't flinch.

Stella nodded. "I'm not all that surprised. Let me guess—he was ripping Funzi off, and Funzi found out."

"He, um. Yeah."

"Tell me how."

Patrick licked his cracked lips. "Funzi had him driving weed up to Kansas City. He'd go pick it up from these Vietnamese guys in Bolivar that Funzi's got growin' the shit in their basement."

"He start skimming, is that it?"

"Yeah . . . outta the bales, a little here and there, but then he took a whole brick, you know? Hard to miss that. Funzi's not stupid."

"What'd he want to do, sell it?"

"I guess. Thing is, he, ah . . ." Patrick glanced miserably at Chrissy. "I mean, I'm sorry if you didn't know, Mrs. Shaw, Roy Dean had a girl—"

"That fucktard," Chrissy spat. "Yeah, I knew."

"So I guess they were gonna sell it or, I don't know, he gave it to her or whatever but by the time Funzi had Beez and Gus mess him up, it was gone."

"So Funzi killed him?"

"Not right then. They gave him a week to come up with a couple thousand bucks."

Chrissy barked a short laugh.

"That was after they beat him up?" Stella asked.

"Yeah."

Stella looked to Chrissy. "What do you think? Was Roy Dean looking for money that week?"

"Was he ever *not* looking for money? Shit, Stella, he'd turn over the couch cushions every time before he went to the bar. But he knew I didn't have none, so it wasn't like he'd ask me."

"Arthur Junior didn't say anything about Roy Dean hitting him up either."

"Well hell, he was fixing to trade my baby away, I guess he didn't think he needed it," Chrissy said. "If he wasn't dead, I'd kill him myself."

"That what happened, Patrick?" Stella asked. "Roy Dean come in here with Tucker?"

"Yeah." If it was possible to look any more uncomfortable than he already was, with a leaking hole in his leg, Patrick did. "He was supposed to have the money Friday night, but he showed up here Saturday with the, uh, with your boy."

"Oh!" Chrissy said. "That little . . . I went out to my friend Tiffany's house Friday night to play cards, and Tucker was with me."

"He was planning to take Tucker out to Benning's that night," Stella guessed.

"No shit! All along he meant to—he had it *planned*." Chrissy was trembling from her fury, and Stella put her hand on her back and patted gently. Righteous anger was good, but she had to keep it under control.

"So?" she prompted Patrick.

"So, um, Benning has Roy Dean go wait in the shed and he calls Funzi, and, and Funzi was headed down to the lake house with Gus and Beez and Reggie, so they all turned around and came back up here."

"How long did it take Funzi and them to get there?"

"Not long, maybe fifteen minutes. Me'n Roy Dean, we were kind of talking some, and the kid was on the floor playin' with some little stuffed dog—"

"Pup-pup," Chrissy interjected. "That's his favorite. Oh, God—"

"Okay," Stella said, giving Chrissy a one-arm hug, a firm one, to get her to focus. "We got to listen to the rest of this, hon."

Chrissy gulped and nodded.

Patrick's breathing had gone short and fast. He looked back and forth between them, his eyes unfocused. "So when Funzi and them came in the kid had shit his pants and Roy Dean couldn't get him to shut up. Funzi's all, Where's the money, you got my money? And then Roy Dean tells Funzi, look here, you can have the kid and that'll settle us up, and Funzi looks at him like he's out of his mind and then he goes nuts. Tells Roy Dean, Is he fucking crazy? . . . And then he smacks him around a little, keeps asking where the fuck his money is, and then all of a sudden he just stops. He, uh, tells Gus to take the kid and drive him down to the lake house, you know, where his wife is. And Roy Dean's looking all happy because, like, he figures Funzi went for it and all, but the second Gus walks out the door with the kid Funzi tells me and Beez, go outside and guard the place and don't go nowhere until he comes and gets us. So we go out, and it wasn't more than a minute or two after they locked the doors again, we heard a shot. And I knew Funzi shot Roy Dean."

Patrick swallowed hard. Stella had a pretty good idea it was the first time Patrick had heard something like that, despite all his swagger.

"Okay," she said gently. "He killed Roy Dean. Maybe he figured he couldn't keep him around, knowing where the kid was. What happened to the body?"

"Well, shit, we were like—I mean, Funzi tells me, go get some plastic and a chain saw from Benning, and I, and I, I did that, and Beez stayed and guarded the shed, and when I got back I knocked on the door and gave the stuff to Funzi and then a minute later we heard them fire it up."

"Funzi and Rollieri . . .?"

"Yeah."

"Holy mother," Stella said. "A chain saw, didn't that make a hell of a mess?"

"Yeah," Patrick said, his voice a hoarse whisper. Stella noticed a smell coming off him, acrid fear mixed with blood and body odor. "Funzi, uh, didn't make us help with the, uh, sawing. He told us to stay outside and, you know, we did. But later, when we were cleaning up . . . Jesus."

"So you and Beez helped take care of the body when it was done?"

"No. Funzi gave me the chain saw and said, clean it off, and I wiped it down and all that, and Beez went and helped Benning close up and Funzi said, wait for him in the house so we . . . we, um, did."

"How long did that take?"

"I don't know . . . maybe like . . . half an hour? More maybe, we were, uh, sitting around at the house, and, and finally Funzi called on the cell. He said for me and Beez to come back up to the shed and, like, the pieces of, of Roy Dean were wrapped in plastic and Funzi told us to carry it all out to the burn barrel. Reggie had headed back to the city, so it was just me and Beez done it."

Stella grimaced, thinking of the grisly task. Chrissy looked a little green herself. "Where's the burn barrel?"

"Out behind the shed on the back side," Patrick said, lifting a limp arm to point back across the property.

"Then what did you do?"

"We, uh, laid in some newspaper and shit to get it started and then we put the, uh, you know, Roy Dean in there. Plastic and all, Funzi wanted it all burned. Poured on the kerosene but we waited until dark to light it up."

"Did it catch right off?"

"Yeah, but it took all night to burn down. The smell . . . it nearly killed us. In the morning, there was, there was a few pieces of bone or something with the plastic burned onto it.

Gus was back by then, and Funzi made us dig, like, five or six holes and put the shit in."

"Was it all destroyed? Other than the bone pieces?"

"There was some little bits of cloth around the barrel that must've come out of the flames or something. And what didn't burn . . . I think there were teeth, like that." Patrick stared miserably at the ground.

"Could you find those holes again?"

"Yeah. Since I had to do most of the digging. Funzi had me put the dirt back and drive the front loader over the top when I was done."

"Okay." Stella sat back on her haunches for a minute, thinking over the story. She glanced at Chrissy, whose anger seemed to have dissipated some, though she kept the gun loosely trained on Patrick. "Patrick, where exactly is Funzi on the old mob totem pole?"

"Kinda low, I guess," Patrick said. "I mean, he's got just Gus and Beez and Reggie. And me. He reports up to Donny Calabasas, and then after Donny, it's Justin Frank—he's got the whole south end of Kansas City."

"Okay, I get the picture," Stella said. "He's a pissant and Gus and Beez and Reggie are little pissants and you're just a teeny little baby pissant. That about the size of it?"

Patrick barely nodded. His eyelids were slowly sliding down, and Stella was worried he was about to pass out. "Look here, can you tell me how to get to the lake house?"

"Yeah . . . it's the biggest-ass house on the north shore. It's in that new development down past the U-Store-It where Route 4 hits the shore road."

"On that private drive they put in?"

"Yeah, there's maybe six, eight houses on a cul-de-sac."

"And you're sure that's where they got the kid?"

Patrick looked uncertain. "Well . . . probably. I mean, Mrs. Angelini spends most of the summer there, and now she's got the kid—"

"*My* kid," Chrissy interrupted, and Patrick swallowed.

"Sorry . . . yeah, I'm like ninety percent sure that's where they are."

"All of them? Funzi and Gus and Beez?"

"No, Funzi had Gus run something up to the city, some delivery for Donny Calabasas. So it's just him and Beez."

Stella still didn't like those odds. Ordinarily she wouldn't move until she was certain. But there wasn't anything she could do about it now.

"How long until someone figures out you're gone?"

Patrick shrugged. "Depends. If Benning and Larissa are partying, sometimes he don't even come down."

"But the rest of the time?"

"The rest of the time he's down here around eleven, eleven thirty. Midnight maybe."

Stella checked her watch: ten. Shit. "And where's Funzi and them tonight?"

"At the lake house, I guess. Unless they went into town, to the bars . . . I don't know. They don't check in with me. Benning would know, but—"

"Yeah."

For a moment Stella considered heading up to the house and scaring the crap out of Benning and his girlfriend, but that was introducing all kinds of opportunities to fuck things up.

If they left now, there was a chance they could get to the lake house and figure out how to get Tucker without Funzi knowing they were coming.

If Funzi had warning, Stella was pretty sure things would end in disaster. She and Chrissy wouldn't stand a chance against two armed thugs. Plus Funzi's wife. She wasn't sure what the body count would be, or who would be left standing, but she wouldn't put money on any kind of mother-and-child reunion.

"We gotta move," she said decisively. "Sorry, Patrick, but you're gonna have to haul your ass down to the road. We'll help you, but I don't want to hear any whining. I'll get the car and then you're gonna give Chrissy here the best directions you ever gave while I drive you over to my friend's house, hear? He'll take good care of you while Chrissy and I go get the job done."

Patrick nodded miserably. Stella noticed with admiration that he made almost no sound at all as they helped him stagger to his one good leg and gimp his way to the road.

SEVEN

. . . .

Stella considered having Chrissy keep her gun on Patrick once they got in the car, but since it was going to have to happen eventually anyway, she decided they might as well take care of him now.

She left the car idling while they got Patrick settled into the back seat. Stella helped hoist his bad leg up on the seat, a pile of rags from the trunk spread out underneath to catch the thin stream of blood that ran from the wound.

"Sorry you have to see this," she told him apologetically, leaning into the car. It was awkward to crawl in, her knees on the floor of the car, but she needed to get close to his face.

"See what?" Patrick asked.

"This." Stella hit him fast and hard on the chin, the way she'd learned from watching boxing videos on YouTube, channeling Muhammad Ali from when he took Sonny Liston down. She backed her way out of the car and slipped the brass knucks off her hand and returned them to her purse, pleased to see that Patrick was breathing well, his head leaning back against the door.

"At's a shame," Chrissy said, shaking her head. "I was startin' to like that one a little bit."

"Don't like him too much. He stood by while they killed your husband."

Chrissy snorted. "Somebody ought to give him a medal for that."

"Well, but he watched them haul your kid out of there, didn't he? Would have put a gun on us, too, if we hadn't got to it first."

"Wouldn't a shot us, though."

"The hell you say."

"He didn't have it in him, Stella. Come on, it was obvious."

"Well, until today I wouldn't have figured you for cold-blooded shootin' either, but you sure nailed those two crazy mutts."

Chrissy didn't respond. Stella got into the driver's seat and buckled herself in. Her body ached dully all over, and she figured it was a delayed muscular response to the beating she'd taken the night before. Well, she'd just have to power through the next hour or so and hope she had the juice for another round.

Either way, she'd be in for a long rest after this night was over. She just hoped it wasn't permanent.

Stella made the U-turn and drove slowly back past Benning's, glancing over at the trailer. The blue glow from the television was the only light visible inside, though the pole lights still illuminated the grounds. If Benning or his girl-friend looked out the window, Patrick's post, with its abandoned camp chair and boom box, would be obviously empty. The thought made her want to drive a little faster, but she waited until Benning's was out of sight in the rearview mirror before putting the pedal down.

The inside of the Jeep was quiet as Stella made the drive back through Prosper and out to Goat's. She slowed on the final stretch of gravel drive before pulling up in front of the house, a tidy little wood-sided foursquare that had been empty for a few years before Goat moved in.

Stella pulled the Jeep into the yard, cut the headlights and turned off the ignition, and coasted the last twenty yards, praying Goat was a heavy sleeper. Off to the side of the house, his service sedan was pulled up square next to his truck, a battered Toyota. A single light burned somewhere in the house, its soft glow pale gold in the windows. Through the gaps in the sheer curtains Stella could make out the shapes of furniture, the outline of the staircase, a picture hung on the wall.

She felt an odd tug, a longing that she couldn't at first identify. She wanted to go inside and look around, pick up objects off the tables and hold them in her hands, examine the photographs. She wanted to look in the fridge and the medicine cabinet and the bookshelves. She wanted to know all about the man who'd taken up residence in a protected corner of her mind.

Upstairs, out of sight, Goat was undoubtedly sleeping, dreaming maybe. Stella imagined his bedside table: there would be reading glasses, of course—a person didn't get to be their age without them—and maybe a glass of water. An alarm clock, though Stella would bet Goat was the kind of man who woke up a minute before it went off. A book—maybe a biography, or a World War II history. The clicker—or maybe not. Maybe he didn't like a television in the bedroom. They said it distracted—that your sex life suffered from its presence.

That was about enough of *that,* Stella chided herself. She opened the car door as quietly as she could and got out, Chrissy following suit. Then she opened the passenger door in back and stared down at Patrick.

He didn't make for a very threatening captive, unconscious in the back seat, his lips parted and his long lashes casting moon shadows on his smooth cheeks. He looked about twelve years old, in fact.

"Well, let's get it done," Stella said, grabbing one of his feet and indicating that Chrissy should take the other. They pulled him out, Stella grabbing his head and barely preventing it from glancing off the door well and banging into the ground. "This fellow's too damn big. I'm getting tired of hauling him around."

"We can just drag him, I guess," Chrissy said. "You clipped him pretty good. I don't think he's gonna wake up anytime soon."

"Yeah. Too bad we couldn't just put a timer on him. A pop-up timer like you stick in a turkey. I don't want Goat finding him too soon. We need to get in there, you know—"

"Without the law," Chrissy finished her sentence for her. "Well, we could hit him again, I guess."

They staggered across the lawn, up the steps, and then lurched onto the porch and dropped Patrick into one of the Adirondack chairs—nice ones, looked like Goat had made them himself—on the porch. They stretched Patrick out as comfortably as they could. Stella went back to the car for the rope and tied Patrick's ankles together. She checked the wound, which had nearly stopped bleeding and was drying to a crust around the edges.

The ankle of the shot leg was looking pretty pale, and it felt cold to the touch. The skin had a little too much give, like chicken skin on a butcher fryer. Stella wondered if she ought to loosen the rope she'd tied above the knee.

Then she remembered Patrick—sweet baby face and all—stalking toward them with that gun slung across his body, hand caressing the trigger. And left the rope right where it was.

Chrissy stepped back and examined their handiwork. "He looks kinda funny," she said.

"I guess maybe we ought to leave some sort of note," Stella said. "Hang on."

She went to the car, got her case notebook, and tore out a sheet. With the car's dome light for illumination, she wrote a quick note:

Goat, don't untie this boy until you got some other way to keep him down. It's one of Alphonse Angelini's boys—he tried to shoot us. Tell you all about it later.

She looked at what she'd written, chewed on the pen.

There was a chance that things were going to go spectacularly wrong. She and Chrissy were about to go looking for a pair of coldhearted gangsters who had a whole lot of firepower between them. Neither of whom, presumably, were chubby or beat up or schooled only in shooting squirrels—and now, of course, dogs. As far as weapons went, Stella didn't even want to think how outgunned they were.

Still, if today was her day to go out, so be it. Stella sighed, and added to the note, "If you don't hear from me by tomorrow afternoon, *find Tucker.*"

She looked down at the note and couldn't help feeling like she hadn't quite written everything she wanted to say to the man. But there wasn't time to worry about that now.

Back outside the car, she noticed that the moon was climbing higher in the sky and plumping itself up into a respectable shiner, lighting up the close-mown lawn and some flower beds Goat had carved out along the edges and filled with petunias and marigolds.

On the porch, Chrissy was fussing with Patrick, wedging a chair cushion behind his head. Stella set the note on the little side table next to the chair and weighed it down with a rock.

"Okay, say good-bye to your boyfriend there," Stella said. "Time to hit the road."

Chrissy gave a brief, nervous giggle and waggled her fingers at the unconscious boy, who now looked as though he was taking a noontime siesta, with his hands clasped in front of him and his ankles crossed.

They made the drive to the lake mostly in silence, Chrissy piping up now and then to read from the directions Patrick gave her. The roads were practically empty; they passed only three other cars on the way.

"What're we gonna do if these directions take us to a Pizza Hut or something?" Chrissy asked as they got close. "Or if the address don't exist? I mean, we didn't exactly get any guarantees out of Patrick."

"That would be a problem," Stella admitted. "But do you really think he's feeling the love for those guys right now? If he has half a brain he's probably hoping we take them all out."

"That what we're going to do, Stella?" Chrissy asked, her voice whisper-quiet. "Take 'em all out?"

Stella said nothing for a moment. Then she gave the only answer that she felt she could: "We'll do exactly what we need to. No more, and no less."

When Chrissy didn't say anything more, Stella figured she'd better stop her from getting too far ahead of herself.

"Stop worrying about what you can't control," she said. "Trust me, I know. I've been there before. What you want to do is stay in the moment, deal with all the shit as it comes down the pike. Then later you can think about how you might have done things different. Over a beer or twelve."

Chrissy nodded. "Okay. Hey, that's our turn. Loblolly Pines Road."

Stella eased past a pair of stone pillars with fancy iron fencing sticking out at angles on either side. There was a brass plate on either column bearing the words LAKEVIEW MANOR ESTATES. The road was smooth asphalt, with a median strip planted with young redbud and dogwood trees.

"I'm surprised they don't have them a little house here with some tight-ass guard ready to blow away any riffraff that comes along."

Chrissy sniffed. "Riffraff's already got in. Funzi'n them ain't exactly quality folks theirselves."

Stella laughed softly. "Well said, darlin'. Okay, let's see what we got."

She cut the lights and rolled slowly down the road. After a

hundred yards or so, the street curved gently to the left, and there in front of them lay the lake, shimmering in the moonlight.

It was so beautiful it made Stella's chest tighten up. The little ripples on the water's surface danced silver and black. The crescent moon was reflected in the water, a flickering slice of pale light. Stars had come out, just a smattering, and they sparkled their way down the horizon until it looked as if they were bits of sugar dusted down from some heavenly shaker.

Reluctantly, she turned away from the water. It wasn't a night for beauty.

Up ahead she could see the lights of an enormous house, and beyond that another, and another.

"I'd drive on past," Stella said, "check out the situation, but there's no telling what Funzi's got in the way of manpower up at this hour. If he's got one of his guys outside on some sort of watch—"

She glanced at the dashboard clock. One fifteen. Late enough that presumably everyone but the insomniacs would be asleep for the night. If Funzi had someone posted outside the house, a car driving by at this hour would draw attention, putting them on alert.

"Tucker's prob'ly been asleep for hours," Chrissy said. "You know, Stella, don't laugh, but I got a feeling that he's right close by."

Stella didn't laugh. She eased the car over to the side of the road and let the engine idle, and considered Chrissy carefully. "Yeah, what do you mean?"

"Well, I don't know, I guess it sounds kind of dumb, but I get a sense about things sometimes. I just got this *feeling,* see?"

She held up her hands, turned them over, and looked at her fingers. "Like a little tingly feeling. I can just—oh, Stella, I can just *feel* Tucker, you know, under my fingers, his little cheeks and his hair and his little baby butt when I hold him. I'm tellin' you, he's *here*."

Stella took a slow, easy U-turn in the broad street, still well back from the first house, and drove slowly back to the gated entrance at the turnoff. Back on the main road, she drove a few moments until she found what she was looking for, a turn-in for farm vehicles, with a padlocked gate over a cattle guard. She parked off the road and cut the engine, then turned on the map light and looked at her partner.

"Well, honey girl, what's this sixth sense of yours tell you about what we're about to do?"

Chrissy put her fingers lightly to her face, tapping on her chin, and closed her eyes. She focused hard for a minute, her eyebrows knit in concentration, and then her eyes popped open.

"Oh!"

"What?"

"I don't know—I had this, like, swirly feeling and then kind of a like a mini fireworks in my head."

"Is that good?"

"I—I'm not sure. Yes. Wait. Yes, it's good, I'm getting a good feeling, but there's all this trouble first—that's what I'm sensing."

"Well, that sounds about right."

Stella reached in the back seat for her backpack. She took out the flashlights again and handed one to Chrissy.

"You better reload," she said. She dug in the backpack for

the Makarov's spare magazine. Stella slid the other one out expertly and replaced it, sending the slide home with a satisfying snap.

"This old piece turned out okay, I guess," Chrissy said, tucking it back in the holster. "Thanks to Uncle Fred. So what's the plan?"

"Unfortunately, I don't have much of one. Kind of goes like this: sneak in, don't get caught, and get Tucker. Then we can get the hell out of here and call the sheriff."

Chrissy put her hand on the door latch and nodded as if Stella had given her a detailed strategy. "Okay."

She got out of the Jeep and Stella followed suit, slipping the backpack onto her sore shoulders. They kept off the street a few yards. On the lake side, there were clumps of cattails and the occasional stand of willows, which made for good cover, so Stella felt confident they wouldn't be spotted even by someone on the street.

As they passed the first two houses, a motion light went on. She grabbed Chrissy's arm and scrambled out of the illuminated arc, close to the bank that sloped down to the water.

They stood motionless for a few moments, waiting for a reaction from inside the house. Stella could feel Chrissy's pulse, rapid and strong, through her sleeve. Her own heart was pounding just as fast. After a few minutes they ventured ahead, staying close to the bank of the lake. At the edge of Funzi's lawn, they paused.

Ahead loomed the enormous house, three stories of pale stucco topped with a tile roof like it was in the middle of the damn Mediterranean. There were arched windows all along the back of the house, and sets of French doors, and little balconies sticking out from the upstairs rooms, like some kind of *Romeo and Juliet* stage set. Stella was a little surprised to see that some of the windows were open; she expected them to have the air-conditioning blasting on a night as hot as this.

Stella glanced at Chrissy and saw that she had drawn the Makarov and held it ready, her hands steady.

"Thinking about dogs?" she whispered.

"Hell, yes."

"Maybe the Angelinis aren't pet people."

In answer Chrissy only snorted.

"So here's what I'm thinking," Stella said. "The place has got to be alarmed every which way, right? We try to break in, even through a screen, they'll be on us before we have time to turn around. Plus they'll have the advantage of knowing exactly where we are."

"Yeah . . . so?"

"What we need is, we need one of *them* to come *out*. Then I figure it's a fair fight."

Chrissy scratched her chin with her free hand and gave Stella a quizzical look. "Well, how are you gonna manage that? Ring the doorbell? Pretend you brung 'em a pizza?"

Searching for ideas, Stella looked carefully from the vine-covered trellis that ran from the front overhang along the side of the house, around to the back where a wooden pergola had been built over a huge tiled patio. Extending out from the patio, a stone path bisected the backyard, continuing to a set of steps that led down to the water, where a number of boats were docked.

She briefly considered climbing up the trellis to the second floor, where she figured the master bedroom faced out over the water. It would be possible to get from the trellis to the balcony, and it looked like the French doors were open, so she could slip into the room, possibly surprising Funzi and his wife in their sleep, getting a gun on them before they had time to react.

It would be possible . . . if she were Tarzan. She doubted the trellis would hold her weight, and even if it did, climbing the wooden structure was a little different from the climbing wall she occasionally worked out on at the gym.

She studied the pergola. It had no hand- or footholds, and the vine on it was still young, its strands thin and weak. No help there.

So she wasn't going to be able to get in. There had to be a way to get someone to come out. Some way to cause a distraction in the backyard so that someone investigating would leave the door open behind him, letting one of them get inside.

"Okay," she finally said. "Down on the docks, see?"

Chrissy looked where Stella was pointing. "Yeah, they got a speedboat. Couple a those Wave Runner things. What do you want to do, hop on one and drive it up on the lawn?"

"No, not exactly . . . do you know where they put the gas in on one of those things?

"I guess. I been Wave-Running with my cousin Kip, and we pulled up along the pumps at the marina to get gas. There's a gas cap up there near the front, just like on a car."

"Huh. Okay, I think I have an idea."

"A good idea?"

"Not really, kind of a piss-poor one, but we don't have a lot of options."

Or a lot of time, either. Stella considered checking her

watch and decided she was nervous enough already. She got the bolt cutters out of the backpack and knelt at the edge of the flower bed, rummaging through the impatiens with her hands until she found what she wanted. She gave the irrigation system's drip line a yank and came up with a loop of black tubing, then pulled carefully and followed where it snaked along the edge of the bed, back along the fence, and toward the host pipe. She snipped off a six-foot section and wrapped it around her palm.

"What the hell are you up to?" Chrissy demanded.

"You'll see in a minute." She got two water bottles out of her pack and twisted off the caps. She handed one to Chrissy. "Drink up now because you won't have another chance."

After Chrissy obliged, Stella took the bottle back and up-ended both, pouring the water out on the lawn.

"What'ja do that for?"

"We need the bottles," Stella said. "Come on."

In the moonlight she took the stairs, slowly and carefully. To the sides of the steps, long grasses and weeds stirred as they went past, making an otherworldly whispering sound.

At the bottom Stella took a breath and set one foot on the dock, nearly jumping back when the thing swayed under her weight. "Shit," she said. "If I fall in, pull me out, girl. I can't swim."

Chrissy snorted. "Know how my dad taught me to swim?"

Stella made her way gingerly toward the closer of the two Wave Runners, a sharp little craft that looked as if it would seat a couple of bikini-clad nymphets. "No, how?"

"Took me down to the reservoir and threw me in when I was eight years old. I set to dog-paddlin' for my life. Made it to the side and swore I'd never forgive him, but when I managed to haul myself out he was standin' there with tears in his eye telling me how proud I'd made him."

"Wow, sounds like a setup for hundreds of hours of therapy if I ever heard one."

"Ain't no Lardner ever had therapy," Chrissy said, with a note of pride.

Stella figured that was a discussion for another time. She found the gas cap right on top, conveniently located where she didn't even need to lean far over the open water. She twisted it off and slipped one end of the black plastic tubing inside.

"Let's hope they left the tank full," she said. She let the hose loop down so that it touched the deck, then lifted the other end up to her lips and made a face.

"Wow, I've sucked all kinds of stuff in my day," Chrissy said, giving Stella a leering grin, "but I'm glad that's you about to put that in your mouth and not me."

"Well, honey, the idea is not to get any in your mouth."

"How you gonna manage that?"

"It's a physics thing." She sucked on the hose until she figured the liquid had traveled as far as the dock, then pulled her lips away and whispered, "Here goes nothing."

After giving the gas a minute to make its way through the tube to level, she put the open end in one of the water bottles and then held the bottle down along the side of the dock.

Liquid began to fill the bottle.

"Yes!" Stella exclaimed, pleased, a little surprised the technique actually worked.

"Damn," Chrissy said with admiration. "That's quite a trick, but it smells nasty."

"Well, we're a couple of nasty girls," Stella said as she filled the second bottle.

When it was full, she coiled up the tubing and dropped it on the deck. She handed a bottle to Chrissy and they started back up the steps.

"So now what, we ask them fellas to drink this shit and hope they pass out?" Chrissy asked when they got back up to the lawn.

"No, darlin', we're gonna set this place on fire." She led the way to the side of the house, running her fingers along the stucco and the trim, trying to judge flammability.

"Stella, I don't think we better burn the house down," Chrissy whispered, clearly worried. "I mean, Tucker's in there. And if, you know, if we get blown away or something, I still want him to get out. Even if it's with, you know . . . them."

Stella turned to Chrissy and saw moonlight creamy on her pale, broad cheeks, eyes miserable with worry. That was a mama for you, putting aside thoughts of her own safety, her own life even, for her baby. It gave Stella an extra little burst of determination. "Ain't gonna happen," she promised. "No one's getting blown away today—at least, none of the good guys. Besides, I'm talking about a little bitty fire, just on the outside of the house. Just enough to set off the alarms and get their attention."

She settled on a stretch of flower bed that ran along the back of the house. A row of shrubs had been planted out of reach of the sprinkler system and had died and dried up into sticks. Stella slowly poured the gasoline out of the bottles onto the shrubs and the wood trim, and up along the side of the house. She wasn't sure what stucco was made of these days—probably Styrofoam—and hoped to hell it would burn.

"Okay," she said. "Moment of truth."

She dug her lighter out of the bottom of the backpack and then reached for Chrissy's hand and gave it a squeeze.

Chrissy squeezed back. "What are we going to do when it lights?"

"Well, first of all, try not to set ourselves on fire. Then I guess let's stay close to the house, maybe around the corner. That way we can see around but we'll be out of the fire. This ought to smoke up good, so it should set off the alarm and they'll be able to see it out the windows. You gotta figure they're gonna come out the back to see what happened."

"But what if they go out the front?"

"Well . . . whoever comes out, it's going to be my job to take them down, so all you need to worry about is getting in. Don't wait around to see, just go. If no one shows up back here, I guess I'll go check on the front door. But I got to think they'll come around to the back once they see nothing's burning out front, don't you think?"

"Sounds like a lot of guessin' and hopin' to me," Chrissy said.

"'Fraid so. But I'm plum out of alternatives."

"Okay. So you get the guy outside, I go in and find Tucker—"

"Upstairs, I'm thinking. There's probably three, four different bedrooms up there. I'll be right behind you, soon as I can, and I'll try to cover you. But there's a chance you're gonna be on your own until you find him. So you just concentrate on finding him and then you grab him and go. I'm not kidding, Chrissy, you come out of there and you *fly*. Back to the Jeep, unless you get hurt or something, then I guess you'll have to get to a neighbor's house and call the cops."

Shot, she meant, or stabbed or clubbed or any other manner of violent reckoning—and then it would be a matter of great good luck if Chrissy got out of there at all.

But Chrissy just nodded calmly. "Then what?"

"Throw Tucker in the Jeep and *go*. Don't wait on me. Here, you're going to need these." She got her car keys and Patrick's phone out of the backpack and handed them to Chrissy. "Give me a call when you're safe. I'll take care of myself until I hear from you, okay?"

Chrissy took the keys and stuck them in her pocket, then flipped open the phone. "Okay. Give me your number."

As she recited it and Chrissy keyed it into the phone, Stella tried not to think about how flawed the plan was. What if the fire didn't catch? What if the flames outdoors weren't enough to set off the alarms? Or if the smoke detectors were out of batteries—they were always going on about that on the news, how people let their batteries run down and ended up cooked in their beds.

Or what if the fire just took off and sent the whole house up in a ball of flame? Unlikely; they probably coated that Styrofoam stucco with the stuff they made kids' pajamas out of before the house got a coat of paint.

What if they all came out—Funzi and his wife and Beez. That would be three against two, and then—

Stella forced herself to stop. That kind of thinking wasn't going to help.

She zipped the backpack shut and slipped it on her shoulders. The pain and fatigue she had been feeling earlier was gone, replaced by a nervous tension that hummed through her whole body.

Chrissy snapped the phone shut and slipped it into her pocket. "Well, what're ya waiting for?" she demanded.

"Right," Stella muttered, and flicked her Bic.

She held the flame down to the trim around the window, and there was a sputtering and a strong smell of burning chemicals, but no fire. Stella realized she was holding her breath as her fingertips grew increasingly hot. Right when she thought she was going to have to drop the lighter, a tiny lick of flame went up and over the edge of the painted wooden trim and spread its way down the board. A fraction of an inch at first, and then another one . . . and then in a whoosh a finger of flame tracked down a rivulet of gasoline that dripped from the stucco and grew into a sizable flame.

"I think we're in business," Stella said.

She stepped back and slid the lighter into her pocket. She grabbed Chrissy's hand and led her away from the growing fire. Chrissy gave her a businesslike nod and sprinted to the back porch, where she took up position on the side of the door, flattened against the house, gun hand bent at the elbow, looking plenty ready to blow the head off anyone who even looked at her sideways.

Stella took the other side of the door, copying Chrissy's stance, the Ruger drawn and ready. Her fingers felt faintly sweaty on the warm ivory grip, and her heart was keeping up a pretty good pace.

It felt like an hour, but Stella guessed it was another three or four minutes before the flame spread itself out along the trail of gasoline that had dribbled down to the base of the house's siding, and was burning well in the dried vegetation. The fire leapt along a stretch of wall, growing taller by the second. Flames licked at the bottom of the second-story windows, and the smell of smoke was thick.

Chrissy coughed gently and Stella put her sleeve up to her nose, breathing through the fabric.

Then they heard the bleep of the fire alarm from inside the house.

The thought that came unexpectedly to Stella's mind was: *cooking*. That damn alarm that Ollie had installed right in the middle of the kitchen, after Stella tried to convince him to put it in the hall, like it said to do on the box—but you couldn't tell the man anything.

The thing would go off whenever Stella sautéed or fried or even baked a pizza, and Ollie would come stand in the door, scratching his belly and demanding, "Burning something again?"

Hell, *yeah*, she was burning something, Stella thought. Almost wished the fucker was there to see it for himself.

Inside, Stella heard someone knocking around upstairs, and imagined Funzi and the other men lurching out of bedrooms, bleary with sleep, looking around and trying to figure out what was on fire.

Probably wondering if it was a false alarm, or if they'd left a cigarette smoldering in an ashtray or a pan of Bagel Bites in the oven.

Above her a window was suddenly yanked open.

"Holy fuck, Marie, there's a damn fire out back of the house!"

Stella shrank as close to the house as she could manage, praying that whoever was looking out—Funzi, presumably— wouldn't look down and see her there. There was a growing cloud of thick smoke, swirling blackened bits of charred crap through the air, and she struggled not to cough, the air acrid and poisonous even through the soft fabric of her shirt.

She felt, rather than heard, the reverberations of feet running along the hallway upstairs. A couple of moments later there was a sharp percussive slap on the inside of the door they were guarding, and then the sounds of someone rattling the knob, throwing the bolt.

Stella stared straight into Chrissy's eyes and was comforted to see that the girl looked just as unafraid and determined as she had a few minutes earlier. She turned back to the door as it sprang open—and nearly fainted from shock.

The man who came bursting out of the house was Roy Dean Shaw.

EIGHT

. . . .

Roy Dean wore boxer shorts and a muscle T-shirt with the sleeves cut off, and while there was little evidence of his having been recently dismembered and burned, he was far from a robust-looking specimen of humanity. His greasy brown hair lay flat on one side of his head and stuck straight out on the other, his pale sloped shoulders were pocked with acne scabs, and his narrow eyes were bloodshot.

"You bastard!" Chrissy yelped. "You're supposed to be dead!"

"Don't worry about him, just get on in there," Stella said, giving the girl a shove, and Chrissy slipped past him into the house.

Roy Dean started to wheel in a circle toward the flames, his feet scrambling on the ground. It was kind of comical, like a cartoon of Wile E. Coyote when he ran off a cliff, legs pinwheeling for a moment in midair before he fell.

Stella took one big step toward him and raised her gun hand, realizing just in time that the trajectory of his outstretched arm was going to connect about at her wrist, knocking the Ruger out of her grip.

She pivoted forward instead so that Roy Dean connected full on with her, his whole mass slamming into her torso at full speed. The impact knocked her back, and she could feel it in her bones, in her teeth, but it stopped him coming and he tripped and fell forward on top of her, arms flailing.

No gun.

Roy Dean had no gun—that was Stella's thought as she rolled away from him, tipping a stone planter off its base, the broken shards cutting into her flesh as she scrambled out of the way.

Then she realized that she didn't have a gun either as she watched the Ruger skitter across the slick patio surface toward the lawn.

For a second her eyes locked on Roy Dean's homely face above her. There were red lines in his flesh from his pillow, and she could smell his breath and sweat, and then he pushed off her, propelling his body along the ground toward her gun. He managed to grab it and had it up and trained on her in what seemed like half a second.

"Bet you're wishing you'd been a little nicer to me now, aintcha," he said, leering.

Stella felt her heart lurch: she'd let Roy Dean take her gun like he was taking a lollipop from a baby. Chrissy had made it inside, but now she was on her own, and after Roy Dean shot Stella he'd go right back inside and alert everyone else.

Chrissy didn't have a chance.

The thought pissed Stella off mightily. She got to her knees, hair escaping the ponytail holder and falling in her face, obscuring her vision. Her hands scrabbled in the dark behind her, finding the largest piece of the pot, what was left of the bottom, with a thick layer of potting soil matted to it.

"Surprise, surprise, here you are back from the dead," she said, stalling for time. "So who did you all kill in the shed?"

"Rollieri," he said. "Who else? Only I didn't kill him. I ain't no killer. Funzi done that hisself."

Stella thought back to what Patrick told them: *Reggie'd gone back to the city.* Funzi and Roy Dean and Rollieri were alone in the shed while Patrick and Beez waited outside. Funzi must have shot Rollieri instead of Roy Dean. But why?

"What'd he do, anyway?"

Roy Dean snorted. "He was skimming the take on the book. Funzi figured it out a while ago, but he had to wait for Donny Calabasas to give him the go-ahead."

"Why'd you all lie to Patrick and Beez?"

Roy Dean blinked, his brow furrowing. "How do you know Patrick?"

"We're old friends. Quilting bees."

"Fuck you, Stella. Anyway, we didn't lie, we just couldn't tell 'em until Funzi sent proof back up to Donny it was done." Roy Dean giggled, looking like a little boy caught with a cookie. "We sent up Reggie's hand that had the spider tattoo—that was my idea."

"Brilliant," Stella said. "Sure seems like there was a lot of 'we' in that story. How come Funzi's trusting you all of a sudden? The way I heard it, you were skimming off your *own* deliveries. You were cheating Funzi, too."

"I wasn't." Roy Dean reddened with anger, and the gun wavered in his hands. Stella was tempted to reach out and grab the barrel, take her chances with him getting off a wild shot, but he stood just out of reach. "I *paid* my debt," he finally spat. "And that was all mostly just a misunderstanding anyway. What Rollieri did—now that was just *wrong*. Funzi couldn't let that go."

"You didn't pay anything," Stella protested, enraged. "You gave away a baby that wasn't even yours. A *baby*. How could you do that—even a scum-sucking bottom-dweller like you?"

"Hey, Chrissy ain't fit to be a mother," Roy Dean said, his watery eyes narrowing, a vein throbbing on his temple. "She's no better'n a whore. It's her as brought this down on herself."

That was just the reminder Stella needed of Roy Dean's essential worthlessness. Enraged, she screwed up her face into an expression of exquisite pain—not such a stretch, given the beating her fresh stitches and recent bruises had taken.

"Ohh," she wailed, reaching a shaking hand down to her legs, which were bent beneath her. "I think you broke my ankle."

Roy Dean danced from one foot to another. "Shut up, Stella, or I'll waste you right here."

But he hesitated—Stella could see him do it. Worthless human being that he was, he'd been right about one thing—he was no killer. He'd fallen for the old lady ruse, and that gave her just the fraction of a second, the opening that she needed. She gave one more weak moan for good measure and stumbled to her feet like she might collapse from the effort.

Roy Dean stutter-stepped out of the way, as though the thought of 180 pounds of AARP-eligible female falling on him was simply too much, and Stella recovered her balance at the last second and pushed off her left foot—pain shooting up into her bad hip—and swung the heavy piece of pot up around and smashed it against his forehead.

Roy Dean went down without even a grunt, collapsing into an awkward pile of splayed limbs, his head bouncing off the slate patio with a thud Stella could feel through her feet.

"Ouch," she exclaimed. That would have hurt plenty, if Roy Dean wasn't already out.

Stella took her gun out of his hand, his fingers twitching slightly as she pried them off the grip. She jammed the Ruger back in the holster and dusted off her knees, and then, before she straightened up, she put two fingers to Roy Dean's neck, finding a fluttery pulse.

"You know what your mistake was," Stella whispered, backing away. "You hesitated. You thought you had me because you're young. But badass comes in all ages."

She spun toward the house, her heart pounding from exertion as well as fear. How long had her encounter with Roy Dean taken? Three minutes? Four? It was miraculous that no one had come out to check on him. Stella opened the door and slipped into the house, flattening herself against the wall to the right of the door and swinging her gun arm to the left and the right, trying to adjust to the dark of the room. The only light came from under the counters in the colossal kitchen that opened up to the left of the family room.

A hall led from the far side of the family room straight through the center of the house, and Stella could see that the front door was open up ahead. Someone—Funzi or his wife or Beez—must have gone to check out front. When they didn't find anything amiss, they would circle around to the back—and find Roy Dean laid out cold.

Stella darted down the hall toward an ornate staircase on the right, an enormous wood-railed affair that curved upward. She grabbed the rail and hauled herself up the stairs, trying to keep her steps light, but thoughts of Chrissy and Tucker propelled her forward. At the top of the stairs she could see a darkened bathroom with its door ajar, and she dove across the hallway and into the bath, skidding on the polished marble floor, and went into a crouch facing out to the hall.

Cautiously, she peered out: the hall was empty. To the left it opened into a huge loft room dominated by a big sectional sofa, the floor littered with electronics: a PlayStation and Wii controls and a plastic guitar, plus stacks of DVD cases and some crumpled soda cans.

To the right, the hall stretched twenty feet and ended at a set of carved double doors. These were open a fraction of an inch, not wide enough to see anything inside. Along the hall on either side were other doors, all closed, leading to bedrooms, no doubt, and possibly more bathrooms.

Shit. Each of those doors presented a threat. Each one of them could have someone on the other side, poised and ready to shoot. Not to mention whoever was outside, who at any moment would come tearing back up the stairs.

Sweating and hyperventilating, Stella, counted the doors to the right. Five, not including the master.

The wife was probably still in the master bedroom, Stella thought, unless she'd run to the baby when the alarm first went off. Would she do that? Would the last few days with Tucker have been enough to make her start thinking like a mother?

Stella ran that scenario through her mind. If Chrissy had

managed to get up here fast enough, if she found the nursery right away, maybe got there at the same moment as Funzi's wife—Stella had no doubt about who'd prevail in that conflict—or maybe been lucky enough to get in and out before anyone discovered her . . . was there any chance that Chrissy could have made her way back down the stairs and out the front door with Tucker? Could she be back at the Jeep already, putting it into gear and roaring back out onto the highway?

As Stella considered this hopeful possibility, she heard a sound from one of the doors on the right side of the hallway, a footstep or something heavy being moved. She realized her hopes were wildly unrealistic: Chrissy hadn't got away. If she had managed to grab Tucker, Funzi and Beez would be in pursuit, the wife hysterical. Instead, they'd shut themselves in the rooms—and they had Chrissy and the baby with them.

Her instincts propelled her, and she burst out of the bathroom and across the hall and into the door, smashing into it with all her force.

It wasn't locked, and she went flying into the room, knocking into a bed frame, her shins slamming painfully against the brass, her gut jarring against the rail. Staggering back, with nausea rocketing through her, she noticed the other person in the room.

Stella thought for a moment she was staring at a ghost, illuminated by a dainty ceramic lamp on a bedside table. Wearing a nightgown of sheer flower-sprigged cotton, an impossibly thin woman with lifeless blond hair hanging down past her shoulders stood hugging her arms to herself. Her eyes were rimmed red, with huge purple circles underneath. She looked terrified.

But Stella knew better—appearances could be deceiving.

She seized the woman's arm and twisted it behind her back, doubling her over. She trained her gun on the woman's head, pressing the barrel to her forehead. The woman made a small mewling sound, like a kicked puppy, but didn't protest further.

"Where's the baby?" Stella demanded.

The only sound the woman made was a strangled sob, and Stella yanked harder. She heard something pop in the area of the woman's shoulder.

The woman screamed.

A thundering sound came from down the hall, and a bulky figure burst into the room, coming to a lurching halt in front of Stella. Funzi. The man who'd watched from the comfort of a park bench while his goons beat the shit out of her. A doughy man in his late forties, he wore striped cotton pajamas, thick black chest hair peeking out of the V neckline. His hair was slicked back on top of his head, in the style of a fifties crooner.

The gun he had trained on her made their entire cache of weapons look like toys from a cereal box. Stella figured it for a streetsweeper, a fully automatic shotgun that could shoot six hundred rounds a minute.

"I'll shoot her," she yelled.

"Oh, I don't doubt it," Funzi said, slow and deadly. "That you'd shoot Marie here. The question is, would it be worth it, for a chance to put a bullet in your brain?"

Stella's finger on the gun twitched involuntarily, and she realized Funzi had just unwittingly saved his wife.

She couldn't shoot the woman now, knowing that Marie's

own husband was willing to stand there and watch her die. There was the evidence of what mattered to him. There was the balance of power. There was a drama Stella had seen played out a few times too often.

She relaxed her grip on Marie Angelini's arm, and the woman fell to the floor, whimpering with pain and clutching her arm. Stella pointed the Ruger at Funzi.

"You'll take me out with that thing," she said, voice hard, "but can you be sure I won't get off a shot, too? I'm not a bad shot, and right now I'm sighting right up your hairy nostrils."

Funzi laughed, a horrible sound laced with what sounded like genuine mirth. "Yeah, you might. And if you do, know what'll happen next?"

Stella said nothing, dread growing in her gut; From down the hall she heard a huffing cry: Tucker.

"Beez, come on down here," Funzi called. "Bring our guest."

Funzi stepped lightly aside, never taking the gun off Stella, and a second later Chrissy's battered face appeared in the doorway. She was being shoved along by a compact, muscular dark-haired man in his twenties who was wearing a T-shirt smudged with blood and a pair of cotton lounge pants with beer cans screen-printed on them.

Chrissy's hands were bound behind her, and she'd taken a couple of good slugs to the face. One eye was rapidly swelling shut, and as she opened her mouth to speak, Stella could see that a couple of her front teeth had been broken off.

"You look about like I feel right now," Stella said, trying to keep her voice from wavering, but the situation was impossible now. They were doomed.

Chrissy gave her a small nod, but her eyes glinted with fury. Down, Stella thought, but not out. There was still some fight left in the girl.

"Did you nail Roy Dean?" Chrissy asked, her voice thick and slurred through the busted teeth.

"Yeah, I did," Stella said. Though a fat lot of good it was going to do. "I knocked him out. Now I'm gonna take down this jerk."

"You shoot me, Beez here will put a bullet in your girl's brain and then, depending how pissed off he is, he just might go put one in the kid, too."

Chrissy went rigid at his words, her eyes wide, her muscles straining as she worked against her restraints. Her lips moved and she spat at Funzi; the bloody glob landed on his cheek. Marie whimpered from the floor.

Gus yanked upward on Chrissy's restraints, making her gasp with pain, but she didn't cry out. Funzi picked up a little decorative pillow from a chintz armchair and wiped Chrissy's saliva slowly and deliberately from his face. Then he tossed the pillow to the floor.

"I think you'll be sorry you did that," he said. He turned to Stella. "Okay, you ugly sack of flesh, how 'bout you give me that gun and come along like a good little girl."

Reluctantly, Stella lowered her gun and handed it to Funzi, who stuck it in a pocket of his lounge pants. He came forward and yanked her shirt up, revealing the empty holster below. He took it off her with a vicious yank and threw the thing in the corner of the room.

"What you got here?" he demanded, reaching down to her ankle holster. He pulled out the scissors and laughed, then tossed them in the corner, too. "What were you going to do, snip me to death?"

Stella focused her attention on Chrissy, never taking her eyes off the girl's face. "How's Tucker?" she asked quietly.

Chrissy nodded once, firmly. Good: so the boy was all right. For now.

She had to believe Funzi had been bluffing about shooting the kid, but it was too risky to try anything now. Especially given the odds: two large, armed, and muscular men against the two of them, unarmed and beat to shit.

"Get up, Marie," Funzi growled to the woman on the floor. Slowly, painfully, she got to her feet.

Stella heard something. A faint sound, a wail that gradually got louder. A siren.

Someone had called the fire department. Or—was it possible?—maybe the next-door neighbors had been looking out their window and seen her struggle in the back of the house with Roy Dean. Maybe the cops were on their way. Suddenly, the idea of being arrested sounded pretty damn appealing, since it would mean Chrissy and Tucker's safety.

Down the hall Tucker's hiccuping whine escalated to a wailing cry. Chrissy bit her lip and squeezed her eyes shut for a second.

"Beez," Funzi barked. "Go see what happened to Roy Dean. I'll deal with these two."

Beez bolted from the room and down the stairs. Stella hoped Roy Dean had bled rivers from the gash on his forehead, a blood pool so big and wide the cops or fire rescue couldn't miss it.

"In the room," Funzi said to Chrissy, getting behind her

and giving her a shove. The girl stumbled forward and sat down hard on the bed.

"You," Funzi said to Stella. "Next to her."

Stella sat down on the bed, close to Chrissy, and put her arm around the girl. "It's okay," she whispered fiercely.

Whether it was or not might be up in the air, but Chrissy leaned into the hug. "I know," she whispered back. It clearly hurt to talk, given the hit she'd taken to the mouth.

"Marie, get your ass in gear and get the rope," Funzi ordered his wife. "And the tape. Move!"

Holding her arm painfully to her side, Marie slipped past him without a word. The blood had drained from her face, leaving her skin white and lifeless, and Stella figured the shoulder was dislocated and hurting like a bitch.

Too damn bad.

Marie was back in moments with a coil of orange plastic rope looped over her good arm. She also held a roll of duct tape. Outside, the sirens had grown in volume until they were practically earsplitting; then, abruptly, they stopped. Stella heard men's voices and the clop of heavy boots on the drive, a pounding on the front door—Beez must have shut the door when he went down to deal with Roy Dean.

Funzi took the rope from his wife and, with surprising speed, tied Stella's hands behind her and then looped the rope through Chrissy's arms and secured the ends of the rope to the bed frame.

"Marie, get that kid and shut him up for Christ's sake," Funzi said.

Marie backed out of the room, but at the doorway she hesitated.

"He has a name," she said, her voice quiet but with a faint echo of something at the heart of it.

"Yeah. Alphonse Junior. Now move your ass."

"No," Marie corrected him. "It's *Tucker*." And she was gone.

Stella felt Chrissy tense next to her, but before she could say anything, Funzi grabbed the roll of duct tape and tore off a huge strip. He slapped it across her mouth, winding the ends around her head a couple of times. Stella had to work hard to keep the panic from making her hyperventilate, and she breathed hard through her nose as Funzi repeated the process on Chrissy.

The pounding downstairs grew louder, and Stella willed the firefighters to break the door down, to come in primed for action—but instead she heard Beez's voice, slightly winded, speaking calmly.

"Hey, guys. Thanks for coming out."

"Sir, we have a report of a fire at this address."

"Yeah. Yeah, damndest thing. I think I just got it put out. I've had the hose on it out back."

Funzi stepped away from the bed and gave his handiwork a once-over. Stella glared at him as hard as she could. Funzi wiped his hands on his pants and straightened the collar of his polo shirt and shot her a thumbs-up before he disappeared around the corner.

Tucker's cries had diminished to a cranky whimper, with a rhythmic pattern to it, and Stella figured Marie had picked him up and was bouncing him quiet, much as she'd done for No-elle all those years ago.

Of course, she'd never done it with a dislocated shoulder. Grudgingly, she raised her opinion of Marie a few notches.

"Gentlemen," Funzi's voice boomed heartily from downstairs. "So glad you all came out. Me'n my buddy here can't figure out what happened out back. Why don't you all come on this way. . . ."

She could hear their voices at the back of the house but couldn't make out the words. She strained her wrists against the rope, but flexing her muscles just made it bind more tightly against her skin, cutting in painfully. She wondered if she and Chrissy could maneuver themselves so their hands touched, whether one of them might be able to free the other's wrists. But there was no way to make the suggestion, not with their mouths taped shut.

Stella fought against the panic in her chest. Was there any way to get to the scissors? She could see them across the room, where Funzi had thrown them against the wall, but they were four feet past the end of the bed, too far away to do any good.

That's when she remembered the rotary cutter. Rocking her hips, she worked her loose camo pants around, twisting them against the shiny bedspread, until she could touch the top of the pocket with her fingertips. She tried to communicate to Chrissy with her eyes, to let her know what she was trying to do, and though the girl looked confused, she leaned as close as she could to give Stella as much slack in the rope as possible.

She strained against the rope and managed to touch the top of the rotary cutter's handle, but it was smooth curved plastic, and she couldn't get a grip on it. She bent backward, forcing her shoulders back and straining her fingers as far as she could, until they slid down the handle far enough to get a grip. Stella grasped the cutter and worked it out of her pocket.

Comprehension dawned in Chrissy's eyes, and she nodded sharply and looked down at her bound hands. Stella followed the path of her gaze and saw that she was opening and closing her fist, and realized what the girl was trying to communicate: she had more freedom of movement in her hands than Stella did. She wanted Stella to give her the cutter.

Stella didn't hesitate. She managed to turn the tool in her hands, and pointed it toward Chrissy. She felt the girl take it from her and then she heard a beautiful sound: the snick of the safety being released.

She looked at Chrissy and for a moment their eyes held and she tried to communicate everything she was feeling: encouragement, resilience, and sheer ass-kicking vengeance. Chrissy blinked twice and then she leaned back and Stella felt the pressure of the blade against her restraints.

The blade was wicked sharp, and it spun free, making it hard to control. It was meant to be held firmly against a flat cutting surface. Used against an uneven surface like the knots, it could easily slip off, slicing into the vulnerable flesh of Stella's hands or wrist.

She held as still as she could, but even so, twice she felt the blade slip and sink into her skin. She tried not to react, knowing that Chrissy needed all her focus for the task, but she felt blood dripping down her hands and pooling in her curled fingers. She'd cut herself with the rotary cutter before, and it was like a cut with a straight razor—so clean and so fast that you didn't feel the pain at first.

The voices in the back yard faded and then came back louder as the men returned to the house. Stella could hear them in the downstairs hall, laughing now, all worries about the fire put to rest, and her heart sank. So Beez had managed to obliterate all her hard work with Roy Dean—the unconscious body, the puddle of blood. Well, it wouldn't have been hard, with a few minutes' blasting with the hose.

She felt one of the strands of rope strain against the blade, and suddenly it snapped free, the frayed end hitting her fingers. Stella made a sound in her throat, of surprise and gratitude. Chrissy murmured in response, and Stella could feel her tugging at the loosened rope.

Funzi and Beez led the firefighters to the front door, and their voices carried easily up to the bedroom. They sounded almost jovial, like a bunch of guys going to the bar after a softball game.

"I think I'll have my wife and son go stay in a hotel for the night. You know, don't want the little guy breathing that smoke," Funzi said.

Chrissy paused and Stella wished she could pat her shoulder or comfort her in some way, but after a second Chrissy attacked the knots with renewed vigor.

"Not a bad idea, sir. If you call the station tomorrow they can give you the name of a couple of outfits that deal in smoke damage. You know, for the drapes and what-all."

"Yeah, I guess the rest of it'll keep us busy for the weekend. So much for fishing."

"That's a damn shame." Another voice. "Hope to see you back on the water soon."

"I'll look forward to it."

Just then, Stella felt Chrissy pull the loosened strands free, shoving them out of the way with her fingers, and Stella opened and closed her fists a couple of times to get the feeling back, noting with dismay that they were slick with her own blood.

She closed her fingers over the handle of the rotary cutter just as Funzi and Beez stomped up the stairs and into the room. She prayed they wouldn't see the blood seeping under her hands, staining the bedspread beneath her and Chrissy.

Funzi stood in the doorway and leered in. He looked almost maniacal, a grin stretched across his otherwise grim features.

"Isn't that great?" he said. "Nice to see your tax dollars at work like that, huh?"

Behind him, Beez tagged along. He didn't look one bit happy. Stella could sympathize. The evening wasn't exactly a smashing success for anyone so far.

"Ought to rip your head off right now," Beez muttered.

"You nearly screwed us with what you did to Roy Dean," Funzi said, his manic voice edging higher. "Leaving him lying out on the ground for anyone to see. Good thing Beez got down there fast. He put Roy Dean into the cushion box. Big old Rubbermaid thing we keep the cushions for the outdoor furniture in? I mean, the thing was perfect, like it was made for holding a body. Only Roy Dean started to wake up. Fucking beat that. He starts to wake up and what's Beez supposed to do, we got the fuckin' fire department down our shorts, can't have Roy Dean making noise and pounding on the box, now, can we? So Beez had to put a bullet in his brain."

Beez looked away, his face darkening, and Stella felt her face go rigid with horror. She remembered the feel of Roy Dean's pulse under her fingers, and she couldn't help thinking that he had been *alive,* he'd still been breathing when she left him lying on the patio.

She hadn't killed him. But he was dead anyway, and he wouldn't be if it wasn't for her. Did that make her guilty? Did it matter? Before the night was out, more people were going to be dead. Probably her and Chrissy—but not if she had anything to say about it.

"You might as well been the one who pulled the trigger," Funzi added, as though he were reading Stella's thoughts. He prodded her tied ankles with a meaty hand. "You cost me one of my men. I might have to, you know, express my displeasure with you before I shoot you."

Stella looked at the pale skin of Funzi's stomach, a band of which hung over the elastic waist of his pajama bottoms. She imagined sinking the rotary blade in right there, rolling a nice big slice out of him. Now wasn't the time, though, not with both of them focused on her and Chrissy. She needed to get one of them alone.

"Marie! Get down here!" Funzi hollered down the hall. His wife appeared in the doorway, holding Tucker in her good arm, with a diaper bag over her shoulder.

Chrissy strained against the ropes and grunted frantically against the tape against her mouth. The sound was heartbreaking. Tucker heard it, and his little blond head whipped around and he arched away from Marie, leaning out with his arms and screaming.

The boy recognized his mama, even with her battered face and tape over her mouth.

Stella figured her heart was going to break right there.

Then she made herself take all that anguish and turn it into honed, sharp fury, pictured it swirling in her gut, ready to burst out and take down all the evil in the room.

Marie struggled to get the boy under control with her good arm, the bag slipping to her elbow and dangling there. Tucker wasn't a dainty child. He was pink and round and big, and Stella figured it would be a miracle if he didn't wiggle out of her one-arm grasp, Marie red-faced with the effort of hanging on to him.

Marie didn't look toward the bed. Stella wanted to scream at her: *Look here, right here, this is Tucker's real mother. The woman your husband is going to shoot down like a dog, just so you can playact at being Mommy.* She willed Marie to look, but the woman turned away.

"Jesus fuck, Marie, get him out of here," Funzi said, pulling a set of keys out of his pocket. "Take the Escalade. Go to the town house. I'll be there later today. Move."

He gave his wife a perfunctory peck on the cheek and a little shove, and she staggered down the hall without a backward glance.

That peck on the cheek—noisy, brief—Ollie used to kiss Stella like that, but only if there were other people around. She'd be standing with a group of women at the Knights of Columbus barbecue and he'd come over, flush with a few beers, bringing the conversation to a halt with his lurching, leering presence. The women would all watch as he winked broadly and kissed Stella. Sometimes he'd pat her butt, too. And then he'd wander off to find his buddies and another beer, and there would be this little silence before the conversation started up again, and even though it was a matter of seconds, it was excruciating, and Stella knew what they were all thinking.

That she was a saint to put up with Ollie Hardesty. And that somebody ought to stop him from doing what they all knew he did.

And then someone would mention that her niece was having surgery for a fibroid the size of a tennis ball, and Stella would stand quietly with the trace of the kiss burning an invisible scar on her cheek.

Stella felt a little sorry for Marie. It was going to be a tough drive, wherever she was going, probably up to the city, fifty or sixty miles with her arm screaming in pain. Maybe they'd get pulled over for not having a car seat—but what would that accomplish? If she and Chrissy didn't walk out of this place, even if Tucker somehow escaped Funzi and his wife, he'd be headed straight for social services. Foster care. The start of a whole other kind of no-good life.

There were no two ways about it: she and Chrissy *had* to come out of this alive.

Funzi gestured at the women. "So Beez, what do you think of taking the ladies out for a boat ride?"

"Sure," Beez said, but he still looked pretty crabby.

"Go get the keys, I think they're still on the cooler out in the garage. Or maybe on the hook in the game room. Somewhere down there, anyway."

Beez left the room.

"Here's the thing, girls," Funzi said, going to the corner of the room where he had thrown Stella's holster. He picked up the scissors, examined them carefully, admiring the curve of the blades. Then he came over and sat next to Stella on the bed. "You ladies are the plus-size variety. That's a problem. Beez and I are gonna have a hard time carrying a couple of heifers like yourselves out of here, so you're going to have to cooperate."

Stella glared at Funzi. He was enjoying this. Having fun at their expense. As if to confirm her suspicion, he pulled the hair away from her face, almost delicately, and put the tip of the scissors to the edge of the duct tape gag. Slowly, carefully, he worked the blade under the edge of the tape and cut through it. He was cutting into her skin, too, Stella was pretty sure, given the sharp pain she felt.

Once he got the cut started, he picked at a corner of the tape with his thumb and forefinger. He leaned in close to her face, and Stella could smell him: sweat and body odor and traces of some fruity aftershave.

There was a ripping sound and suddenly her face was a world of pain. Funzi had yanked the tape away in one furious motion, and it felt like it had taken a couple of her stitches out and opened up all her gashes again and stripped a few layers of skin as well. Her lip dribbled blood, no doubt split further than before. She gasped involuntarily and then worked her jaw back and forth, trying to get some sensation back into it.

"Not much of a looker, is she?" Funzi laughed, addressing Chrissy and pointing to Stella with the scissors. "They say she took out her husband. Poor guy, he probably wasn't sticking it to her enough. That what got you so mad, Stella? Huh?"

He chuckled at his own humor, and Stella squeezed the rotary cutter hard, the handle sticky with her blood.

"But it's kind of hard to blame him. I mean, even without the shit kicked out of you, it's not like you're gonna win the

Miss World title, you know? Now *you*—" pointing at Chrissy with thumb and forefinger cocked, gun-style. "You got some potential. I hope I didn't hurt your feelings, calling you a heifer. You see my wife? See how damn skinny she is? Man, she ain't had anything decent to eat in years. Drives me bat-shit. I'm like, Marie, have a fucking French fry, for Christ's sake."

More mirth. Funzi was able to amuse himself pretty easily. "Yeah, but I like you. I do," Funzi said softly, letting his gaze travel up and down Chrissy. "Nice and soft, probably feel pretty good to sink into, and you'd have plenty to hang onto, you know?"

He leered suggestively, but Chrissy shot him a glance that Stella figured made it pretty clear what she thought of the idea. Good girl, she thought. *Stay angry.*

"You're not her type," Stella muttered through her bloody lips. "You ain't anybody's type, 'cept your own. Too bad you couldn't just fuck yourself so you could be with someone who loves you back."

Funzi's eyebrows shot up, and then he was laughing, but his laughter had a hard, mean edge to it now.

"Now see, there's that bitterness again. Woman, you are desperately in need of a good screwing, but I'm sorry, that's just not going to happen. Maybe in your next life."

The humorous tone was gone now. He had lost his patience; he was done playing with them, and Stella tensed, sensing the moment was near.

"You know," he said, pointing at Chrissy again, "you ought to be thanking me. Your boy's gonna have things you'd never have been able to give him. Private school, soccer and baseball, decent clothes, a car on his sixteenth birthday. And you know what?"

He leaned across Stella, getting as close to Chrissy's face as he could, and it was clear that he was enjoying her pain, enjoying dishing out the cruelty.

"He won't remember you," he said, voice soft and silky. "Don't fool yourself about that little episode a few minutes ago. This time next week he'll be calling me Daddy."

Stella found herself staring into his ear, a fleshy, large, knobby thing with hair on the inside. As she swung her arm from behind, up and over in an arc, she was able to make a detailed observation of Funzi's ear hair—it was one of those moments that seems to stretch on forever, even though it lasted a mere fraction of a second. Evidently Funzi hadn't done any personal grooming in a while, because the bristly black hairs were a quarter of an inch long, as though he was growing a wire brush inside his ear, and as Stella brought the rotary cutter down across his neck and blood came flying out of the severed artery in a spray whose volume surprised even Stella, Stella who'd brought forth the blood of a dozen men before, Stella who'd knocked the life blow by blow from her husband's cruel eyes, the thought that went through her head in slow motion was that she might not be beautiful, but because of her, the world was going to be short one truly ugly son of a bitch.

Funzi jerked back, hands flying to his neck, blood pumping between his scrabbling fingers as he tried to scoop it back in. His eyes widened and his lips moved, and some of the blood splashed across Stella's face and more of it landed on her shirt as she instinctively pulled away. There was blood on her lips, she sputtered as some of it got in her mouth, spat out the blood of the man who'd wanted to kill her, and she pulled her bound ankles in toward her body as far as she could and then kicked them hard and Funzi was shoved off the bed onto the floor, making choking sounds of horror all the way down.

From her peripheral vision Stella saw Beez burst into the room, watched his glance fly from her to Chrissy, who was struggling to get up off the bed, and Funzi on the floor in his bath of blood, twitching now, fingers extended out stiffly, eyes rolled back in his head.

Beez had his gun up and got off a shot before Stella could react, and Chrissy jerked back against the headboard. A neat hole blossomed red in her chest and then she started to tilt slowly to the side.

Stella dove off the bed on top of Funzi, reaching for the scissors that had fallen from his grasp onto the white carpet. Her fingers brushed against the blades as the sound of another shot exploded way too close. As she grasped the handles there was another shot and she felt a giant wallop in her left shoulder and thought *holy shit he got me*—but she palmed the scissors, rolling over onto her back on top of Funzi as Beez seemed to fly through the air toward her. She grabbed the handle with both her bloody hands and held the scissors in front of her.

For a fraction of a second she saw Beez's eyes widen as he flew toward her, and then he crashed on top of her as the gun went off once more and the scissor handles jabbed hard into her sternum and knocked the wind out of her. Stella struggled against his weight, trying to figure out if that last shot had connected, but she was still moving, her shoulder burned but she was moving, she was kicking and clawing and holy mother she wanted to be out from under him, and then she was, crab-scuttling away on her one good arm and only then did she see that the scissors were sunk into his throat and blood was leaking out fast, Beez lying now halfway on top of his boss, on Funzi, the two of them going still and cold even as their blood continued to leak out.

If they weren't dead yet they would be soon but what good was it going to do with Chrissy dead and Stella shot twice shot *twice* oh shit how had she been so lucky for so long how had it worked out that a washed-up fucked-over dried-out shell of a disappointed woman had managed to keep it going as long as she had -

- and as her hands found the holes in her flesh, felt her own blood leaking out, heard her own whimpering, Stella knew the answer, knew it as sure as she'd known anything in her entire life:

- she'd had the luck of someone who just didn't care, who didn't much give a damn if she lived another day, who didn't believe life had any more gifts to give her, who believed that death would be every bit as satisfying as rattling around that empty house, as waking up in the early morning hours and feeling loneliness like a huge weight pressing on her chest—

- and then she'd gone and done the one thing that she'd never thought she could do again—she had *cared*.

And caring was what had got her dead.

Sweet fucking irony. Stella fell down in degrees, feeling her strength ebb out as she grabbed for the bed frame, felt it slip out of her fingers, unable to hold on. She felt woozy, circling clouds of hot red in the outskirts of her vision.

There was no more movement from the men on the floor. With an effort that felt like it took about a year, Stella forced herself away from them, catching sight of Funzi's staring eyes, no longer mean, just empty.

Slowly, painfully, she pushed herself to her forearms and looked over the bed.

Chrissy lay on her side, turned toward the wall away from Stella. Her cap had come off and her pale, curly hair spilled out prettily. Stella couldn't see the wound from here. Couldn't see the blood.

Stella dragged herself the rest of the way up, until she was almost sitting. The crime scene guys were going to have a field day in here—four bodies, all bleeding out. By the time the cops came, no one would be left to tell what happened. And Goat—would they call him? Was he going to have to see her like this, banged up and wearing the blood of too many other people? Was that going to be what he remembered years from now when somebody happened to mention her name in passing?

From somewhere in the vicinity of her heart, Stella thought *no.*

It was a small notion, but as she sat on Funzi's floor with a couple of holes in her, it bloomed and grew until the word itself crowded out all her other thoughts and rang in her ears: *No.* It was too much. It was just too damn much. *NO.*

She'd been humiliated, beaten, taunted, and now shot, but no one, not even the entire Kansas City mob, was going to leave little Tucker motherless and take away Stella's chance to get her hands on Sheriff Goat Jones on the same day.

"God . . . damn . . . ," she mouthed as she edged her way along the bed, pulling at the frame with her fingers, until the side-table phone was in reach.

It took a couple of tries to get the receiver off the base, and then Stella sank back down on the floor, exhausted from the effort of trying to stay upright. She brought the phone close to her face, and as the numbers swam blurrily, she tried to remember where the hell she'd left her reading glasses this time.

But she could see just well enough to press the buttons. It took a while, and she went slow, because she wasn't sure she had the energy to do it twice if she messed up, but then she heard Goat's voice, Goat's sleepy deep sweet voice saying hello, and Stella closed her eyes and breathed through a smile:

"Come and get me, big boy."

And then she let the clouds swirl on in.

NINE

. . . .

When Stella woke up she didn't open her eyes at first. Didn't quite feel up to the job, with her head fuzzy as if it had been stuffed with fluffy cotton, and the rest of her body suspended in a kind of swimmy grogginess.

Then the pain made its appearance. What it lacked in immediacy, it made up for with sheer intensity. It felt as though there were a burning ember on the left side of her stomach, and a dull ache that radiated out from her shoulder. Her entire torso felt as if it had been stomped on by someone wearing heavy boots.

It took her only a few seconds to decide she wasn't dead. Whatever the afterlife held, and Stella didn't have any special convictions on the subject, she did believe that it probably wouldn't include all this pain and sweaty nausea. But what really convinced her was the smell: a combination of industrial disinfectant, bleach, burned Salisbury steak, and an undercurrent of floral preservative.

Had to be the hospital again.

Goat must have come and got her. That thought sparkled into her brain like silvery glitter, bringing with it a little hoppity-skip sensation in her gut. She remembered dialing his number, but it had taken a long time.

Thoughts and images flashed by and Stella tried to seize them and make sense of them, but her thought processes seemed a bit compromised. No doubt they had her pumped up full of all kinds of drugs, which were preventing her from using all her powers of logic. But a few things stood out, now that she thought about it, like the fact that she'd been shot. Twice. And hadn't she left most of her blood on the pale carpeting of Funzi's lake house?

The scene came back to her in fits and starts until, after a dreamy little while, Stella remembered everything. She moved her fingers, under the hospital blanket, to her stomach, where the second bullet had slammed into her. Wasn't all that surprised to find a thick layer of bandages. She tapped it experimentally and grimaced from the pain.

Hopefully they'd dug that sucker out. It, and its twin, lodged somewhere around her shoulder, a location that seemed like too much trouble to explore right now. Didn't they leave the bullets in sometimes? Like if they were too close to an organ or something? Stella did not at all relish the thought of carrying around any souvenirs of the last few days.

Something to ask the doctor about.

Sighing, Stella opened her eyes. The left one seemed more eager than the right, but a little effort unstuck it, and she found herself looking around at a room very similar to the one she'd been in—what was it, two nights ago? It felt like a hundred years had gone by.

This time, Chrissy wouldn't be arriving to spring her, a thought that made her heart hurt. She'd be all alone in her room in Sawyer County Regional Hospital, a place she'd visited dozens of times over the years. Funny how the humble act of everyday living brought her through the doors of this place from time to time: everything from Noelle's stitches when she fell off a swing set, to Ollie's emergency appendectomy, to friends' and neighbors' gallbladder surgeries and hysterectomies and cancers and strokes and basic human frailty.

But before this week, the only time she herself had been a patient was when Noelle was born. Almost three decades ago.

Stella remembered that the curtains had been yellow then, thick-woven polyester things, and the floor tiles had flecks of green in them, and the trays they brought the food on were turquoise plastic. She'd stayed three days, dozing and nursing and hobbling to the bathroom, marveling all the while at the tiny little life she'd brought into the world.

It had felt like a solo effort. Lots of men stayed in the waiting room during childbirth back then, but Ollie seemed uncomfortable not only with the baby's arrival but with everything else about Noelle. He made only one appearance per day, hands in pockets, shifting from foot to foot uncomfortably and staring out the window, declining to hold his daughter.

Back then, Stella's room had a view of the parking lot. Now, her view was of the tops of trees, so she knew she'd scored a room on the other side of the hospital complex, the side that overlooked the little park where patients were taken in their wheelchairs to get some sun.

She was moving up in the world.

An IV cart stood next to the bed, with a line that led under the covers. Stella flexed her fingers—tried to, at any rate, but they were covered with something. She pulled her hands out from under the covers and saw that they both had been bandaged and wrapped, the right one with enough layers that it looked like a mitten, the left wearing a wide band of dressing around the palm. The IV entered her arm in a neat little taped hole.

Gingerly, Stella tried to move her legs. They felt as if they had fallen asleep, but she saw the blanket shift a little on the bed. That was good news: she guessed it meant that neither bullet had nailed her spine. Sometimes bullets did all manner of pinball-style ricocheting around in the flesh, if the TV shows were to be believed. She wondered if the little bits of metal had punched through any of her organs or sliced up a lung, but decided she'd be hooked up to more than just an IV if that were the case.

The longer she was awake, the more Stella was beginning to realize she didn't feel all that horrible. She was going to pull through. No doubt all that exercise had helped, her body too strong and stubborn to succumb to a mere double shooting. In fact, if she'd started Weight Watchers like she meant to six months ago, she'd probably be feeling even better. But hey, maybe this would be her wake-up call. They always talked about "wake-up calls" on the late-night weight-loss infomercials. "My reunion was coming up, and I weighed eighty pounds more than I did my senior year," some little stick-thin gal would gush. Or "My doctor said I was headed straight for type-two diabetes if I didn't make some changes."

Stella pictured herself sitting in an armchair, staring into the camera, with an unctuous host sticking a microphone in front of her. She'd say, "I got my face pounded to a pulp, and then I got shot a couple times and nearly bled to death in the middle of a hotbed of organized crime." Some wake-up call that would be. The thought made her frown.

Frowning, it turned out, hurt like a bitch. Sharp pain seared along the tender skin of her lips and around her forehead, and along the lines of her stitches. Hell, she probably had a whole new set of stitches by now; she probably looked like she was sporting zippers in every direction across her face. Or maybe they just took a staple gun to her, pushed that flap of skin in place and let fly. Why not? Might as well save the nitpicky detail work for a case where they could actually make a difference. Stella put the fingers of her left hand gingerly to her face and made an exploration, and it felt as if she hadn't been far off: the ridges and bumps and sharp little knots were an unfamiliar landscape, with bulges and valleys nowhere near where they ought to be.

Stella sighed and put her hands back on top of the cool sheets. So her face was wrecked. So what. It would heal. She was trying so hard not to think of the other thing, the thing that had been slinking along the edges of her mind ever since she first woke up, the thought she'd taken down with her as she first sank into unconsciousness and which had featured in her hazy, troubled dreams as she came out of anesthesia.

There was no keeping it at bay any longer.

Chrissy.

Chrissy, braver than Stella had ever imagined, fearless to the end. Beautiful in her fury, rosebud lips focused in a deadly frown of concentration, those cornflower blue eyes glinting with fearless determination. Stella knew that even as she took the bullet, even as she fell, Chrissy hadn't faltered.

Stella's grief welled up, and it was stronger than any of the other emotions she'd experienced so far. She'd sworn she would never again endanger a woman while doing her job, but somehow along the way the task of finding Tucker had seized them both and thrown them together on this desperate journey, and it was only together that they had been able to get as far as they had. Stella didn't regret taking the girl along with her—it was no more an option for Chrissy to stay home than it was for Stella to turn away when Chrissy had first arrived at her door.

They'd given their all: she was sure of that. Stella knew that neither of them had held anything back, that they'd put fear behind them and barreled ahead, knowing the situation could end up like this.

If only things had worked out differently.

The fact that Chrissy was the one to go down and stay down—it didn't seem right. Stella should have been the one who died. No one needed her; no one waited for her. And besides, she'd rolled the dice more than most people ever had a chance to, taking risks, scraping through situations that by all rights should have ended in disaster.

Why couldn't Chrissy have been the lucky one this time?

Stella heard soft voices in the hall, and then the door to her room was pushed open wide and a young woman with spiked magenta hair came into the room, dropped the paper cup she was holding, and burst into tears.

Noelle.

"Baby girl," Stella said, surprised to find that her voice was nothing more than a scratchy whisper, and she held out her arms and her sweet grown-up angel girl rushed straight into them, laying her head on Stella's chest and immediately jerking back with a shriek, which might have been a good thing on balance since the pressure of the embrace felt like an axe cleaving Stella's flesh. But she needed to hold her daughter, and she grasped Noelle's hands and tugged her back.

Very gently Noelle knelt down next to the bed and laid her cheek on Stella's arm, blinking tears from her big violet eyes. "Mama," she said, "what on earth have you gone and done?"

She sounded so distraught, so dismayed, that Stella had to laugh. It was a hurtin' little laugh, bumpy and rough, but it felt good. "Just makin' trouble, sugar. I'm sorry to say it, but I can't seem to stay away from it."

"Oh, mama," Noelle said. "You look just awful. You had me so scared. When the sheriff called me I—"

"Sheriff Jones?"

"Yes, he called this morning when I was getting ready to go to the shop. He said you were trying to rescue a kidnapped baby and got all shot up."

"Did they find him?" Stella asked quickly. "The baby?"

Noelle's pretty, worried face flashed confusion and she shook her head. "There wasn't any baby, Mama. Nobody found anything like that, the sheriff said. He seemed mighty concerned about that part."

Stella's heart, which had been thrumming along with renewed vigor to see Noelle, gave a lurch. So: after all this, poor Tucker was still missing.

They'd failed.

If it hadn't been for her daughter, warm and real and close enough to touch, Stella might have rolled over and prayed her way back to numb unconscious. Instead, she forced a ghost of a smile onto her lips and told a mother's lie: "That's all right, sweetheart."

"Sheriff offered to send somebody over to get me," Noelle said, "but I just jumped in the car and came straight here. Mama, I been here for hours, waitin' on you to wake up. And now all's I did was go get a cup of coffee, and I wasn't gone but a minute and look at you, wakin' up when I was out of the room."

This brought a fresh onslaught of tears, and Stella reached to brush them off Noelle's cheek. Her daughter's skin was soft and creamy, as beautiful as it had always been, and Stella let her fingers linger there, her heart swelling with the knowledge that one thing she'd done, anyway, had turned out better than she ever could have dreamed.

"How long have I been out, anyway?" she asked. It was hard to tell if the light in the room signaled morning or afternoon. "What time is it?"

"It's almost three. They took you to surgery as soon as they got you in here, but time I got over here, you were in recovery."

Stella thought of the thick dressing on her stomach, the pain in her shoulder. "How bad am I?" she asked.

"Oh, Mama, they said you were just incredibly lucky," Noelle exclaimed. "It was small-caliber bullets, and the one in your shoulder just chipped your clavicle. The bullet came out the other side, so they didn't have to hunt for it, but they had to dig around in there for the little bone pieces. But they did it arther—arther—"

"Arthroscopically?"

"Right, I just can't seem to get that out. So you just got a few stitches there. And the one in your stomach, why, all's it did was kind of bounce off your spleen, is what the doctor told me. They had to take out the bullet and repair some blood vessels, but they say your spleen'll fix itself right back up. You're just going to be mighty tender there for a while."

"Yeah, I can tell," Stella said, grimacing. "Do I have to stay here much longer?"

"Just a few days, Mama, and then I'm going to take you home and take care of you and make sure you don't go jumping up trying to do too much before the doctor says it's okay."

Noelle's declaration was so lovely and so unexpected that Stella couldn't think of any kind of response. Noelle coming home, even if it was just for a while, was a gift she'd stopped hoping for long ago.

"That's some hairdo you got there, baby girl," she said instead.

The last time she'd seen Noelle, at the Sawyer county fair last September, her daughter had a yellow-blond bob with long pieces coming down past her chin and the back trimmed up short to the nape of her neck. In Stella's view, her daughter would be gorgeous even shaved bald, but Noelle did manage to come up with unusual things to do to her hair.

That day at the fair, Stella stopped in the middle of the throng of people, unable to move forward, her friend Dotty Edwards chattering on about how she'd been robbed in the jam competition, and Noelle had turned in the bright early autumn sun and caught sight of her mother. For a fraction of a second the two women had stared at each other across the crowd of fairgoers, amid the screeches from the midway and the sweet-hay smell from the animal barns, and then Noelle had dashed off, looking stricken, and Stella had made her excuses to Dotty and gone home with a headache.

All those months ago, months that had gone by without seeing her daughter, without talking to her, without having a chance to hug her and hold her. The loss of it seized up in Stella's throat, and she realized that no matter what, she was going to do whatever it took to stay in her girl's life.

Noelle touched the spiky top of her head self-consciously. "I got an award, Mama," she said shyly. "I did this competition up in Kansas City, with this new amino glycine color process? And I got the Judge's Choice. I mean, it didn't come with any cash or anything, but I got two hundred dollars in product and my picture's going to be in *Midwest Salon* magazine."

"Oh, that's wonderful, sweetie," Stella said, pride swelling up in her battered chest. "Could I—when it comes out—do you think I could have a copy?"

The leaky tears Noelle had already produced were nothing compared to the torrent she unleashed then. Her face crumpled, and she buried it into the crook of Stella's elbow and sobbed.

"Mama . . . I've been so terrible to you . . . and I just missed you so much and I don't know why I was that way . . . just everything that happened, you know, and I—I—"

She finally pulled away, her face damp and splotchy and smeared with mascara, and went for the tissue box and snuffled and wiped at herself until she had most of her composure back. Stella waited patiently, choking back a tear or two herself.

"I'm sorry, Noelle," she said. "You haven't had an easy go of it. And I haven't been, you know, Mother of the Year."

Noelle shook her head. "Don't, Mama. Let's not even talk about the past, okay? It's just—I mean . . ."

Stella reached for the girl's hand and squeezed it. Noelle picked at the blanket for a minute, frowning.

"Mama," she said. "I'm not seeing Gerald anymore. That guy, you know, my boyfriend."

Relief and surprise flooded Stella, but she was careful not to react. She'd made the mistake of throwing in her two cents a few times too often to risk doing it now.

"Are you all right with that, sugar?" she asked.

Noelle snorted in disgust. "More than okay. Just—I just wanted you to know. I mean, I don't know if I'm even going to date at all anymore, you know? It's all so . . ."

She made a helpless gesture and glanced at her mother tentatively. Stella's heart contracted. She knew all too well how it felt when you realized that the man who shared your bed wasn't who you thought he was, how it felt when your hopes and illusions slowly shriveled and died. All that trust, all that hard work going into the hopeless project of making a broken relationship keep rolling along on sprung wheels.

Rejecting the whole mess might be a sign of sanity. But still, the thought of Noelle, barely a grown woman, shutting herself off from love hurt Stella to the core.

"Maybe don't give up completely," she suggested.

"Oh! I forgot. The sheriff's out in the waiting room, Mama. He wanted me to come get him the minute you woke up."

"He is?"

"Yeah, he's been here almost the whole time. He had to go on some call or something, and he's been in to see that other girl a bunch of times, but—"

"Wait," Stella said, grabbing Noelle's arm. "What other girl?"

"That got shot with you, you know, that Lardner girl—"

"Chrissy's alive?" Stella's heart did a somersault, her throat dry. She didn't dare hope, but—

"Um . . . I mean, she's alive but they—but—Mama, I'm so sorry, they don't know if she's going to make it. She barely had a pulse when they got there, and the bullet went through her lung and there was some problems with her heart and they got her on all these machines."

Slowly Stella relaxed her grip on Noelle's arm. She nodded once. All right. Chrissy had made it this far. *Good girl,* she thought fiercely. There probably wasn't a betting pool in the hospital, but if there were, Stella would put all her chips on Chrissy.

"She's a good kid," she said. "I think you'll like her."

For a moment Noelle's expression wavered, her smile slipping, her eyes going a little opaque, and Stella realized something surprising: Noelle was jealous. Just a tiny bit, maybe she wasn't even aware of it, but it was there nonetheless.

"I *know* you'll like her," Stella said quickly. "She's not smart like a whip, the way you are, and she's still got some growing up to do, but I think she's got potential."

Noelle nodded, and the worried expression relaxed. "Well, maybe when this is all over, I mean, when you get out of here, I can bring you to visit her. Or something."

"Yeah," Stella said. "I'd like that."

There was a silence, but it was a nice one.

"I think I'm supposed to tell the nurse you're awake," Noelle said after a while. "And, you know, fetch Sheriff Jones."

"Speaking of that," Stella said. "Look, I don't know how to put this exactly, but I imagine I look pretty terrible, and with you being an expert and all, do you think you could do a little fixing up before he comes in here? I mean, strictly for practical reasons," she added hastily. "I'm going to come out of this with a lot of explaining to do, and I'll probably end up in court or jail or something and, you know, seems like I ought to get off on the right foot with Goat . . . uh, with the sheriff."

"Jail?" Noelle demanded, eyes widening. "Mama, they can't put you in jail. Those guys were the worst kind of criminal! The sheriff told me—I mean, they're like the *mafia*, Mama, up in the city."

"Sheriff told you that?" Stella asked hopefully.

"Yeah. And what's with—" Noelle broke off and studied her mother carefully. The scrutiny was uncomfortable; Stella flinched at Noelle's unwavering examination. Suddenly her daughter raised one eyebrow and cracked a small grin.

"Huh. Well. I got my makeup kit in my purse. Let's see what we can do."

He stared.

Stella kept the determined smile fixed on her face, trying to ignore the uncomfortable tugging of her stitches, the warm buttery weight of the concealer and foundation and whatever else Noelle had dabbed on her, and waited for Goat to say something.

But he just kept staring. He'd walked into the room, two, three steps, then sputtered to a halt a good three feet away from the bed. His big hand went to the back of his neck, as though to brace himself, and he grimaced, eyes crinkling up to glinty ice-blue slits.

"Damn it, Goat," Stella finally said. "Could you say something, please? I just got done taking two bullets. I don't think I'm up for carrying the conversation, you know?"

Goat snapped to life as though a switch had been turned on. His look of detached horror was replaced by a weak smile. He grabbed the visitor's chair and spun it around backward, straddling it with his long legs jutting out at angles and his arms draped across the chair back.

"I'm glad you're not dead."

Stella gave the smile one last surge and then let it collapse, her facial muscles crying out in protest. "Yeah, me too."

"You had me worried."

"Uh." Stella licked her lips, tasting breath mints and the waxy gloss Noelle had brushed on. "So when I called you from Funzi's . . ."

"We got it traced to the lake house right away, and Ogden County responded lights and sirens. They made it in less than ten minutes. I was probably fifteen minutes behind—I gotta tell you, I burned rubber." Goat blinked hard and a pink flush warmed his cheeks. "It was some kind of mess, Stella. When it went out on the scanner, fire service picked it up, and they came on back. I don't even know how many paramedics there were. And the coroner, and the crime scene techs—I've never seen anything like it."

"What about, you know . . . the scene in the bedroom?"

"I couldn't get anywhere close until the EMTs got you and Chrissy on the bus. They had to move the other bodies to get the stretchers in and get you and Chrissy tubed and loaded up. So by the time the first guys on the scene and the paramedics had been in and out of that room, it wasn't much of a crime scene anymore, if you know what I mean."

"Was there any sign of Tucker at all?"

"No, except it looks like they had him sleeping in one of the guest rooms. There was some toys, all new stuff, a few new outfits in a drawer—some even still had the tags on. Did you see him in the house at all?"

Stella gave him an edited version of Marie leaving the house with Tucker in her arms, and passed along the few details she'd overheard: the Escalade, the town house.

"I'll get the word out," Goat promised, "but she could be anywhere by now."

"I know," Stella said sadly. She was silent for a moment, considering how little there was to go on. "Did they retrieve . . . anything useful?"

Goat wrinkled his forehead. "They took quite a few things out of there. Took 'em forever just to bag and tag it all. They just let me stay as a courtesy, you know, so I couldn't give you the specifics. Let's see, there were all the guns. There was a knife . . . and some sort of sewing implement. I know they're having a devil of a time trying to figure out what went with who."

Stella swallowed hard and tried to arrange her face in an expression of confusion. "I just wish I could remember what happened. You know? It's just all so hazy."

Goat regarded her solemnly for what seemed like hours. Stella was aware of Noelle standing off to the side, looking from one of them to the other like a spectator at a tennis match. The poor girl was no doubt bewildered.

"So . . . ," Goat finally said. "Why don't you just tell me about what you *do* remember. Going back to when they kidnapped you and Chrissy."

Stella started to correct him, but that's when she noticed the eyebrows. Goat's beautiful expressive eyebrows were tilted askew, which along with his faint grin gave him a rakish expression. As she was trying to puzzle out his meaning, he winked at her.

Kidnapped . . . by Funzi.

"In my own car," she said, and then elaborated, making it up as she went. "Um, from my house. Chrissy took me back to the house after she sprung me from the hospital, and, you know, we just rested the rest of the day. We were getting ready to watch a little TV and I guess I, uh, left the back door open and suddenly there they were. I mean, Chrissy and I didn't stand a chance."

"That," Goat said carefully, "must have been terrifying."

"You're telling me. Why, there was nothing to do but go along with them, not make a fuss, them being armed and all."

"I mean, the weapons they found at the scene . . . knives and handguns and pistols and I don't know what-all," Goat said. "It was just a real wide range of firepower, you know?"

Stella shrugged. "I guess maybe Funzi was a, what do you call it, gun fancier?"

Goat snorted. Okay, that might have been pushing it a little.

"If mine and Chrissy's prints were to show up on any of those . . . ," she said carefully.

"Yeah, now, that was a concern of mine, frankly," Goat said. "But I figure, you all obviously gave them quite a battle, grabbing at everything in sight, who knows what you would have touched? Besides, there was a hell of a lot of matter on everything. It's not clear whether the evidence is going to give up much in the way of prints."

Stella swallowed. She remembered trying to hang on to the handle of the rotary cutter with her hands slick with blood. Remembered looking up into the snub barrel of Funzi's handgun.

"Now the scene in the back yard, that's sure got everyone scratching their heads."

"Oh?" Stella said. "Um, what did they find—what happened in the back yard?"

"Well, it's a puzzler. There was a struggle back there, that's for sure. Lots of blood trace, though somebody hosed it down. See, there was a fire earlier in the evening, like I mentioned, with the fire department called out and all, just a little structure fire on the back side. It got put out pretty quick. Duty boys barely logged it. But get this, we found Roy Dean Shaw shot dead and stuffed in a landscape box."

"No kidding," Stella said faintly. "How on earth, I wonder?"

"I mean, he must have done something to piss off Funzi,"

Goat said. "But we just can't figure what it was. You know? I mean, maybe it was some sort of double-dealing—we got some leads that he was doing work for that outfit. Oh, by the way, there's a team out at Benning's now, digging up pieces of a body. Must be somebody else that ticked him off. There's a thousand things, when you get down to it, that can get you in bad with the boss, you know?"

"I—I just wish I could remember," Stella said. "I mean, if I could remember what happened after they took us to that house—"

"Yeah, that would sure clear up some things," Goat said. "But if it ain't happenin', it ain't happenin'. The brain is a mysterious thing."

"Yeah," Stella agreed. "Very mysterious."

"And you know, that wasn't the only strange thing about today," Goat said. "I found something real interesting sitting on my doorstep when I went home to take a shower awhile ago."

Shit! Stella had forgotten all about Patrick. The kid had been laid out on the chaise since the middle of last night. He would have woken up at some point with a hell of a headache, wondering where he was and how he got there.

"Was he—was it—"

"I think somebody left it there by accident," he continued, ignoring her. "Clearly this thing didn't belong there. And it was in kinda bad shape. I fixed it up as good as I could, put a fresh shine on it, and took it back to its rightful owner."

He put extra emphasis on the last words, fixing her with an intent stare.

And then he winked.

And the corner of his mouth twitched.

And under all the layers of gauze and bandages and tape and antiseptic gel, Stella felt a little stirring. A little warmth. A little reminder that there was at least one darn good reason to hurry up and get better.

"And did she . . . the rightful owner"—Patrick's mother, it had to be. "Was the owner happy to have this thing back?"

"Yup. I think it's safe to say she's gonna take real, real good care of it. Not let it out of her sight, you know?"

Stella tried to absorb what Goat was telling her. He'd been hinting pretty broadly that he was ignoring and willfully misinterpreting the evidence laid out at the Funzi place. That was bad enough. But freeing Patrick had to add up to evidence tampering. Or worse, if he'd told the boy to keep his mouth shut—that might be considered a threat.

Goat was riding straight into a storm without an umbrella.

And he was doing it for her. Her gut flip-flopped over again.

"That trick with the rotary cutter—that was really something," Goat continued.

"Oh. Uh, now that you mention it, seems like I might have had that on me."

"Took us a little while to figure out. You know, it has that retractable blade and all. Plus, it was pink. We had to call a gal from Jo-Ann Fabrics up in Fayette to explain that one."

They stared at each other and then Goat gave a little chuckle. Nothing more than relief, it sounded like, but it was contagious, and Stella couldn't help joining in, though she had to be careful because of the pain in her stomach.

"It benefits breast cancer research," she finally said. "We carry a whole line of pink accessories down at the shop."

"I'll make a note," Goat said. "Maybe I ought to come check it out. You know, the whole . . . sewing thing."

"Goat Jones," Stella said coquettishly, batting her eyelids as well as she could, given the fact that they were swollen nearly shut and gluey with Noelle's eye shadow and mascara. "Are you one of these pathetic men who can't sew on a button to save his life?"

As she watched, Goat's broad, handsome face slowly reddened, starting at his cheeks and spreading out to his ears and up to his lovely smooth scalp. He opened his mouth to say something and closed it again.

Then he shrugged. "Guilty."

"Well, about time we take care of that, don't you think?"

"You offerin' me sewing lessons, Stella Hardesty?"

Stella smiled for real this time, searing pain in her lips be damned.

"I might be," she said. "What have you got to trade?"

Goat grinned back. "I don't know, Stella," he said, his voice low and rough, just the way she liked it. "I have half a mind to paddle you out to this little spot I know."

TEN

. . . .

S tella was trying to nap the next morning, breathing the cloying scent of flowers and wishing evil on the nurses, who'd come in every few hours during the night to poke and prod her. With any luck she'd be out of here in another couple of days, but she planned to return, fortified with snacks and celebrity magazines, to set up camp in Chrissy's room.

Apparently Chrissy had woken up for a few minutes early in the morning. Stella was torn between dismay at not having been there and enormous relief when the shift nurse described how Chrissy looked around the room and asked where she was.

The doctor said it would probably go like that for a while, little lucid periods and lots of sleep, while Chrissy's body made up its mind to start rebuilding the destruction the bullet had wreaked on her innards.

Stella let her eyes flutter slowly open and noticed that there were even more flowers than when last she drifted off. Lots of her well-wishers had remained anonymous: Stella figured her past clients had heard about her troubles.

But the biggest arrangement was from Goat. It was a funny-looking thing, giant pink and green caladium leaves with white roses, delphinium, and Shasta daisies. "All my favorites," he'd confided, embarrassed, when he stopped last night as he was heading home for the day. "I had 'em make it up special."

Then they'd stared at each other for a while, not saying much, while Noelle watched from her chair, a knowing little smile on her face.

Noelle had finally gone home this morning after spending the night on a cot. She said she'd be back after a shower—with doughnuts.

Stella pressed the button to lift the back of the bed, slowly gliding to a more upright position. Her stomach, if possible, hurt worse today, but the shoulder throbbed a little bit less and her face was more itchy than anything. Noelle had removed the makeup carefully, dabbing with swabs and cotton squares, and then spent forever massaging cream in between the stitches. Stella hoped she wasn't having some sort of allergic reaction; there'd be hell to pay with her doctor, who'd practically blown a gasket when she saw the makeup.

Stella was reaching for the clicker, figuring she'd see what the fuss over *The View* was about these days, when Noelle walked in the door.

Carrying a baby.

Stella's mind did a loop-de-loop and then she recognized the familiar shock of white-blond fluffy hair and said, "Is that who I think it is?"

Noelle turned the little guy around in her arms. He was

rubbing at sleepy eyes with a fist, yawning, showing a pair of tiny white teeth.

"Mama, a lady came by the house this morning and dropped this little fella off. She said I should bring him to you."

"Holy shit." Stella breathed, her heart leaping.

"Mama! Not in front of a child," Noelle scolded, covering one of Tucker's perfect little shell ears with her hand.

While they made their way down the hall, Stella going as fast as she could while limping and dragging her IV drip, Noelle said the lady looked as if she hadn't had a decent meal in a year but was dressed nice and driving a new Escalade, and that she said Stella would know what to do.

"Where was she going?" Stella asked.

"I didn't ask her," Noelle said, exasperated. "I was still trying to figure out what to do with this guy, you know?"

Stella shut her mouth, but not before noticing that Noelle seemed to be finding her way around a baby without too much trouble.

Maybe she'd make Stella a grandma someday. The notion wasn't entirely unpleasant.

Stella pushed open the door to Chrissy's room, and Tucker took one look at the sleeping woman and made a sound that was half burp and half exclamation and then he leaned out of Noelle's arms like he wanted to fly through the air to his mother.

Noelle sat gingerly on the bed just as Chrissy's eyes fluttered open and then she saw her baby and cracked a smile that couldn't have been lovelier if she'd been the Mona Lisa herself.

Stella, watching from the foot of the bed, holding her gown shut with one hand and the IV pole with the other, beaten and bruised and smelling of a couple hard days, got a little sniffly and figured she'd never seen anything prettier.

Good job, she congratulated herself.

There was nothing quite as satisfying as honest hard work.